THE CHEERIO KILLINGS

C THE HEERIO KILLINGS

DOUGLAS ALLYN

A · THOMAS · DUNNE BOOK

St. Martin's Press   New York

To Jerry Reed Hubbard,
whose dark talent inspired it.

THE CHEERIO KILLINGS. Copyright © 1989 by Douglas Allyn. All rights reserved.
Printed in the United States of America. No part of this book may be used or
reproduced in any manner whatsoever without written permission except in
the case of brief quotations embodied in critical articles or reviews. For
information, address St. Martin's Press, 175 Fifth Avenue, New York, N.Y.
10010.

Design by Amelia Mayone

Library of Congress Cataloging-in-Publication Data

Allyn, Doug.
    The cheerio killings / Doug Allyn.
        p.   cm.
    "A Thomas Dunne book."
    ISBN 0-312-03302-8
    I   Title.
    PS3551.L49C47   1989
    813'.54—dc20   89-34842
                                                          CIP

First Edition

10 9 8 7 6 5 4 3 2 1

CHAPTER 1

THE SLED SNAGGED ON A PATCH OF ROUGH ICE, NEARLY JERKING the towrope out of Lamont's grasp. He glanced back to make sure Toby hadn't tumbled off. Nope, still aboard, grimly clutching the side rails with both mittens, a bundle of grubby snowsuit with a runny nose. And frozen to the sled, from the look of him. Not that he'd ever admit it.

"Get up and stomp around a minute, Tobe, get your blood pumpin'."

Lamont tried to shake some feeling back into his own arms, numbed by the December wind and the weight of the sled. He'd hiked a lot farther than he'd intended, hauling the kid in a wide circle across the ice on the Detroit River, almost to the Canadian side and back again. The river was a mile wide, shore to shore, a crystal wonderland glistening in the late afternoon sun. The walk back seemed longer and definitely a heckuva lot colder, but the diamond-dusted icescape was worth every step.

Toby was doing a reluctant shuffle, halfheartedly tapping the toes of his red galoshes on the ice.

1

"C'mon, Toby, don't be a wimp about it, *stomp* 'em. Do like those cloggers on 'Hee-Haw,' let's see a buck-and-wing, or a little Cotton-eyed Joe." Lamont tucked his fists under his armpits and began leaping around like a crazed stork. Toby hesitated a moment, then grinned and joined in, the two of them capering around the sled in an arctic war dance, their breath showing white in the wintry air.

Lamont gave out first. The chill was stinging his throat and he could feel the shock from his numbed feet all the way up to his shoulders. "Saddle up, Toby Red. We got a ways to hike yet."

"Papa, I'm still a little cold," Toby said, not complaining, just saying it.

"Then we'd better get haulin'. Tell ya what, we'll stop by a bar on the way home and I'll buy us a couple cold beers."

"Do they have cocoa there?"

"I don't think so, but I bet they got ice cream. How's that grab ya? A big bowl of ice cream with frozen strawberries on top. Or maybe a frozen pizza. We won't even thaw the sucker out. We'll just break off chunks and wash 'em down with a nice cold milkshake. Whaddya think?"

"I think your brain must be frozen." Toby sighed.

"I think you're right." Lamont tugged gently on the towrope and began walking again, shifting the rope from hand to hand every few steps, flexing his numbed fingers. The cold was getting to him now. He wasn't really dressed for it in his denim jacket and jeans, but as long as he kept moving it wasn't too bad. His cowboy boots were his biggest mistake. They offered poor traction on the ice and no protection against the cold. His legs felt like they belonged to somebody else. He shifted the rope again without missing a step.

The throaty roar of a couple of snowmobiles playing tag on the ice downriver drifted by on the wind. Not much farther now, a hundred yards or so to the shore, and the truck.

He paused, letting the sled glide to a halt behind him. Where was the truck? He scanned the jumble of drifts along the riverbank, squinting against the glare. Where had he parked the damn pickup?

Voices. Somebody was shouting. Two figures were silhouetted on the bank, bundled like Eskimos, waving at him, yelling something. What—?

"Papa?" Toby said.

Lamont glanced back at him. Water. The sled was sitting in a shallow puddle. Sweet Jesus! More was seeping up through fissures in the ice, lapping at the sled runners. He stared at it for a moment, paralyzed, then lunged forward, trying to drag the sled clear of the widening pool.

His left foot broke through the surface plate and the frozen slush clamped it like a vise. He tried to jerk his foot free, lost his balance, and stumbled to his knees in the puddle. It was spreading, gurgling up through the ice even faster now. He reached forward as far as he could, both wrists in the icy water, straining desperately for some leverage—and then the pack moaned and collapsed, plunging him into the freezing dark.

The bone-chilling shock of the river surging through his clothing drove the breath from him. The current was alive beneath the surface, tugging at him, sucking him down. Toby! Couldn't see him. He glimpsed blurred light glinting through the jumble of ice somewhere above him. He thrust himself toward it with one last despairing lunge, senses fading, going dark, legs faltering. The towrope slipped through his numbed fingers. One last push toward the light . . .

"Papa?"

Lamont jerked upright in the bed, the stab from the IV unit in his wrist snapping him instantly, painfully awake. Emergency room? No, not anymore. He remembered being moved. His bed was in an open ward now, a long, narrow room like a prison barrack, dimly lit, with beds on both sides of the aisle, some curtained off with green sheets, some not. The old cop and the faggot chaplain had visited him here—how long ago? Hours. It must have been hours ago. No Toby. They hadn't found Toby Red. He was still down in the dark water. Under the ice. My God. My—

"Hey, mister?"

3

A teenaged face was peering at him solemnly from beneath the partially lifted curtain on the next bed. Dark eyes, dark hair. A wetback maybe.

"Hey, they told me about what happened," the kid said softly. "I'm really sorry—"

"Butt the fuck out," Lamont hissed.

"I just wanted to . . ." The boy's voice wavered and trailed off, silenced by Lamont's icy stare. The curtain fell back into place.

Lamont slumped to his pillow, then immediately straightened again, gagging on the rush of bile that surged in his throat. The taste of the river, oily and foul. He was sitting up, swallowing rapidly, when he heard voices.

A choir. Singing.

People were singing out in the hallway at the end of the ward. Not a radio or TV. People.

Blacks.

What the hell? In the middle of the goddam night?

"Hey, kid," Lamont said quietly, "what's goin' on out there? What's all the noise?"

If the boy in the next bed heard him, he gave no sign.

Lamont listened intently for several minutes. The singing continued, echoing hollowly through the shadowy ward.

Throwing his blankets aside, he swung his legs carefully over the side of the bed and stood up. A mistake. The ward tilted sharply on its axis and the cool tile floor seemed to shudder and flex beneath his bare feet.

He waited a moment for the room to steady, then tried a tentative step. The IV unit tugged sharply at his wrist, tethering him to the bed. He ripped off the adhesive pad, yanked the needle out, and threw it aside, sending the bottle and its support stand crashing to the floor. Then he staggered off down the aisle toward the open doorway, leaving a trail of crimson droplets behind him like a wounded animal.

CHAPTER 2

"**S**IGH-A-LENT NIGHT, HOOOLY NIGHT . . ." THE SALVATION army trio bellowed, in excruciating harmony. Their heavy woolen uniforms were rimed with street salt sprayed by passing traffic, and they were ruddy-faced from trying to outshout the canned carols blaring from the Sears store entrance behind them. Still, they hung in there gamely, and Garcia admired their tenacity if not their tenor. He dropped a couple of bucks into the red charity bucket as he passed, then eased casually into the shadows by the store entrance, keeping the singers between himself and the four whores working the bus stop on the corner.

He'd been eyeing the hookers for ten minutes or so, waiting. They were definitely pros, two blacks and two whites, dressed to the nines in miniskirts, thigh-high boots, and fake furs, but cool about it. No outright propositions, just a look, maybe a cocked hip, a raised eyebrow at a passing car or a likely john. Enough to get the message across without attracting Sears security people. And if a prowl car happened to cruise by, the girls were just Christmas shoppers waiting for the bus.

5

Traffic was heavy on the strip tonight, suburbanites braving the light snowfall to try a little downtown shopping, college kids on Christmas break checking the action, maybe trolling for crack or a walk on the wild side. Garcia flipped up the collar of his leather trenchcoat, hunching his shoulders against the icy wind off the Detroit, wishing to Christ he'd worn some earmuffs. And then he spotted Cordell, shouldering his way through the strollers, wearing a bulky navy peacoat with a watch cap pulled low over his ears.

Cordell paused beside Garcia in the shadows, shook out a pack of Marlboros, and lit up.

"Nice you could drop by," Garcia said.

"Got hung up in traffic." Cordell grunted, his chiseled features an ebony mask in the flare of his Bic. "You make him yet?"

"I think he's one of the hookers working the bus stop."

Cordell half-turned, gave the ladies the once-over, then shook his head. "You gotta be shittin' me. One of them honeys is Harvey?"

"So I'm told. When I busted him four years ago he was just a fruit hustler, but he's supposed to be a full-time transvestite now. Dresses like a fox, gives head and hand jobs right in the car, and the johns never guess. Unless of course they try to get *really* romantic. At which time Harvey flashes a straight razor. Gotta be a helluva rush, especially if he's holdin' your shlong at the time."

"So which one you figure he is?"

"I'm not sure," Garcia said. "He's black, so that narrows it down a little. Maybe the one in the red dress and the phony leopard coat. The build's about right."

Cordell glanced over at the bus stop again. "Red dress? The tall, skinny one? You sure?"

"Hell, no, I'm not sure. The one in the white plastic raincoat's the right size too, and the last time I saw the guy he was still wearing a goatee."

"He sure as hell don't have one now," Cordell said, "least not where it shows. So whaddya think? You want a closer look?"

"I don't know if it'd help. Without the goatee and wearing makeup . . ." Garcia shrugged. "Tell you what, how about you

6

stroll past and wait on the corner. I'll ease on up, say hello, and if he rabbits, he'll run right into your arms."

"He better. I don't wanna be chasin' anybody in this slop."

"How fast can a guy run in spike heels?" Garcia said. "Go ahead on."

Cordell eased his bulk into the flow of pedestrians. He kept his head down as he passed the bus stop, avoiding eye contact with the hookers. Garcia waited until the big man was in place, then sauntered over. A heavyset white mama in a fake rabbit fur coat and Tina Turner wig eyed him hopefully as he ambled up, then sniffed and turned away as he tapped the slender hooker in the red dress lightly on the shoulder.

"So, Harvey," Garcia said softly, "how you been doin'?"

The woman glanced around, startled, and Garcia knew instantly he'd made a mistake. She wasn't Harvey. But the hooker in the wet-look white raincoat flashed him a startled glance, let out a wail, and sprinted past him toward the store entrance, kicking off her shoes on the way.

The heavy mama in the rabbit fur clamped onto Garcia's arm. "Hold on, sucker, whatchu think—?"

Garcia tried to push her off, slipped in the slush, and they both went down in a tangled heap. Cursing, red-dress swung her purse at his head, catching him flush on the cheek, spinning him half off his feet as he pulled free and stumbled into the crowd after Harvey, with Cordell only a few paces behind.

He caught a flash of white raincoat as he bulled through the crush at the store entrance. Juking around a red babushka'd grandmother with an aluminum walker, he broke into a lope, bobbing and weaving through the shoppers like an NFL half-back. Up ahead, Harvey lunged onto the down escalator and vaulted up the steps three at a time screaming, *"Heelllp! Raaape!"* at the top of his lungs.

A pudgy salesman in a green blazer stepped tentatively into the aisle, blocking Garcia's path. "Hold on a minute, you—"

"Police!" Garcia snapped. "Get out of the way!" He stiff-armed the guy aside harder than he'd intended, with a forearm shot that sent him reeling off-balance into a pyramid wristwatch display, toppling the tower of Timexes across a plate-glass jewelry counter in an explosion of rhinestones and crystal splinters. Shoppers and clerks were shouting now, competing with Miss Peggy Lee on the PA, Peace on earth, goodwill to men.

A few steps from the top of the escalator, Harvey was blocked by a fashionably frowsy yuppie matron with one baby in a backpack and another in a stroller beside her. He tried to vault over the stroller but his long legs tangled in the frame and he went down hard, gashing his forehead on the steel-ribbed steps. Cursing, he kicked free, tumbling the stroller down the escalator at Garcia, who barely managed to block it with his chest, tasting blood and steel as the metal handle caught him sharply in the mouth.

Garcia jammed the stroller handle into the hands of a startled teenybopper, charged past the screaming mother, and leaped into space as he cleared the top of the escalator. His outstretched fingers barely brushed Harvey's slim ankle, but it was enough to sweep the hooker's feet from beneath him, sending him skidding headlong down the aisle.

Garcia scrambled after Harvey like a dog, on his hands and knees, sprawling on top of him, fumbling for his wrists, and ducking as the hooker slashed at his face with blood-red finger-nails.

"*Heelllp! Raape! Somebody help me, pleease!*" Harvey's wail cut through the hubbub like an air raid siren as Garcia struggled to pin one hand behind his back. "*Raaape!*"

"Awright, freeze, asshole! Get your hands in the air and get offa her!"

Garcia risked a quick glance, still grappling with Harvey. A pasty-faced security guard, all of twenty years old in an oversized uniform, was crouched in a perfect combat stance off to his left. The kid's .38 was aimed right at Garcia's head, its muzzle so close he could count the soft-nosed slugs in the cylinder.

"Police," Garcia said, gasping. "This man's a murder suspect. He—" Garcia ducked as Harvey tried to rake his throat.

"Goddammit, I said get offa her!" the guard yelled. "Now do it!"

"You stupid bastard, put your damn gun away! I'm a cop!" Garcia freed one of Harvey's wrists long enough to reach for his badge.

"Keep your hands where I can see 'em!" the guard screeched, wild-eyed, earing back the hammer on his .38.

"How the fuck can I show you a badge if—?" Harvey's elbow caught Garcia full in the mouth, snapping his head around. "Dammit!" Garcia backhanded Harvey, then snaked a forearm around the hooker's throat and jerked him upright, wrestling him into the security cop's line of fire. "You wanna shoot now, asshole, be my guest! But you're gonna be in a world of shit! Now listen, I'm a police officer, Detective Sergeant Garcia, Metro Homicide. This guy's wanted for quest—"

"He's lyin'!" Harvey screamed. "He's crazy! Tryin' to rape me! You seen him! You're my witness!"

"Mi-mister," the guard stammered, shifting his position to line up his weapon on Garcia's head, "I don't know what the fuck you're tryna pull, but you better let that woman go, right now! And get your hands in the air!"

"Jesus Christ, if I let him go he'll rabbit, and I just chased him halfway— Look, just hang loose, okay? My partner'll be here in a second. *Cordell! Come on*, goddammit!"

"No!" Harvey wailed. "Don't listen to him!"

"Police officer! Out of the way!" Cordell shouldered through the jam at the head of the escalator, and took in the situation at a glance. "Okay, okay! Now everybody cool out. We're police officers." He eased his ID out of his peacoat pocket and walked slowly toward the guard, showing him his bronze. "Now, boy, you ease that hammer down before you hurt somebody."

"Don't do it!" Harvey pleaded. "He crazy! They both crazy rape-os. They kill us all!"

The guard was sweating, his eyes blinking rapidly. He swung his weapon to cover Cordell. "Get over by your friend," he said, swallowing, "and tell him to get off the woman. Somebody call the police!"

"Dammit, we are the police!" Garcia shouted. "And this turkey isn't a woman, you dumb fuck! Look, I'll prove it, okay! You

9

know the difference between boys and girls, asshole? Well, check this out!" He grabbed the shoulders of Harvey's red dress and ripped downward, stripping the hooker to the waist. And bared two perfectly formed cantaloupe-sized breasts, dark-nippled and quivering, the surgical implant scars neatly camouflaged by a faint trace of body makeup.

"*Raape!*" Harvey shrieked, trying to cover himself.

"Terrific." Garcia sighed, feeling the muzzle of the rent-a-cop's .38 press against his temple. "Just terrific."

CHAPTER 3

S OMEBODY WAS WHISTLING "THE STRIPPER" AS GARCIA AND CORDELL stalked into the squad room to a smattering of applause. Garcia scanned the forty-by-forty grimy crackerbox office but couldn't spot the whistler. It didn't matter. He had the feeling he'd be hearing the song again. Often.

The squad room was half empty, thank God. Marv Cream was hammering away on his IBM, Bobby Pilarski was refilling the coffee machine, the U of Detroit preppies, Keller and Wilk, were batting the breeze with a reporter from the *News*, probably comparing squash scores. Garcia slumped into his swivel chair at the battered, gunmetal gray desk he shared with Cordell, put his feet up, and then promptly took them down again as the captain's office door opened and Joad came storming out, headed in their direction. Even angry, the guy couldn't resist pausing at Lt. Al Fielder's desk for a courtesy call, or giving Marv Cream a backslap as he passed. Just one of the troops, with his too-good-to-be-true custom toop and seven-hundred-dollar suit.

Garcia glanced across the cluttered desk at Cordell. His partner

11

was rumpled, his paisley tie was askew, his gray-streaked Afro needed a trim, and he was at least thirty pounds over departmental guidelines. But a far better cop than Joad had ever been. And with the instincts of a born survivor, Cordell was already looking busy, banging away on his Selectric with his two-finger hunt-and-peck system. Garcia considered following his example, but decided the hell with it. Maybe if he frowned, it'd pass for deep thought.

"Gentlemen," Joad said coolly, perching a fleshy thigh on the edge of the desk, "I won't ask what happened. I was getting detailed complaints about it before your suspect had his dress back on, a dress, I might add, that's coming out of your checks. So what's the bottom line on him? Is he a live one or not?"

"No, sir." Cordell sighed. "Don't look like it. He's in a halfway house program for guys havin' sex changes. Got rock-solid alibis for at least two of the killings. He was at support group meetings with ten witnesses. Looks like he's clean."

"Which means I'll be hearing from his lawyer shortly, right?"

"Harvey can't sue anybody, Captain," Cordell said patiently. "He's still on parole. If he gives us any static, we can violate him for hookin' and he knows it."

"Well, that's something, at least. Now all I have to do is figure a way to explain your Keystone Kops routine to the press. And speaking of the press, your little peepshow last night may be the least of our problems. Chas Mullery was in to see me this morning. It seems the *Free Press* is planning a feature on these killings. I tried to talk him out of it, but he's got his orders. What can you feed him?"

"Feed him?" Garcia echoed. "Captain, we only got plugged into this thing last week. We've barely had time to hit the scenes and read the damn reports—"

"Look, nobody's asking you to walk on water, Garcia, but Mullery's going to write *something*, and we'd better hope to hell it isn't another Motown/Murder City piece, or we'll all be directing traffic down on the Corridor. Give me a quick rundown on exactly what you've got."

"Captain, we can't give the Freep a thing that's gonna look any way but bad," Garcia said. "Three homicides in the past three weeks. Victims: female, throats slashed in their cars after dark, one each in East Detroit, Romulus, and Dearborn Heights. No robbery or rape, though their underclothing was cut up, possibly so the perp could fondle them. Except for elevated blood alcohol levels, the victims didn't have much in common, different ages, backgrounds, et cetera. No witnesses."

"What about suspects?"

"We've got suspects up the ying, a shit list with about sixty names on it. Marv Cream's taking A through L, Cordell and I've got M through Z. We've got five or six live ones, guys with priors or who were suspects in similar homicides."

"Progress?"

"Well, we got one less suspect than we had yesterday," Cordell offered.

"Not funny, mister," Joad snapped. "And you're not going to find my comments on your E-vals funny either. Now listen up. If Mullery talks to you two, you tell him the investigation's proceeding blah, blah, the usual."

"He won't buy it," Garcia said, "especially not from me."

"Maybe not, but he's a pretty good troop, and maybe he'll print it anyway. So if he asks, arrests are imminent, right?"

"Sure." Cordell sighed. "Any day now."

"Good, And I've got a name to add to your list. At the top." Joad flipped a memo onto the jumble of reports on Garcia's desk. "I got a call this morning from the community relations director at U Hospital. We golf occasionally, so he laid this situation on me, hoping we could help. Did you read about a guy and his kid falling through the ice near River Rouge yesterday? They hauled the man out but the boy drowned?"

"What were they doin' out there?" Cordell frowned. "The ice is usually posted near the river mouth."

"I gather they were just walking around, didn't see the signs. The guy's from Tennessee, what's he supposed to know about ice? Anyway, they took him to U emergency, and patched him up. This morning, one A.M., they find him in an elderly woman's room, yelling about something. They hustled him back to his

13

own bed, but meanwhile, the old lady expires, apparently of natural causes."

"So?" Garcia said.

"So as they're clearing up, they noticed her oxygen had been turned off. And they're not clear on when it happened."

"And they think the guy may have snuffed her?" Garcia asked.

"They're . . . concerned," Joad said. "If the guy did cut off her oxygen for some reason, and confesses to it later, the hospital might have a problem."

"Every hospital's got that problem. It's called liability lotto. Too bad. What's it got to do with us?"

"There's more. I had Wilk run an LEIN check on the gentleman in question, a Mr. Lamont Stacy Yarborough. It seems Mr. Yarborough did time, at Brushy Mountain. For murdering a woman."

"Who'd he kill? Wife?"

"That's right. Shotgun, I believe."

"Captain, that hardly makes him a candidate for our list," Garcia said carefully. "As I'm sure you're aware, spouse killers rarely repeat."

"I think the death of his son and the old lady changes that. In any case I want you to look into it."

"Let me see if I've got this straight," Garcia said. "You're asking us to help out your golfing buddy by having a little talk with this Yarborough, on the off chance he's gonna cop to pulling the old lady's plug? Because unless he confesses, there's no case against him at all."

"That's about the size of it," Joad conceded coolly, "except for the 'asking' part."

"Terrific. Well, you're the man in charge. Is this guy still in the hospital?"

"No, he checked himself out first thing this morning. Sounds like a fairly sturdy individual, doesn't he?"

"Or maybe he didn't have his Blue Cross paid up," Cordell offered.

Garcia glanced at the address on the memo. Harry's Riverview Trailer Court. "Two to one on no insurance," he said.

Harry's Riverview was nearly a mile from the Detroit River, and the only view it offered was of a couple of support columns for a Fisher Freeway overpass. It looked like an elephant's graveyard where old mobile homes rolled off to die, a dozen rows of decaying hulks with sagging roofs and rust-streaked walls. The address on Joad's memo was for the last trailer at the end of a rutted, unpaved lane, the end of the line in more ways than one. A late-model Ford pickup truck, metallic brown with oversize tires, was parked next to a battered blue Chevette in front of the trailer. Garcia swung his grubby gray city Chrylser in beside the pickup.

"What do you think?" Cordell said. "You want the front door or the back?"

"There's no point in both of us going. We can't roust the guy, and if he did hard time at Brushy Mountain he's probably not into interracial harmony. Why don't I just talk to him for about thirty seconds and we'll grab some lunch someplace."

"Okay by me." Cordell eased back in his seat. "But if you run into a problem, like maybe this ladykiller ex-con doesn't feel like talkin' to a cop the day after his kid drowns, you just holler. 'Course, you might wanna holler real loud. I'll be catchin' some z's."

"Terrific. Just don't let some kid pop the wheels off this heap, okay? I got a date tonight."

"You're takin' this on a date?"

"My 'bird's in for service."

"You want me to keep the motor runnin' in case you need a fast getaway?"

"Nah, go ahead and zonk. If the guy's super-bad I'll probably just beat feet home. I'll try to remember to rap on your window on my way by."

"Good," Cordell said, folding his arms and resting his head against the passenger window, "you do that."

A woman answered Garcia's knock, and his spirits dropped a notch. She'd recently suffered a few knocks of her own. She was

15

nearly as tall as he was, just under six feet, a raw-boned woman, mid-thirtyish, with dark, steady brown eyes and a thick mane of unevenly rinsed red hair. She was wearing a faded blue flannel shirt and jeans. Her left eye was swollen and she had a nasty bruise along her jawline.

"Mrs. Yarborough?"

"No." She frowned. "There ain't no Mrs. Yarborough. You a reporter?"

"Police, ma'am," Garcia said, showing her his shield. "I'm Sergeant Garcia. Is there a Lamont Yarborough living here?"

"Did you find the body?"

"The body?"

"Toby's body. Is that why you're here?"

"No, I'm afraid I don't know anything about that, ma'am. I, ah, just need to talk to Mr. Yarborough. Is he here?"

"You just need to talk to him?" she echoed dully. "Well, what the hell, everybody else has. Thing is, I don't think he feels much like talkin' anymore."

"It'll only take a minute."

"Might not even take that long. You wanna talk to him, you go on ahead. He's in back playin' his damn guitar, but for God's sake try not to rile him, okay? Place is enough of a mess as it is."

"I'll do my best, ma'am." Garcia sighed, picturing Joad roasting slowly on a spit over white-hot coals. "Believe me, I don't want to, ah, rile anybody."

The mobile home's interior was a little nicer than Garcia expected. The decor was Early Salvation Army, but it was clean. There were brightly patterned plastic curtains on the windows and yellow artificial carnations in a bowl on the kitchen table. Somebody cared about the place, but it still looked like the employees' lounge at a scrap yard.

Garcia followed the sound of the guitar down the narrow hallway that ran the length of the trailer. The song was a melancholy country blues, played with surprising skill.

The door at the end of the hall was closed. Garcia knocked once and pushed it open. The room was a small den, a rack of stereo equipment against one wall with albums scattered on the

16

floor around it, a homemade gun rack with a 30/30 carbine and a couple of shotguns in one corner, a portable TV in the other. Lamont Yarborough was sitting at a black vinyl studio bar on an unsteady chrome bar stool, cradling a maroon electric guitar in his arms, his fingers dancing lightly over steel strings.

He was a few inches over six feet, Garcia guessed, fortyish maybe, lean as a crowbar, and prison-yard hard. He was barefoot, wearing worn denims and a faded blue Willie Nelson T-shirt. A dark shock of hair hung in his eyes. A black eagle tattoo glared from his left bicep. Lost in the song, he didn't notice Garcia at first. Then he paused in midphrase to reach for a nearly empty fifth of Jack Daniels on the bar. Neither man spoke for a moment, sizing each other up across the littered room.

"That was, ah, nice," Garcia said at last. "You play very well."

"It's what I do," Lamont said. He picked up a roll-your-own cigarette from the ashtray on the bar, took a deep drag, and let it out slowly, squinting at Garcia through the smoke. "Who the fuck are you anyway?"

"My name's Garcia. I used to play a little guitar myself, back in high school, you know, parties and stuff. That's a nice old guitar. A Gretsch, isn't it?"

"A Country Gentleman," Lamont said, nodding. "And you're a cop. Don't bother flashin' a badge at me. I can tell by the jailhouse smell. So what do you want? Am I busted?"

"Busted? For what?"

"For killin' Toby. Willa Mae had me arrested once for back child support. I imagine she'll try to get me lynched for lettin' the kid drown."

"Willa Mae's your ex-wife?"

"One of 'em."

"The only one still breathing?"

Yarborough stared blearily at him a moment, then shrugged. "Matter of fact she is," he said at last. He fumbled for the ashtray, missed it, and ground his cigarette out on the bar. "Got a Smith and Wesson divorce from my first. Probably shoulda ex-ed Willa the same way, but she wasn't worth doin' the time for. Nothin' is. Liked that boy though, Toby." He picked up the fifth and took a

17

long deep pull straight from the bottle, swaying a little on the stool, and wiped his mouth with the back of his hand. "That's Toby on the wall there."

Garcia threaded his way through the albums on the floor to a group of photographs above the stereo, turning casually to avoid showing Yarborough his back. There were only two snapshots, one of a younger Lamont wearing bib overalls, standing with a grizzled old man in front of a tarpaper shack. Beside it was a color photograph of a frail, red-haired eight-year-old staring uncomfortably at him from a plastic K Mart frame.

"He looks a lot like you."

"Don't know why he should, bein' I'm not his father. Hell, Willa probably couldn't guess who his father was if ya gave her the guy's initials. I adopted him though. Gave him a name. Boy's gotta have a name. Even paid child support when I could after me and Willa split. Nice kid. Quiet. Never had to whup him much. Toby Red I called him, 'cause of his hair. He—" He coughed and took another pull from the bottle. "He'd stay with me summers and holidays and such. We always had us a good time. I been teachin' him guitar. Pretty good little picker too. That's his guitar over there in the corner, the three-quarter size Gibson. My woman, Jobeth, bought it for him. He played it real nice. 'Wildwood Flower,' songs like that, he . . ." Lamont looked away, clenching his jaw, trying to clamp off the trembling in his voice. "You don't care about any of this," he said abruptly. "What do you want?"

"Mr. Yarborough, I'm sorry about your boy."

"I told you he wasn't mine and this ain't no social call," Lamont said, laying his guitar aside on the bar. "Now I asked you what you want. I ain't askin' again."

Garcia hesitated, sensing violence smoldering in Lamont only one wrong word away. The booze was making it worse, but it would be there anytime, like a gas leak in a smokers' lounge.

"Mr. Yarborough, last night at University Hospital, you were found in a woman's room. They said you were . . . shouting. You want to tell me about that?"

18

"Tell you—? That's what you're here about," Lamont said, astonished, "the blacks?"

"What blacks?"

"Singin'. In the old lady's room. I could hear 'em clear down in the ward. Nurses said I musta had a dream, maybe tripped out from the downers they gave me, hell, I don't know. It wasn't about nothin' anyway. I just told 'em to knock it off is all."

"Told who to knock it off?"

"The people singing. The blacks."

"You mean you were sleepwalking or—"

"No, goddammit, I was awake! Or I thought I was. Look, I ain't real clear on what happened and I don't really give a shit. Toby Red's in the damn river and you're hasslin' me about this crap? Mister, you'd best be movin' along."

"I suppose so." Garcia nodded. "Look, I'm sorry I had to bother you, I know it's a bad time . . ." But Lamont wasn't listening. He'd picked up his guitar and began playing again, the same mournful blues.

"That really is nice," Garcia said quietly. "You do good work."

"You dig it so much you can come hear me down to Roy's Country Crossing out in Romulus. I'm doin' six nights a week there with Sonny Earle. Might wanna call first, though." He glanced up, his empty blue eyes meeting Garcia's. "I ain't sure they serve spicks."

"Maybe I'll drop by some night," Garcia said evenly, "or maybe I'll come back here. On business. Either way, the next time I see your woman, I hope she's looking better. It's not her fault you're hurting."

"No," Lamont said, releasing a long ragged breath, "I know it's not. And I didn't beat on her, if that's what you think. A man don't hit women, or at least I don't. That's not what they're for."

"Right." Garcia nodded. "By the way, what's that song you're playing? I don't think I know it."

"You don't. I'm just workin' it up. Probably won't amount to much. Most of my stuff doesn't. You know that old song where the guy finds his woman dead in a long black limousine? This one's gonna be somethin' like that. It's called 'Blood Red

19

Cadillac.' Don't sound likely to get a barroom full of people goin'
wahoo, does it?"

"Maybe not," Garcia said, "but it's still good."

The woman was washing dishes in the kitchen sink, up to her
elbows in soapy water, dull-eyed, wisps of hair trailing over her
ears. She didn't even look up when Garcia touched her gently on
the shoulder.

"Look, ah, Jobeth, maybe it's none of my business, but have
you got somewhere to go if things get out of hand here? Friends
you can stay with, maybe?"

She shook her head, scrubbing away like an automaton. "I got
no reason to go. Nothing happened that was his fault, and I can't
leave him now. Not now."

"You know, there's a crisis center that—look, I'll tell you what,
if you need help, you call me. Here's my card, okay? Day or
night, you call me."

She glanced up for a moment, measuring him with her eyes.
"You figure you can handle him?"

"I don't know. I can try."

CHAPTER 4

"**D**O YOU THINK SHE'LL ACTUALLY CALL YOU SOMETIME?" Linda Kerry asked. She was wandering casually around the kitchen of Garcia's apartment, sipping a glass of Chablis blanc, wearing a severe navy blue dress that would have passed muster at a convent. A bright, blond, lanky lady, one you'd want on your side in a semifriendly touch football game. Or any other time.

"I hope not." Garcia retrieved a head of lettuce from the grocery bag on the counter, peeled and discarded the outer leaves, and began tearing the rest. "One, I don't think she'd call unless she was in big trouble; two, the guy's bigger than I am, mean as a snake and an ex-con to boot; plus, when you interfere in a family hassle, you never know which side who's on, and she's nearly as big as he is."

"But if she's asked for help?"

"Women call for help in a family fight when they're angry, or afraid, or hurt, but the key word's 'family.' If you try to restrain or arrest the guy, you can wind up waltzing around with everybody. Maybe it's the maternal instinct, I don't know. How are your maternal instincts?"

21

"Solid enough, I think. But if the goon squad came to haul you off I could probably hold myself in check. I'd miss your cooking, though."

"And rightly so. Do you like your tomatoes sliced, or quartered?"

"Sliced, then quartered. And there was something in your tone when you said he was an ex-con."

"Maybe I'm catching a cold."

"You know what I mean. Do you automatically distrust ex-convicts? I mean, after they've served their sentences aren't they supposed to be more or less square with society?"

"Technically maybe. You know, you try not to get a hard—ah, not to develop a negative attitude about cons, the same way you try not to let inner-city street duty turn you into a racist, but it's hard sometimes. They've already survived the worst society can do to them, and a lot of 'em would rather die than go back. Very touchy people. I'd rather roust Girl Scouts anytime."

"Then why did you leave the lady your card?"

"Damned if I know. She was washing dishes, you know, by hand? In the sink. Had a mouse under her eye. How heavy do you like the garlic in your garlic bread?"

"You're the chef. Season to taste, I think the phrase is. I probably won't do it justice anyway. Ten pounds to lose."

"I don't think you need to lose ten pounds. Or any pounds. You look fine to me."

"Two points for tact, minus three for dishonesty."

"Mary Travers," he said.

"Who?"

"Mary Travers. 'Blowin' in the Wind'? Before your time, like almost everybody else I like. You ever listen to folk music? Peter, Paul, and Mary? You remind me a little of Mary Travers, a very classy lady."

"I remember her. Chubby Mary, we used to call her. She needed to lose ten pounds too. And you're not that much older than I am. You're what, early thirties?"

"Almost forty, and no cracks, okay? I haven't had my midlife crisis yet. I've been meaning to, just haven't had time."

"You're kidding. You're really forty?"

"Thirty-eight. You want to cancel dinner?"

"Don't be so touchy. I would have guessed you were . . . much younger, that's all. Count your blessings. You're tall, dark, and presentable, certainly too young for a midlife crisis. And you don't have ten pounds to lose either."

"If you want to starve, be my guest. More munchies for me. Be less of you to love though." He felt the temperature in the room drop two or three degrees. He concentrated on slicing the tomatoes to perfection.

"Mmmm. Look, Garcia, we've known each other, what, a couple of weeks?" She moved very close behind him, almost touching his left shoulder. "And I'm less than six months out of . . . a bad marriage. I'd rather that word didn't get bandied about."

"Which word? Starve?"

"Don't be a jerk. Ground rules, okay?"

"Okay. I give you fair warning though, I'm a romantic. Old movies, old cars, poetry that rhymes. You want to shake the salad dressing?"

"Sure." She mixed the vinegar and oil with an easy up and down motion. He steeled himself to keep from staring at her breasts. Delicate situation here. He sensed it the way he sensed violence in some people, or guilt. Or which clown in a crowd of drunks was blitzed enough to take the first swing. It was becoming very important to him not to screw this up.

"Just one further thought, while we're talking rules," he said. "We've talked shop and I've bored you with cop stories, but this thing with Yarborough is the first time we've talked about a case in progress. It stays between you and me, okay? I mean, if you wanted to do a story about it, fine, but I'd want to talk it over first."

"The only stories they're giving me at the Freep are fluff stuff for the Tempo section, movies, fashion shows, all that junk. Is this guy a fashion plate, do you think?"

"Maybe for *Psychology Today*. I'm serious though. Ground rules."

23

"I guess rules are something you're heavy into, right?" she said coolly. "Justice, that sort of thing?"

"No, ma'am. Justice lives in heaven. I do business in Detroit. Any way I can."

"Fair enough. Is scorching the spaghetti sauce a specialty of yours, or is it time to eat?"

Garcia thought the dinner went well. Almost everything edible got eaten, the conversation was good, but not self-consciously so. And at one point she'd cupped his cheek with her palm when he said something nice. He wanted to say it again but her touch seemed to blank his memory. Or maybe it was Alzheimer's.

She wandered out to the sofa after helping him clear up. The evening had an easy, comfortable feel to it, but with a definite tang of musk in the air. Linda relaxed, leaning back into the cushions, slipped off her flats, and rested her feet on the coffee table.

He rummaged through his cassettes, decided on Joni Mitchell, and popped her into the stereo. Humming along with Joni, he carried two snifters of Courvosier into the living room, passed one to Linda, and eased down on the couch beside her, close, but not too. It wasn't the time for the big push. Yet. Easy does it.

"I remember that song. What is it?"

"'Free Man in Paris.' Joni Mitchell."

"Were you ever a free man in Paris?"

"Nope. Only in—ah, nope, I just like the song."

"Only in where? What were you going to say?"

"You're gonna be an ace reporter, you know that?"

"I *am* an ace, they just haven't noticed yet. And you're ducking the question."

"Hong Kong. I was in Hong Kong once."

"Why Hong Kong?"

"Nope, your turn. I cooked, you talk. Fair is fair."

"What about?"

"Anything. Pretend I'm your cat. What do you tell your cat?"

"Everything. More than I'd ever tell you. Or my mother, for that matter. Want to hear me carp and whine about my career?"

24

"Absolutely. Carp away." And he meant it. Listening to Linda was almost a sensual experience. Her voice was husky velvet, like Bacall's in *Key Largo*. He sipped his brandy, feeling the glow spread down from the base of his throat, following her drift without really hearing the words, enveloped in her warmth, her scent, and the sound of her voice. He watched her gently rotate her brandy, warming it, and noticed a spray of freckles on her wrist. He was wondering if she had more of them, and where, when suddenly it dawned on him that it was time for the big move. Or at least a move. And he nuzzled her wrist as she talked, and she pretended not to notice at first, and kept talking, trying to keep from giggling as he nibbled the hollow of her elbow, but failing in the end.

"What do you think you're doing?" She smiled, tugging her arm away, shifting around to face him.

"Dessert? I forgot to make any."

"Is that what I am? The next course?"

"Nope, unless you'd like to volunteer."

"I'm not sure," she said, mock seriously, searching his eyes. "Maybe I might." She leaned forward slowly and kissed him full on the mouth, gently at first, but with a hint of urgency. And then the beeper beside the phone began *meee meee meee*-ing, and blew the moment.

"Does that mean you have to go out?"

"I don't know yet, but I have to call in." He reached across her for the phone on the end table and nearly forgot why he wanted it. Al Fielder took the call and gave him a quick briefing. Garcia checked his watch as he listened. Ten after eleven. Jesus, no wonder Fielder made lieutenant. "I've got to go," he said, hanging up. "They think they've found another woman."

"I'd like to come along, if you wouldn't mind. I won't get in the way," she added hastily, "and I'm an accredited member of the press."

"Look, this isn't going to be something for the Tempo section. It's going to be cold, and if it's like the others, it'll be ugly."

"I did volunteer work in a VA hospital for four years. I've seen

25

things that weren't pretty. And I don't want to be stuck covering flower shows forever. So how about it? Please."

"You'll have to bring your own car," he said. "No civilians in police vehicles. Sorry about that."

"No problem. Can I have two minutes to run up to my apartment and put some slacks on?"

"Take five. There's no rush. The car's still in the river."

CHAPTER 5

THE GLARE OF THE HALOGEN FLOODLIGHTS FROM THE ROOF-RACK of the huge Metro wrecker lit up the riverbank like a moonscape, throwing the jagged ruts where the car had gone over into sharp relief. Two prowl cars, beacons whirling in the dark, were parked at forty-five-degree angles to the site, adding their headlights to the scene. A young patrol cop was tying yellow police-line tapes to portable barricades around the area, while two more waved motorists past with orange-coned flashlights.

The car was nose down in a watery pool of broken ice, with only its roof and part of the trunk visible above the waterline. A team of uniformed crime lab techs was already taking Polaroid photos and measuring distances along the bank.

Garcia and Bennett watched in silence as the wrecker driver scrambled cautiously away from the car after hooking a steel tow cable to its frame. Cursing, with water streaming down the right sleeve of his grimy coveralls, he climbed onto the bed of the wrecker, a shadow figure outlined in the lights. He slammed down the lever engaging the winch. The drum began to rotate slowly, lifting the cable out of the snow, drawing it taut. The wrecker bucked and slid a few inches closer to the river, straining, rocking on its oversized tires, its engine howling in the night.

Then, with an audible sigh, the water seemed to release its hold. The car began backing out of the pool, slithering toward the bank like a dazed prehistoric insect, an inch at a time.

"How did they know it was a woman?" Gracia shouted at Cordell over the roar of the wrecker.

"Two kids driving by, probably looking for a place to park, maybe smoke a joint, you know? They see the car in the river, half in, half out of the ice. Whoever pushed it in probably figured it'd break through and sink right away, but apparently it took a while. Anyway, the boy scrambled out there to take a look, didn't even bother with Emergency Rescue, just told nine-one-one to call us."

"Any tracks?"

"About four hundred sets. Take your choice."

"What do you think? Any chance of the kids as suspects?"

"Don't seem likely. You see that little brown patch on the ice next to the front door? That's where the kid coughed up his cookies when he looked in the window."

Garcia nodded, glancing around the scene. Linda Kerry was huddled with an ashen-faced teenager next to a '74 gold Camaro with primer spots and a jacked rear end. She looked like a snow bunny in her powder blue ski jacket and headband, barely older than the boy, but she was listening intently as he talked, nodding in sympathy and getting it all down in a small reporter's notepad. When Garcia glanced back, the entire trunk section of the death car was clear of the water.

"Sweet Jesus," he said softly, "it's a Cadillac."

"Right," Cordell said, hugging himself, trying to keep warm. "Things are definitely gettin' outa hand. Bad enough the guy's snuffed three women, now he's drownin' Caddies. We don't nail him pretty soon, the pimps'll put a picket line around the station."

"That guy I talked to this afternoon, the redneck? He was working on a song, about a car, a blood red Cadillac."

28

Cordell eyed him doubtfully, then snorted. "You're puttin' me on."

"Nope, that's what the man said. Or played, rather."

"He was playin' a song about a Caddy? What plate number?"

"Look, I'm serious. He called the song 'Blood Red Cadillac.' Now does that car look blood-colored to you?"

"Gee, I dunno," Cordell said, shaking his head. "I'm not sure I'd call it blood-colored exactly. It might be a shade too dark. I think that color's called Saxony red. Now if that cracker'd been singin' about a Saxony red Caddy, then maybe you'd have somethin'."

"You're right. It is a little too dark for blood. I don't know why I brought it up. Why don't we take a look?"

"Aren't you gonna wait for a coroner? Nobody's officially dead yet."

"Fuck it, it's too damn cold to just stand around."

The car was on the bank now, and the wrecker driver slackened tension on the winch, allowing the Cadillac to settle on its wheels, mud and ice oozing slowly down its sides.

Garcia circled the Caddy cautiously, but there was nothing to see. The windows were opaque with condensed moisture. He carefully opened the driver's door, cursing as a couple of gallons of water slopped over his shoes. Crimson water.

The interior of the car had been cream leather. Now it had a random polka dot pattern of blood spatters, front and back, as though the victim had done her best to evenly distribute her ebbing life over it. She lay slumped over on her side, away from the wheel, a dumpy, middle-aged woman with ebony rinsed hair, her mouth drawn back in the rictus of a silent scream. A second, newer mouth had been carved just below her chin.

She was wearing a pale chartreuse leisure suit with blood-soaked cacti embroidered on the shoulders. Her blouse had been slit open and her brassiere cut away, revealing her heavy breasts. Garcia glanced at the backseat. The bra was there, tossed carelessly aside. The body seemed to move, to shift, as if she was trying to sit up, but it was only the auto's interior lights coming slowly to life. Garcia leaned a little farther into the car, trying to

29

read the dashboard gauges without getting blood on his leather overcoat.

"Garcia, what the hell do you think you're doing? Goddammit, you know better than to touch anything before I or somebody from my goddam staff examines the body! Now get the hell out of there!"

"Hi, Doc." Garcia sighed, backing out of the car. "Nice to see you too." He stood aside as Les Klevenger slipped a skintight surgical glove over his right, his only hand. His left had been replaced with a stainless steel prosthesis. You didn't want to cross the old man when he was in a bad mood, and on icy nights, his only moods were bad and worse.

Klevenger was an honest to God relic, one of the few active veterans of the Irish Mafia who ran Motown like a private fief in the decades between the Great War and the '67 riots. He'd also been a defensive tackle at U of M, back in the leather helmet days. He carried less beef on his skeletal frame now, and he'd lost a hand in an auto accident years before, but his attitudes hadn't changed a bit. He was still searching the world for quarterbacks.

Klevenger reached into the car and shifted the body, raising the woman by her hair to examine the wound. His mouth tightened for a moment, then he eased her gently back down to the seat.

"Same as the others," he said, fumbling in his overcoat for his cigarettes. "Her head's been hacked damn near off and she's dead as a lawyer's conscience. So what the hell were you in such a hurry to find out?" Klevenger lit a cigarette, cupping it against the wind.

Garcia didn't answer for a moment, fascinated by the blood smears Klevenger's surgical glove left on his cigarette. "What, ah, what do you figure the time of death was, Doc?"

"Not long. Couple of hours ago, maybe."

"Doc, that can't be right. She must have been here longer than that."

"Why? What time was the vehicle reported?"

"Around ten-thirty, I guess."

"So I'm saying around ten or a little before." Klevenger frowned. "So what's your problem?"

30

"The dashboard clock. It's stopped at seven-twenty. It must have—"

"The clock? You want to determine time of death by a damn clock? An *auto* clock, for chrissake?"

"It's a new car, Doc, a Caddy. The clock would've kept running till the battery shorted—"

"Jesus, spare me your expertise, Garcia," Klevenger snapped, dropping his cigarette and grinding it out in the snow. "I was examining corpses when your daddy was still looking for a shallow spot to wade the Rio Grande, so don't tell me—" Klevenger broke off, peeled off his surgical glove, and stuffed it into his raincoat pocket. "Sorry," he said, taking a deep breath, "but I've already had a long day. Gangbang down on the Corridor, three kids . . ." He shook his head. "So what's the problem about the time? Have you got a suspect in mind for this one?"

"Maybe. I talked to a guy this afternoon who looks interesting."

"I see. But he's got an alibi for ten o'clock?"

"I think he goes to work at nine or nine-thirty."

"Well, to tell you the truth, once a body's been submerged in icewater, it's tough to determine TOD by conventional methods. I'll try to peg the TOD as precisely as I can for you, but that's the best I can do. And, Garcia, don't tell me how to do my damn job again, understand?"

"Right," Garcia muttered glumly as the old man stalked off toward his county station wagon, his overcoat whipping in the wind. "Have a nice night."

Chas Mullery eased his bulk out of a white Ford sedan with a Detroit *Free Press* stencil on the door. With his blocky Astrakhan hat jammed down over his ears, and his heavy, fur-collared overcoat, he looked more like a Russian emissary for agriculture than a reporter. He sauntered casually around the site, dodging the police lab techs and photographers, an island of calm in the chaos, and the only person present who didn't seem to mind the cold. He spotted Linda Kerry talking to one of the patrolmen. She noticed him at the same time, made her excuses to the cop, and walked over. Mullery was watching Garcia and Klevenger as she came up.

"You're Kerry, aren't you?" he said without looking at her. "Tempo section, right? Do you listen to police scanners for kicks? Or are you a cop groupie, or what?"

"I was having dinner with a friend when he got the call. I came along for the ride, that's all. I've got—"

"Which friend would that be?"

"Sergeant Garcia."

"Ahhhh yesss," he said, doing a bad W. C. Fields, "the Cisco Kid. You'd be his type, all right, tall, blond, Anglo. He probably shouldn't be yours though."

"What are you talking about?"

"Your dinner date, Garcia. Lupe. Sergeant now, and probably sergeant forever, if he's lucky. Affirmative Action type, you know, bring in the minorities, move 'em up fast. Vietnam vets, him and Bennett both. Not a bad cop, maybe, but a hothead. Look at him goin' at it with Klevenger now, and Dr. K.'s a bad man to get on the wrong side of. Old boy network and all that."

"Maybe he's more concerned about doing his job than playing politics."

"Politics makes this town perk, girlie, and every other town for that matter. Garcia's problem is he's a cowboy. I pinned that Cisco Kid nickname on him myself, back when he was working Narcotics. Very quick on the draw. Too quick, maybe. Ask him sometime how many people he's blown up. I'd guess four, offhand, but I may have forgotten a few. Rumor has it he was that way in Vietnam too, that he was fragged by one of his own men. Check out the plastic surgery scars around his hairline. He wasn't born with that pretty boy face, you know. It's U.S. government issue."

"A lot of people got hurt in Vietnam. It's no crime to be a vet."

"Of course it isn't. I've worn the uniform myself. But when a fella leaves a trail of bodies in his wake, and then gets bumped up to Homicide so he can investigate other people's corpses instead of vice versa, I wonder about him. And so should you. Definitely not your type."

32

"What would you know about my type?" she asked, angry now, moving around in front of him, facing him.

"Almost everything," he said coolly. "Upper-middle-class WASP divorcée in search of a new career, women's lib chip on her shoulder the size of a two-by-four, head full of Sociology 101 crap about the perfectability of the human animal. Garcia might make an interesting class project for you, but that's about it. Take a fat old man's advice, girlie, find yourself a nice stockbroker, get a house in the suburbs."

"I think you missed your calling, Mullery. You should be doing Dear Abby."

"No, ma'am, I like what I do just fine, thank you, and cops and robbers is what I do. I admire ambition, but there are proper channels for it, and you'd better remember it. I've been on the Freep longer than you've been alive, and I've got more'n enough clout to keep you doin' recipes forever."

"I suppose that's true." She nodded. "You're a legend in the business, Chas. I even studied your stuff in school and thought it was terrific. So why is it that someone who writes so well can be such a total asshole?"

"You shouldn't use language like that, girlie, you haven't the flair for it."

"Look, I talked with the two kids who found the body. My notes are legible and complete. I'm not jumping your beat, I just happened to be here, that's all. You're welcome to my notes, but if you call me 'girlie' one more time, I swear I'll punch your lights out in front of all these people. They call it aversive therapy in Psych 101 now. It's the latest thing."

"Thanks all the same but I prefer to gather my material firsthand. I'm sure a dedicated professional like yourself can understand that."

"Fine. The kids left for home ten minutes ago. Farmington, I think they said. If you hop in your car right now, you might catch 'em." She pushed up her jacket sleeve and checked her watch. "About twenty minutes past deadline for the morning edition. That's assuming their parents agree to let them talk to the press at

33

one A.M., of course. Look, I'm sorry I called you an asshole. Now do you want the notes or not?"

"I suppose I can make this one exception." Mullery sighed, accepting the notepad. "And you needn't apologize. You were absolutely right."

"What the hell was that all about?" Cordell asked. "You know better'n to get in Klevenger's face when he's havin' a bad day, and he don't have any good days."

"Just trying to build up a little goodwill so maybe the old fart won't play mumblety-peg on me if I end up on his table."

"You get us bumped back to traffic I'll put you on his table myself. What was the problem?"

"He set the time of death at no longer than two hours ago. This he deduces by jerking the body around like a sack of potatoes and smoking a cigarette, from what I could see."

"So?"

"So we've got a new Caddy here, pushed into the river by person or persons unknown. The dashboard clock was stopped at seven-twenty, which one might peg as approximately when the car went in, and we can assume the lady was already deceased at that point. I think Klevenger's wrong on this."

"He's been the man a long time."

"Too long, maybe, but even if he's right—"

"Sergeant Garcia? My name's Beamon, Twelfth Precinct. I got somebody here you might wanna talk to."

Beamon was short, black, and battle-scarred, with a Fu Manchu mustache. Heavily built, his bulky nylon uniform jacket made him look even wider, a bowling ball with legs, and just as solid. He had his arm around the shoulders of a stooped, gray-bearded black man with shell-shocked eyes, a derelict, who could have been forty, or seventy. The old man was wearing a rumpled brown pin-stripe suit, with newspapers stuffed in his sleeves and inside the grimy blue sweater beneath his jacket. A Day-Glo orange knit cap was pulled down tightly around his ears. The sour acid stink of him made Garcia flinch and immediately start breathing through his mouth.

34

"Come on, Maish," Beamon prompted gently, "tell 'em what you saw."

"Noo," the old man said, cringing closer to the patrolman, "noo, noo."

"You wanna translate that for us?" Cordell said.

"He's afraid of us," Beamon said. "He says we did it."

"What are you talkin' about? Did what?"

"Look, this is my patrol area," Beamon said. "I know this guy. He's a walkaway from the community clinic over on Jefferson—"

"He's mental?" Garcia interrupted.

"Yeah, but he's harmless. He sleeps over by that warehouse down the line there, next to the wall. Anyway, he told me he saw what happened down there. Said he saw a cop car by the river with the Caddy."

"A cop car?"

"Yeah, a big cop car, or maybe a boat. He's not real clear on that part. Look, the guy's more'n half crazy, and he killed a short dog o' T-bird before he crashed for the night. Still, I thought you oughta know."

"So what do you think?" Garcia said. "You say you know the guy, is this worth anything?"

"I really don't know. Sometimes he's okay, we talk sports and stuff; other times he worries about spaceships tryna steal his brain."

"Terrific," Garcia said. "Well, you did the right thing. Get his statement as best you can, and take him back to the clinic—"

"He won't go," Beamon said, "Not without a lotta hassle."

"Fine, handle it anyway you want," Garcia said, "but— Damn! Cordell, take care of this. I'll be back in a minute."

Linda Kerry was talking to a patrolman near the death car as the paramedics were removing the body. One of the medics slipped as they slid the corpse from the front seat to the stretcher, and the nearly severed head lolled back, exposing the massive, gaping wound, and dribbling spots of congealed blood on the snow.

Linda turned abruptly away and stumbled blindly through the jumbled snow to the river's edge. She stood with her hands

35

stuffed deep in the pockets of her ski jacket, taking long careful breaths, staring sightlessly out at the icescape beyond the pool of light. It could have been the surface of another planet, gleaming with reflected luminescence in the dark.

Garcia touched her arm lightly. "Hey, are you all right?"

"I'm . . . it surprised me, that's all," she said, her voice low, tightly controlled. "I didn't— I'm okay. It just surprised me."

"For what it's worth, nobody gets used to it. I blew my lunch the first time I saw one like this. You're doing fine. Why don't you come over to the car? It's out of the wind, and I can buy you a drink." He took her gently by the elbow and guided her to his unmarked sedan. He opened the door for her, then climbed in and fired up the engine and let it idle, the warmth from the heater gradually taking the edge off the chill.

A moment later Cordell popped the back door open and slid . in. "Well, at least we finally got us a witness." He sighed. "Ol' Maish'll knock 'em dead, we put him on the stand."

"No doubt," Garcia said. "Cordell, this is Linda Kerry, my upstairs neighbor, dinner guest, and reporter for the Freep. Linda, meet Cordell Bennett, my partner and fair-weather friend."

The hellos were polite, but reserved.

"Look, can we take care of business?" Cordell asked. "I got to give a deposition tomorrow at eight."

"I think we can talk in front of Linda."

"Okay, so what was all this about Klevenger and the time of death?"

"I just thought he was wrong about it, that's all, but he said he'd doublecheck, and maybe it won't matter. Maybe our man won't have an alibi either way."

"The redneck, you mean?" Cordell asked. Linda glanced up, interested.

"The same. Look, so far we've had no nexus for these killings, right? Zip. Well, maybe, just maybe, old Lamont is it. Suppose he's a stone wacko, crazy enough to play head games with me about a killing that hadn't happened yet. Maybe even crazy enough to pull the plug on some old lady just because she was

36

convenient and he was in a bad mood. There's something wrong about that guy, Cordell, really wrong."

"Anything else? Other'n him givin' you the creeps, I mean?"

"This victim was wearing a western-style outfit and cowboy boots. As I recall, victim number two, the schoolteacher, was wearing boots too."

"I own a pair of western boots," Linda offered quietly.

"So do half the women in Detroit," Cordell said, his tone neutral. "What do you figure, that he's been pickin' the women up at that bar he plays at? Maybe that'd explain their blood alcohol levels bein' so high, but victim number three was a nun. She a big country music fan too? Comes down to it, your bottom line is some song that guy did about a blood-colored car. Now that's a little weird, I'll admit, but kinda tough to offer as probable cause."

"Maybe the nun was just a target or opportunity, like the old lady at the hospital, I don't know, but I think we oughta take a hard look at him. He's as likely as anybody else we've got. I'll get a picture of this victim and try it where he works. Since he knew what kind of car she'd be driving, maybe he knew her. Maybe somebody'll remember seeing them together. When you get back from court you can start checking with the families of the others to see if any of 'em ever hit the country bars. Show Lamont's picture around, maybe we'll get lucky."

"We'll have to telex Brushy Mountain for his mug shot."

"No, why don't you try to get a shot of him from the *News* or the *Free Press*? They must've gotten pictures when his kid went through the ice and they'll be current. The Mountain was a long time ago."

"Look, Lupe, I don't wanna whiz in your punchbowl here, but you're figuring this guy as a crazy, right? But you got to remember you talked to him the day after his kid drowned and he nearly went down with him."

"He didn't seem particularly broken up about it. His woman was in rougher shape than he was."

"And you didn't like that, did you? So do you really figure he's a live one? Or have you maybe just got a hard-on for the guy?"

37

"He's wrong. I've talked to guys doing triple life in Jackson that didn't feel as wrong to me as this guy does. I want him on the list."

"Okay, then." Cordell nodded. "He's nominated. I'll pick up the pictures and see you tomorrow. Nice meeting you, Linda, and excuse me if my French is a little much. I was a lot classier guy before I got stuck with Loop. You take care now."

"No problem," she said. "Nice meeting you too."

The buzz of the heater seemed very loud after he'd gone.

"It's funny," Linda said thoughtfully. "I suppose I always thought of policemen as being more . . . detached from their work. You take this very personally, don't you?"

"Not always. In Narcotics things get pretty confused sometimes. Shades of gray. But Homicide's different. Basic black and white. This woman's only the second one in the series I've seen, but there were two others before we realized they were related, and took over the case. I see their pictures every day. I've talked to their families. They seem very familiar now, almost like, I don't know, distant relatives? That I'll never meet. So maybe I do take it personally. Is that bad?"

"I don't know," she said, opening her door. "I suppose it depends on the kind of person you are."

"And what kind is that?"

"I'm not sure." She slid out of his car into the night, then leaned back in for a moment. "It might be interesting to find out, though. Thanks for a very educational evening. Call me sometime, okay?"

"Count on it." He sensed an edge in her tone that gave him a vague pang of unease, but by the time he decided he hadn't imagined it, she was already gone.

CHAPTER 6

Romulus is only half an hour from downtown Detroit by freeway, but the drive always seemed too short to Garcia. About fifteen hundred miles too short. The all-white suburb could have been transplanted intact from any county in the rural South, and many of its people had been. George Wallace country. Full of houses that looked like they'd been built by their owners, one room at a time, on low, swampy ground.

Roy's Country Crossing blended in perfectly. It was a big rough-sided barn half a block long that the bulldozers had missed when the town sprawled out over the surrounding farmland. It shared its parking lot with a couple of rundown storefront businesses. Garcia nosed his car into a slot in the service drive between the bar and the Laundromat next to it.

Standing in the doorway, waiting for his eyes to adjust to the gloom, he had a quick flash of a job he'd had as a kid, mucking out stalls at the Hazel Park Racetrack. The horse barns were roughly the same size as Roy's, but they smelled better.

The bar was nearly deserted, too early for the lunch crowd, if the place had one. It was really two rooms, a cavernous dancing area with a darkened bandstand at one end, and a long curved bar of real oak at the other, with a few serious drinkers holding it up. The jukebox was sobbing softly in the background, country music, the white man's blues. A spindly-looking swamper was making halfhearted passes at the dance floor with a mop. The swamper definitely looked familiar. Garcia told himself he'd have to think about him. Things were looking up. Garcia took a stool at the end of the bar, away from the other customers.

Two men were working behind the bar, a rangy, watery-eyed old-timer with a red bow tie washing glasses and a heavyset barrel of a man counting the till. The heavier one had a dark bush of hair and a full beard. With his black western shirt and wide-brimmed hat he looked vaguely like a bear wearing a Hopalong Cassidy outfit. He closed the cash register and ambled over, sizing up Garcia as he came.

"Morning, Officer, something I can help you with?"

"Very astute," Garcia said. "Or did somebody pin a sign on my back? I'm looking for the owner, Roy?"

"I own this place, but there's no Roy. Hasn't been for years. I'm Kanelos Grivas." He offered a hand the size of a catcher's mitt. Garcia accepted it warily.

"A Greek cowboy?"

"No, an American, like you. A citizen. With all the same rights. And don't show me your badge, okay? People talk. What is it you want?"

"Just a little cooperation." Garcia passed the morgue photograph over. "Ever see this woman?"

"Not looking like this, no. Maybe when she was alive. I can't really say from this. We get lotta people in here."

"You employ a guitar player here named Yarborough?"

"Lamont? Sure, he works here, maybe six months now. His boy drowned this week, you know? A terrible thing. Nice boy. Quiet."

"Was Lamont here last night? Working, I mean?"

"Sure. The band plays, Lamont is here."

"From what time to what time?"

40

"Band plays from nine-thirty until two. Lamont's here, maybe twenty minutes before that to tune up his guitar, have a beer."

"So he was here all that time, say from nine until two?"

"Well, now," Grivas said, leaning forward, his elbows on the bar, "that's not so easy to say. You want a beer or something? On the house."

"No, thanks."

"You see, sometimes, if another player is here, he might sit in for a few songs, maybe play a whole set. Lamont was here last night, I seen him, but I couldn't say he didn't step out for a while, maybe smoke a joint, you know? It was busy last night, it's a big room. I can't always be sure who's on stage. Band plays, that's all I care."

"But the other guys in the band would know."

"Sure they know, but they probably not gonna tell you."

"They stick together pretty much, do they?"

"Oh, I don't know. Sometimes band guys are friends, you can tell. But this band . . . I don't think so. Not so much."

"You think his buddies would cover for him if they knew he was an ex-con?"

"Ex-con?" Grivas grinned, shaking his head. "Ex-con? That's a good one. Come on now, we have a beer together. Ex-con." He reached into the cooler beneath the bar and came up with two dripping bottles of Stroh's. He opened the first bottle on the cap of the second, and the second bottle with his teeth. "Not bad, eh?" he said, spitting the cap toward an open garbage can against the wall six feet away. Two points.

"Not bad at all," Garcia admitted, half-smiling in spite of himself. "Now tell me what I said that was so funny."

"You don't know?" Grivas asked, surprised. "You know about country western music?"

"A little. I listen to it sometimes."

"You know Merle Haggard, David Allen Coe? Freddy Fender, maybe?"

"I guess I recognize the names, sure."

"All big country music stars, sell lots of records. All ex-cons. They don't try to hide it. It's like a . . . badge, you know? To

41

show people they know hard times too. The people who listen to their music, who come to my bar, are mostly working men, like me, like you. Many are long ways from home, not much education, like me. And most of them, they don't give a shit what people do before as long as they don't make no trouble here, like me. So if Lamont was in prison once like you say, it won't bother nobody."

"What about murder, Mr. Grivas? That bother you at all?"

"Murder? You mean that woman?" The Greek's smile faded. He took a long, thoughtful pull at his beer, nearly draining the bottle. "It could be," he admitted. "Not saying *is*, only could be. I hear Lamont kill somebody once. A woman, I think maybe his wife. Let me see the picture again." He turned it this way and that in his ham-sized paw, shaking his head. "I still can't say, but I tell you what. These people won't tell you nothing, but they talk to me. You want to know about the woman. I don't want no trouble. Maybe I ask around for you, you know? Without anybody wonders. I can't show the picture of the woman, but I can find out if Lamont go out last night, or if he maybe had woman with him. He's living with a woman now, Jobeth. You know that?"

"I met her. She wasn't looking too well."

"Who can say what happens, man and woman?" Grivas shrugged. "Who can say? Anyway, I ask around for you. I call you . . . maybe tomorrow afternoon, tell you what I hear. Fair enough?"

"Fair enough." Garcia nodded, handing Grivas his card. "My number's on this. You call me tomorrow, hear?"

"I say I would. Lupe Garcia, sergeant, eh? Look, Sergeant, I do this for you, you do something for me?"

"Maybe. If I can."

"You gonna bust Lamont, you think?"

"I really don't know yet. It's way too early to say."

"Well, if you bust him, can you maybe call me, let me know so I got time to find another band? Can't have band with no lead guitar player."

"Maybe I can do that. How much notice will you need?"

"To replace this band?" Grivas shook his head sadly. "I don't know, they're pretty good, you know? Got a big following. Maybe an hour, little more."

"I guess I could manage that. Think you could manage me another beer?"

He'd planned to nurse the beer for an hour. Twenty minutes was all it took. At eleven the place started to fill with shop rats, flannel-shirted, baseball-capped auto workers, stomping the snow from their crepe-soled boots, good-naturedly cursing the cold and each other. Grivas got busy at the grill, frying burgers, franks, and fish patties side by side. The elderly bartender was passing out beer and boilermakers as fast as he could put them on the bar. Then he ran short of change. He motioned the skinny swamper over to the bar, a sallow-faced kid with frizzy blond hair that looked like an overripe dandelion. Garcia watched him hand the kid a fistful of bills, but couldn't hear what was said. The policeman tossed a buck on the bar for the beer and eased off the stool, timing it so he was only a couple of paces behind the kid as he left through the side door.

Garcia caught up halfway across the alley. He grabbed him by the scruff of the neck and jerked him around the corner of the Laundromat, out of sight of the street.

"Hey! What the fuck?"

Garcia pitched him facedown into the garbage-strewn slush of the alley and was on him like a cat, twisting his bony arm up between his shoulder blades while he frisked him. He yanked a cheap, chrome-plated .22 revolver out of the hip pocket of the kid's jeans.

"Hey, c'mon! You're breakin' my back!"

"Quiet, Denny, keep it real quiet. You're busted. I'm gonna let you up now, but don't try and run, okay? I hate fillin' out all those damn forms when I shoot somebody."

"Okay, okay! Just get offa me."

Garcia eased his knee out of the kid's back and released his wrist. He stood up, blocking the mouth of the alley, and thumbed the hammer back on the .22, holding it at arm's length

43

so the muzzle was only half an inch from the kid's nose when he sat up.

"Jesus, what the fuck're you doin'? That thing's loaded!"

"Good, Denny. Glad to hear it. Now we can skip the crap about how you've never seen it before. You remember me?"

"Ahhh, God! Garcia, right?"

"Very good. You've got a good memory. Now let's see how good mine is. Seems to me the last time I saw you, you were getting ready to do a nickel in Jackson for grand theft auto, larceny from an auto, possession of controlled substances . . . I don't remember what else, but I remember you drew five. It's only been, what, three years tops? So are you out already? Or haven't you been yet?"

"I been," Denny said, swallowing rapidly, "I been."

"Hope you liked it. You're going back. How come you're out early anyway? You a real good boy?"

"I, ah, they dropped me to a deuce for good behavior."

"Well, maybe they kept your bed warm for you. In fact, a cute little thing like you, I'll bet there were hard-time cons bangin' their heads against the wall and howlin' like dogs the day you left."

"Look, Garcia, please, I can't go back in there. They lemme out on a medical 'cause I was crackin' up. I just ain't big enough to take care of myself in there. And I been straight. Lookit! Lookit this!" He tore off his cheap cotton jacket, tossed it aside, and pulled up his shirtsleeves, ripping the buttons off in his haste. "See? No tracks. I been out five months and I ain't had nothin' stronger than a couple beers. I been workin' and—"

"So why the gun, Denny, you're such an upright citizen now? You're a felon on parole, you draw a mandatory deuce under the felony firearms law. How come the gun?"

"Griff trusts me, he—"

"Griff?"

"Mr. Grivas. He give me a job, never asked nothin' about whether I done time or nothin', just hired me, you know? Even lets me handle money sometimes. Not like now, when I'm just goin' for change, but like the bank deposits. He sends me

44

sometimes if he's too busy to go. I never looked in the bag, but I get the receipt, and it's usually a couple grand. So I . . . picked up the gun. I just didn't wanna get ripped off, you know? Griff trusts me."

"Hell, you're more likely to blow your hand off with this thing than stop a rip-off. But I guess I can see why you got it. Seems a shame. Piece of junk like this doesn't hardly seem worth two years, does it? It's mandatory though, the deuce, nothing I can do about it."

"Please, Garcia, I'm beggin' ya. I'll fuckin' kill myself before I'll go back. I just . . . can't, I . . . ." Denny's voice had been straining higher and thinner as he fought to keep from crying. He was losing the battle.

"Denny, listen to me now," Garcia said softly. He stuffed the pistol in his coat pocket and slipped an arm around the boy's scrawny shoulders, hugging him close. "Now, dammit, don't come unglued on me. I hate it when a guy cries. I just hate it. Look, maybe we can work something out."

"Anything." Denny hiccoughed. "Anything."

"All right now, just settle down. You know Lamont Yarborough, the guy that plays in the band?"

"Lamont? Sure."

"Okay, I want to know about the women he hangs out with, picks up, talks to, anything." He held the morgue photo in front of the boy's face. "Have you ever seen Lamont with this woman?"

"I don't know. Maybe I could have."

"Look at it, dammit! And don't blow smoke at me. I want to know. Now have you seen this woman or not?"

"Christ, I don't know. I ain't never paid attention to who Lamont was with, and . . . hell, nobody could tell nothin' from this. It could be anybody. Why do ya wanna know about Lamont's women anyway?"

"Yours is not to reason why. Yours is to give me what I want or do your original three plus the deuce."

"What about my gun?"

"What about it? For chrissake, this peashooter's your one-way ticket to Jackson! I'm putting my ass on the line by concealing

45

a felony and you want me to give you the damn gun back? A minute ago it was 'anything, Garcia, anything.' What the fuck happened to that? I oughta just hand this piece to your parole officer and wave good-bye when the bus pulls out."

"You ain't gonna, though," the kid said bitterly, "'cause you want somethin'. Everybody wants somethin'. You want me to pull my pants down for you right here in the alley? You want some head maybe? You're gonna wind up fuckin' me anyway, it might as well be now."

"Hey, what is all this? I'm giving you a break."

"Sure you are. But I'm gonna get fucked. I dunno how yet, but I'm gonna. I been gettin' it all my life and I know it when I see it. And you're it, man."

"Look, you play straight with me, I'll be straight with you. I give you my word. You knew me when I was workin' the street. You ever hear I went back on my word?"

"All I ever heard about you was that people around you wind up dead a lot, Garcia, like you're fuckin' AIDS, or something."

"Well now," Garcia said, gently tousling the boy's frizzy hair, "that's not such a bad thing to keep in mind, you know?"

CHAPTER 7

GARCIA SCOWLED AT THE ADDRESS SCRAWLED IN HIS NOTEBOOK AS he swung the Chrysler into a narrow tenement row street in Melvindale. He'd detoured through the area to check out a name on his way back to the station. The address hadn't registered at the time, but now that he was here he remembered the street, a double row of multistory slum apartment buildings, half of them burned out or abandoned, on a street that dead-ended against the Norfolk and Western tracks.

The last house was a sprawling, three-story tenement with a half-dozen motorcycles parked in the littered front yard. Heavy plywood shutters vented with narrow rifle slits covered the first-floor windows and a barricade of sand-filled oil drums ringed the front porch, each of them spray painted with a double-lightning-bolt SS logo. Satan's Sons, one of the roughest outlaw motorcycle gangs in the state. Terrific. A wasted trip. Because there was no way he was rousting anybody in the biker clubhouse without a small army for backup.

Garcia spun the wheel to the right and gunned into a tight

U-turn. As the car whipped around, he caught a flash of movement at a third-story window of a tenement shell across the street and a few houses down from the clubhouse, a metallic glint of some kind. Sniper? On guard in the middle of the day? He'd heard rumors the Sons were going heavy into the drug trade, but they wouldn't be covering the street during daylight unless . . .

He parked his grubby Chrysler beside a fire hydrant three blocks over from the Sons' clubhouse, and circled back toward it on foot, cutting down an alley and across backyards to the asbestos-sided tenement where he'd spotted the movement. A single set of tracks showed in the snow leading to the back door. He popped the rusty lock with his penknife, eased the door open, and stepped inside.

The only light in the open stairwell came from a broken window facing the street. The stench of urine and rotting garbage hung in the air like a fog, and it seemed much colder inside than out. The first-floor apartment had been trashed years before, the walls kicked in and sprayed with graffiti, light fixtures torn out. Even the cockroaches had probably jumped ship. But the wooden stairway looked solid enough. He transferred his Airweight Smith & Wesson .38 from his waistband to the outside pocket of his leather coat, and started quietly up, staying close to the wall.

There were two apartments off the second-floor landing, one standing open and as demolished as the room below. The door to the second apartment was closed. Garcia considered casing it, but the movement had been on the third floor, and if he made any noise here . . .

He continued up the stairs, moving even more cautiously now, his hand on the butt of his .38, back to the wall, trying to keep both the stairway ahead and the door below in view. There were two apartments on the top floor too, both closed. Garcia guessed the one at the end of the narrow hallway faced the street and began inching toward it. And heard the snick of metal on metal from behind him.

"Hold it, asshole, right there. And lemme see your hands, slow. Now." She'd come out of the second apartment, in her

48

stocking feet, a short, slender black woman, clad in faded denim, with a blue Adidas headband around her braided corn-rowed locks. Her eyes were large and dark, a match for the muzzle of the sawed-off automatic shotgun she held shoulder-high, aimed at his head.

"Hi," he said brightly, turning cautiously, showing her his hands, palms up. "You the lady of the house?"

"Skip the bullshit, and walk to the door down there and knock twice. And don't do anything dumb or you're one dead greaser."

"I'm a police officer. I can—"

"You can knock on that fuckin' door right now, or I can blow your head off," she said coolly. "So what's it gonna be?"

Garcia knocked. He could hear someone inside fumble with the lock, and then the door swung open. A tall, goateed black wearing gray Consumers Power coveralls and holding an army issue .45 looked him over, shook his head sadly, and motioned him in. "Hey, Jimmy," he said, "look what we got here."

"Hey, Loop." Jamail Hamadi grinned, looking up from the spotting scope trained on the clubhouse across the street. "How's it goin'? And how come you got your hands up?"

Garcia glanced behind him. The hallway was empty. He shrugged and shook hands with the giant in the coveralls. "Cooley," he said, "who in the hell was the lady?"

"Davonne Watts," Curtis Cooley said. "We got her from Naptown in a narc swap. Best deal we ever made. 'Cept for maybe gettin' you kicked upstairs. She's really somethin', ain't she?"

"Or maybe you're just gettin' drag-ass in your old age," Hamadi offered. The slightly built narc squad boss was wearing a battered leather bombardier's jacket, engineer's boots, jeans, and a grubby T-shirt. His curly dark hair was cut punk, spiky on top, with red and blond streaks on one side. He was in his mid-thirties, but still got asked for ID every time he tried to buy a beer. "That was you in the city wheels a few minutes ago, right? You park anyplace around here?"

"Three blocks over. I spotted the scope in the window, thought it might be you."

"So what's shakin'? Or did you just drop by for auld lang syne?"

49

"Afraid not," Garcia said, pulling a chair up to the littered table next to Hamadi, "and I think you guys may have a problem. I'm gonna have to roust the Sons. One of them—"

"I don't care what it is," Hamadi interrupted, "it'll have to wait. The Sons are into the coke trade now, supplying muscle and mules for a Colombian mob, and dealing themselves. They're into some heavy shit, Loop, and we've put a lot of time in here."

"Heavier than four murders?" Garcia countered.

"Maybe," Hamadi said. "And don't figure on makin' this a pissin' contest, Loop, because you'll lose. We've got our very own private judge now."

"No kidding? Anybody I know?"

"The honorable Amos P. Welch, from Dearborn. The judge's son scored some bum crack on the Corridor and wound up at Samaritan in a coma. The judge phoned me from the hospital, half out of his tree, wants the dealer busted, in half. As it happened, we knew the guy, and nailed him the same night. Only he tried to rabbit on us, and took a header down a fire escape, swear to God. Got banged up pretty bad. Only the judge thinks we helped the guy down the steps because he asked us to. And he's very grateful. And maybe just a little nervous about it. So we can get warrants, writs, anything we need on fifteen minutes' notice, twenty-four hours a day."

"Of course you told him it was an accident, right?"

"Absolutely." Hamadi grinned. "Only he didn't believe me. He's heard too many stories about what badasses narcs are, most of which got started when you were still on the squad. So maybe I owe you one, Loop, but not enough to let you blow a two-week stake for me."

"Maybe we can trade," Garcia said, copping some potato chips from a torn bag on the table. "I need to check out a guy named Vincent Guzik. He did time at Milan for cutting a couple of hookers six years ago. You know him?"

"Crabs," Hamadi said, "that's his road handle. A real piece of work. What do you want to know?"

"For openers, where he was last night between seven and ten-thirty."

50

"At the clubhouse," Cooley put in. "They all were. Had a beer bust went on half the night."

"Are you sure Guzik was there all night? It's important."

"I got a shot of him takin' a leak off the front porch about ten," Cooley said. "That good enough?"

"Yeah." Garcia sighed. "I'd say so."

Cordell was at his desk, typing furiously, when Garcia ambled into the nearly deserted squad room at two. Al Fielder was sitting in Garcia's chair, feet on his desk, sipping coffee from a Styrofoam cup as he scanned a report. Fielder was a square man, mentally and physically, a balding cement block, barely five-nine and an easy two hundred-plus pounds. In the three years he'd worked for him, Garcia was sure Fielder'd gained as many pounds as Cordell, but it didn't show. While Cordell's rangy, linebacker frame had blurred around the edges and sagged into a pillow-sized paunch, Fielder just seemed to get wider without softening at all. He wore half-lensed glasses to read, and when he glanced over the tops of them, you automatically checked your fly.

"Afternoon, Loop, nice you could stop in."

"I try to touch base now and again when I can fit it into my dance card. What's up?"

"It's not what's up, it's what's on. The captain's on my back. He wants your reports updated today. He's gotta do a luncheon talk for the Detroit Renaissance Alliance tomorrow and he wants something to run with."

"What we've got so far won't do much for their digestion."

"Hell, some of the people in that club swallow whole corporations for breakfast, what's a few murders compared with that? But I think the captain's more concerned about the press conference afterward anyway. Doesn't want any surprises. In any case, he said t-o-d-a-y, as in 'before you leave this afternoon' type today."

"Hey," Cordell said, without looking up, "isn't it some kind of ethnic slur to spell things for members of minority groups?"

"He's just showing off," Garcia said. "You have any luck with the victims' families?"

"I think you could call it luck. Most of 'em weren't home. The

51

only ones I got were the nun's folks, Darlene and Arvo Senchuk. 'Mrs. Senchuk, do you know if your daughter, the late Sister Mary Margaret, liked listening to country music? Of if she ever frequented bars where that sort of music is played?' They didn't think so. Ol' Arvo *really* didn't think so, but he told me some stuff he did think and wanted my badge number so I said I was you. You'll be gettin' a letter from him."

"I can hardly wait."

"Had a prowlie check out the driver's license address on last night's victim. Name, Louise Barrett, maiden name, Louise Lorch. Apparently lived alone and her neighbors didn't know doodley about her. A brother's listed as next of kin, Carl Lorch, Seattle. Contacted him but he didn't seem to know much. Said they'd been out of touch. He's flying in later this week, said he'd call in when he gets here. What did you get?"

"We can scratch Vincent Guzik. Jimmy Hamadi's narcs've got him under surveillance and can alibi him for last night, complete with snapshots of his shlong if we want 'em."

"I'll pass," Cordell said. "How about you, Al?"

"Who needs pictures of a prick when I'm workin' for the real thing?" Fielder grunted.

"I also copped a mild buzz at Roy's Country Crossing," Garcia continued, "a dirty job but somebody had to do it. Only Roy isn't Roy, he's a Greek named Kanelos Grivas. Seems straight enough, even offered to ask around about Yarborough for me. But guess who's working for him in addition to our ladykiller. You remember a car theft ring working Grosse Pointe a few years ago? A kid named Dennis Weitz?"

"Skinny kid?" Fielder frowned. "A hype? Worked in the chop shop?"

"That's him. He's out of Jackson already on a medical, and he's working at Roy's. And for us too. This is his piece." Garcia handed the chromed revolver to Cordell. "Stick it in your lock box. We're gonna hold it for him, and he's going to doublecheck what the Greek tells me."

"Class piece," Fielder observed. "Only thing missing is the picture of Gene Autry on the grips. So you erased Harvey the hooker off the list yesterday, and now Guzik. Which leaves who?"

"We've got four, maybe five other interestin' suspects if you count Loop's redneck," Cordell said. "A full boat."

"Fair enough," Fielder said. "If you need backup or whatever, let me know. Meantime I hate interfering with priority police-work like scarfing free beer and hustling cap guns, but that's how the mop flops. Up-to-date reports. Today. And by the way, that wino you talked to last night? Said he saw a police car at the scene? Is he credible at all?"

"If you check it, he said a police car, or maybe a boat," Garcia said. "He also says he's worried about aliens stealing his brain. That answer your question?"

"Then don't mention him in the captain's report. He lets Mullery read 'em sometimes and it's the kind of thing he might run with, 'Police Suspected in Slasher Murders.' Take him out."

"Yes, sir, Lieutenant. I'll get right on it, as soon as you get your butt out of my chair."

"Right," Fielder said, getting up. "Wouldn't dream of holdin' you up."

"What do you think?" Garcia said, sliding into his chair as Fielder stalked off. "Is old Al going conventional on us? Weight of command and all that?"

"Could be. So how about gettin' on the damn reports. I wanna get outa here tonight. I got business."

"Business? I seem to recall you've got a date with Su Hua."

"That's business," Cordell said pointedly, "*my* business."

"You know, maybe I'm just an old-fashioned guy, but I always figured divorce should be forever."

"Tell somebody who gives a shit what you think, and get typin'. By the way, Mullery's been and gone. I gave him a rundown but he didn't seem too interested. Got enough to run with after last night, I guess. And your little friend called, whatsername, Linda? Wanted you to call her back. Number's on your pad there."

Garcia tapped out the number printed on the memo in Cordell's blunt, square script.

"Tempo section, Kerry."

"Homicide, Garcia."

53

"Oh, hi, you got my message."

Her voice was cool, professional, and he felt suddenly uneasy again. Something wasn't . . .

"I, ah, was just wondering," she said, "if you were going to follow through on that situation you were discussing last night? With Yarborough, I mean?"

"We're blundering along in our own comic fashion, yes."

"Good. How would you like to take me dancing?"

"Dancing? I'm not sure I follow you."

"My editor okayed a Tempo story on country music in the big city, using Yarborough as a starting point, possibly even a focal point depending on how it goes. Since you were nice enough to take me along on a job last night, I thought I'd return the favor. Maybe we could mix business with pleasure?"

"We had business mixed with pleasure last night," he said. "It didn't seem to work out all that well."

"No, I guess it didn't at that. Well, it was just a thought. Another time, maybe."

She was slipping away. He could feel it. "No, it was a good thought. Let's do it. Tonight if you like. Just one thing though. Does your editor know that this guy committed murder once? That he's a possible suspect now?"

"If he does," she said coolly, "he didn't hear it from me. And I'm sorry you asked. Look, this was probably a bad idea—"

"Wrong, it's a great idea, and I apologize for the question. Maybe I've been on this job too long. The band starts at nine-thirty bar time, so—"

"Bar time?"

"Ah, you see how lost you'll be without my expertise? Tell you what, I'll pick you up at nine. Or would you like to have dinner first?"

"No, I'll be working late. I'll meet you at your place at nine."

"Good, see you then." Garcia frowned at the receiver as he dropped it back in its cradle. "Damn, I hate it when they lie about little things," he said absently. "It's usually a bad sign."

"I thought you were just friends anyway."

"Yeah." He sighed. "I thought we were too."

54

CHAPTER 8

"**W**HY DON'T WE START WITH BAR TIME?"

"As good a place as any," Garcia said. They were in his silver
'87 Firebird heading west on Ecorse toward Romulus. He was
proud of the car, a T-top with a Trans-Am package, but he had
a hunch she'd have been more impressed by a Volvo with a ski
rack on the back.

"Local bar time is set ahead, that's all, usually fifteen or twenty
minutes. They have to stop serving at two A.M. and some folks get
amazingly hostile about one last drink. Setting the time ahead
gives the bartenders a little leeway."

"But don't the customers know what time it is?"

"The people fighting to get the last shot at closing aren't usually
all that clear on the time, no. Anyway that's how it works."

"How did you acquire your expertise? Years of careful study?"

"Actually I don't spend much time in bars if I can avoid it.
When I was working prowl cars, emergency calls for bar fights
and family fights were the worst. I'll take an armed robbery in
progress anytime."

"You know, I can't always tell when you're kidding me. Would you mind doing it less, or giving me a wink or something?"

"A wink? Sure." He screwed up half his face into a vaudeville wink and twitched the wheel, wobbling the Firebird back and forth in its lane.

"You're a strange guy." She smiled. "I don't see how you handle your job and keep a sense of humor, rudimentary though it is."

"I don't know how I could cut it without a sense of humor, rudimentary or— Gee, you know, nobody's ever called me that before. Rudimentary. I think I like it."

"I'm so pleased," she said drily. "But about bar fights. Were you kidding or not?"

"No, they're the worst. With an armed robbery at least you know what you're getting into. With a bar fight you don't know if you've got a happy drunk who's been goosing somebody's wife, or a wacko with a gun who's gonna take out the first guy through the door. So you blunder in, two seconds to guess who and what and get things under control, and hope they don't notice you're really not all that big."

"But you're armed, aren't you? Always?"

"Lots of people are armed these days. And a gun doesn't intimidate a drunk or a crazy all that much. Unless you use it, of course."

"And you've used yours," she said carefully, "haven't you?"

"Ahhhh, well," he said slowly, "so that's what it is. I knew there was something. I thought maybe it was just last night."

"I don't know what you mean."

"Sure you do. Sensing people is part of my job. Vibes, hunches, call it what you want, you either get the knack or you don't last long. I felt . . . distance between us this afternoon on the phone. I feel it now."

"I think the word is paranoia."

"Nope, not this time. I guess if I were you I'd be curious too. Perfectly natural. And since you're new in town, you'd ask somebody who'd know. Somebody like Chas Mullery maybe, and he'd say, 'Sure I know that guy, Crazy Lupe, the Cisco Kid.'

I was hoping I'd seen the last of that crap. Did you read the articles he did on me?"

"I . . . yes, I did."

"Terrific. And you believe it?"

She shifted in her seat, turning to face him. "Chas Mullery may be a jerk, but he's a good reporter. Are you saying what he wrote wasn't true?"

"No," he admitted, "it was true, as far as it went. While I was working Narcotics I was involved in . . . some shooting incidents. And Mullery made me look like a trigger-happy showboat. How did it go? 'Not a villain, a tragic symbol of the egregious error of setting standards based on anything less than excellence. Only our best will be good enough.' Thoughtful stuff."

"But you did join the force after Affirmative Action?"

"That's right. I don't know what my scores were and Mullery didn't either, but I think I was probably at least as bright as the Anglos I tested with. The difference was that afterward, my application didn't get lost."

"You sound bitter about it."

"It's tough to be objective when you're the one getting ground up in the machinery." He changed lanes and gunned past a slow-moving semi. "Look, it's history. Let's just forget it."

"I don't want to forget it. I want to understand it. I haven't met many people who kill other people."

"Then you're in for a real treat. You're about to interview one."

"I can at least understand that, a man getting angry enough to kill his wife, or vice versa. I have a tougher time with the idea that it's just part of a job. It wouldn't matter so much if I didn't care about you, but it so happens I do. So how about a little help. Please."

"Jesus," he said softly, "you definitely know how to ask. I'd hate to be a banker if you were a little short at the end of the month. Okay, what do you want to know?"

"About the Cisco Kid."

He glanced at her sharply. She was smiling, and after a moment they both were.

"I, ah, joined the force in seventy-three, right after I got out of the army. And maybe it was too soon, I don't know."

"Chas said you were wounded in Vietnam. Did you have trouble adjusting?"

"Looking back at it now, maybe I did, though I didn't think so at the time. You've got to remember what it was like back then. It was just a few years after the riots, the older guys on the force didn't trust us, Affirmative Action was a dirty word. And we were 'Nam vets to boot, you know? Drugged-out crazies. And the people in the streets. . . . That was during the peak of the antiwar protests, black power, white power, La Raza. And we were 'the pigs.' I did three years as a patrolman, and then got tapped for a detective's slot. Narcotics. Just like that. Thought it was a real break."

"But it wasn't?"

"The guys they moved up were all ethnic types, me, Cordell, nearly a dozen more. They made us narcs. The force had been mostly white for years, and the city was taking heat from the feds to move people up. The drug situation was totally out of control, and here are these new guys who don't wear brushcuts, or bowl, or belong to St. Stan's. Perfect narcs. Send 'em into the ghettos undercover, they'll fit right in. Great idea, Muldoon. Thank you, Captain Kowalski."

"That doesn't seem unreasonable to me. Callous, perhaps—"

"You don't understand. Back then the force was run by a kind of WASP/Irish Mafia, and in some ways it still is. But just because the administration types who lived in Hamtramck or wherever didn't know us doesn't mean nobody did. The areas they were sending us into were neighborhoods, you know? Not suburbs. People there know each other. And nobody's more paranoid than a drug dealer. Nobody. So I'd pass for a while, maybe get into a few things, and then somebody'd bump into somebody who knew me from high school and knew I'd gone on the cops . . . And people would get killed. And not always the bad guys, either. Depending on who you figure the bad guys are."

"The articles said the shootings were—"

"We aren't going to talk about the shootings," he said abruptly.

58

"Sorry, but I don't know you well enough for that. Maybe I don't know anybody well enough."

"I didn't mean to upset you."

"I'm not upset."

"No? So why are we doing seventy-five in a fifty-five zone?"

"Okay," he conceded, easing off on the accelerator, "maybe you did upset me. Or at least the subject did."

"Good."

"Good?"

"I was afraid you were going to give me a cool, professional rationale on how you had no choice but to shoot."

"I didn't have any choice!"

"Maybe not, but it still bothers you, doesn't it?"

"You're damn right it does. It'd bother anybody."

"No, it wouldn't, and you know it. But it bothers you, and I'm glad it does. Sorry if I seemed pushy. It was important to me to know how you felt about it."

"Jesus H. Christ," he said, shaking his head slowly, "you're an interesting date, you know that? Not fun, necessarily, but interesting."

"I'm glad you think so."

"Okay, I've got one question for you, if it doesn't conflict with your professional ethics."

"Go ahead. I think I owe you one."

"Straight out, did you ask Mullery about me? Or did he just happen to tell you?"

"I didn't ask him directly, no."

"I thought that might be it. I'll bet it still bugs him that he did me a favor."

"How do you mean?"

"All that Cisco Kid stuff. It made me too hot to narc anymore, so they moved me up to Homicide. He tried to bury me and got me promoted instead. You think that might still bug him a little?"

"At the moment I'm not sure what I think."

"I think we're here," he said, following a jacked-up four-wheel-drive pickup into the Country Crossing parking lot.

CHAPTER 9

LAMONT SPOTTED THEM AS THEY MOVED THROUGH THE CROWD around the dance floor, the Mexican cop and a very foxy blonde. Looked like it might be an interesting evening. Early crowd, already loose and loud and ready to boogie. He could feel the energy in the room, sense it building in the audience as Gopher finished tuning his ax and nodded an okay to Sonny. Lamont lost sight of the blonde in the crush, then had to listen up as Sonny stepped up to his mike, tipped his black gunfighter Stetson back, and looked over the crowd.

"Hey," he said mildly, "anybody out there ready to party?"

A few whoops, mostly women, and a smattering of applause.

"*Hey! I said is anybody ready to fuckin' party!*" A roared response from the audience this time, a wall of noise, rebel yells, applause, and laughter.

"*Well, all right! You're at the right place!*"

Sonny turned his back to the crowd, finger-popped a quick four and the band pumped into their theme song, a hard-country version of Jerry Reed's "U.S. Male," punched out and outlawed, cranked to the max, balls to the walls.

Sonny belted out the first two verses, talking it up, rapping on the rhythm of the lyrics, and then Lamont took over, claw-picking the solo, cookin' it, feeling the room, the crowd, everything fade away into a silver gray haze, until only the song stretched out ahead of him, gleaming like a ribbon of steel. And he honked on down, a Peterbilt pedal to the metal, smoking like a bullet. And got a whoop and a cymbal crash from Mick Woods, the drummer, a shout of encouragement from Sonny, "Do it again, you got it!" But he barely heard them. He was in the other place now, lost, suspended in space, playing like a man on fire.

They found a table for two with a good view of the stage, on the second tier above the parquet dance floor. The room was ringed with tables and booths on three levels, each a step above the other. The air was already hazy with smoke and thick with the mingled musk of perfume and perspiration. The band was loud, but not deafening, pulsing with a heartbeat that seemed to energize the crowd, swirling them in measured motion on the floor below.

"It's a lot bigger than I expected," Linda said, glancing around, taking it all in. "There must be what, several hundred people here already?"

"The club owner said the group was hot. I guess he wasn't kidding."

The room was still filling, but all of the tables near the dance floor were already taken, mixed couples and singles, dressed in chambray or flannel shirts and jeans, people nodding hellos, backslapping, shaking hands. It looked like a family reunion. A honky-tonk family reunion six nights a week.

"Do you know who any of the guys in the band are?" Linda asked.

"The tall kid doing most of the singing is Sonny Earle. I noticed him on a poster as we came in. Lamont's the one on the end in the black leather vest with the wine-colored guitar. I don't know the others. The big redhead at the center of that first long table is the woman I met at the trailer, Jobeth."

"She, ah, doesn't look too much the worse for wear."

61

"She looked it yesterday."

"I have less trouble understanding why you offered to help. She's really quite attractive in her way."

"I guess she is. I can't say I noticed at the time."

"You know," she said, scanning the crowd, "I think you may be the only man in the room wearing a jacket and tie."

"Yup, looks like everybody rolled out for a rodeo. Maybe that's something you can use."

"What, the way people dress?"

"Sure, blue jeans, boots, cowboy hats. It's almost a uniform. Some of these folks may be refugees from the Wild West, but most of them are from Motown. They work in the plants and they've never been closer to a cow than the meat section at Farmer Jack's. So did they all OD on Randolph Scott movies, or what?"

"Their clothes reflect values they admire, I suppose," she said, "or maybe it's just convenient. I mean, what's so practical about a suit and tie?"

"Not much, I suppose. Just a habit—"

"Mind if I ask the lady for a dance?" A pudgy, crew-cut hulk wearing brown work denims with a Valley Trucks patch on his baseball cap had wandered over from the cluster of stags lining the bar.

"I don't think the lady feels like dancing just now," Garcia said coolly. "Sorry."

"Actually, the lady would like to dance," Linda said, getting up abruptly, "that is, if either one of you care what the lady thinks. I was just waiting for someone to ask." She turned and threaded her way between the tables toward the crowded dance floor. Valley Trucks stared after her a moment, confused, then shrugged sheepishly in Garcia's direction and followed her.

The song was a mournful waltz. The trucker held Linda in a distant, formal embrace, primly avoiding body contact, circling the floor in a stolid march.

Garcia had no trouble keeping track of them in the crowd. Even in jeans and a simple white blouse, there was a glow about Linda, an elegance. She was easily the most attractive woman in the room, perhaps one of the loveliest he'd ever met. He had a flash of the night before, the warmth of her palm against his cheek, her smile at something he'd said . . . And then they'd gone down to the river, and something went wrong. And it was still going wrong, barreling along with a negative inertia of its own. Damn! He slammed his fist on the table, making the ashtray jump, drawing a startled look from a waitress in a yellow fringed blouse. He motioned her over.

"You know Lamont Yarborough, the guitar player?" he asked, holding out a five. "Would you ask him to join us when he goes on break, please? I'd like to buy him a drink." He glanced up as the girl took the money and caught Lamont's eyes, watching him over the heads of the dancers.

At the end of the song, Valley Trucks escorted Linda back to the table, thanked her for the dance, thanked Garcia for the dance, and wandered back to the bar.

"You dance very well," Garcia said coolly as Linda seated herself. "You're even fun to watch."

"I would have preferred to dance with you," Linda said, meeting his glance, "but I would also prefer to be consulted about things that affect me. Is that so unreasonable?"

"Not ordinarily, no, but in a place like this—"

"I'd still liked to be asked. Reasonable or not, it's very important to me. Okay?"

"All right," Garcia said. "I guess if it's that important to you, then it's important to me too. Would it be too soon to ask, do you think?"

"Absolutely not," she said, rising and offering her hand. "Sir, would you honor me with this dance?"

He stared at her a moment, then rose, slowly shaking his head. "I'd be delighted, ma'am," he said with a mock bow. "And reasonable or not, you are a very, very interesting date."

After the set Lamont took a moment to retune his guitar, then made his way through the crowd to their table.

"Hi," he said, nodding at Garcia. "The waitress said you were buyin'."

63

"The department is. Have a seat."

He eased into the seat next to Linda. "I already know who he is. Who might you be?"

"My name's Linda Kerry," she said, offering him her hand. "I'm a reporter. Detriot *Free Press.*"

"It's a pleasure to meet you, Linda," he said, taking her hand, holding it, "but if you're here on business, I, ah, don't have anything to say about . . . what happened."

"I write about entertainment," she said, withdrawing her hand, "music, that sort of thing. Can we talk about that? I don't know much about country music, but I liked what you were playing, and it's certainly easy to dance to." She gave Garcia a bland smile.

"I guess we can talk about music if you like. Be a pleasant change."

"Good," Garcia said. "Why don't we talk about that song you played for me the other day."

"What song was that?"

"The one about the car. The 'Blood Red Cadillac.'"

"Car?" Lamont frowned. "Tell you true, I was so wrecked when you were at Jo's place I don't remember much about you bein' there. I, ah, don't handle booze too well, it kinda handles me, so if I was workin' on a song, I guess I musta forgot it."

"I don't know why you'd do that. It made quite an impression on me."

"I write a lot of songs. We play a few, peddle a few, but the majority of 'em get trashed."

"Still, it was an interesting idea, a blood red car. How'd you happen to come up with it?"

"The idea? Hell, I don't know where songs come from. Sometimes you work 'em out a word at a time, sometimes they just come out of the air, like somebody already wrote 'em for you. Sometimes I even dream 'em. Look, what's this all about anyway?"

"Songs," Garcia said, "and cars. A red Caddy's kind of a funny subject for a song, wouldn't you say?"

"Songs can be about anything. Love, death, puppy dogs,

anything that feels right. Even cars sometimes. You know, I think you're the first music critic cop I ever met."

"And you've met quite a few cops, haven't you?"

"A few," Lamont admitted. "Knew one at the Mountain who used to collect socks."

"Socks?" Linda said.

"Right. If you wanted out of a work detail or somethin', you could bribe this guy with a couple dirty socks. Somebody told me he slept with 'em. Had a fetish thing about 'em. You ever sleep with socks, Garcia?"

"Nope, I'm just a music lover who's very interested in your work. All of it."

"Well, tell you what, if writin' lame songs is against some kinda law now, I'm in deep trouble. Triple life at least."

"If you do more time, Lamont, it won't be for songwriting. You music's fine. What bothers me is the mortality rate in your vicinity when you're *off*stage."

"Have you ever sold any of your songs," Linda interjected before Lamont could speak, "or have any been recorded?"

"A few," Lamont said, ignoring Garcia. "Charlie Daniels cut one on an album, and Waylon Jennings optioned another but hasn't cut it yet. We've had feelers from a studio here to do some demos, and something may come of that."

"You don't seem very excited about the idea."

"I, ah, I guess maybe I should be but somehow it doesn't seem too important right now. Too much . . ." He seemed to lose his train of thought for a moment, then glanced up at them, blinking, almost dazed. "Sorry, where was I?"

"You were talking about doing some recordings," Linda said.

"Or not doin' 'em." He shrugged. "I'd like it to happen, but I'll survive if it doesn't. This is what I do," he said, nodding at the stage. "I'm a minstrel. An electronic one maybe, but the job's the same as it's always been. I write songs, and we play 'em for people. It's what I do."

"You've done other things," Garcia said softly, "like time."

"That was a long time ago. You know you could wear on a person, Mex. And I'd like to continue this little interview or whatever, but I gotta go back to work. You gonna stay another set?"

"I'm afraid not," Garcia said. "I've got an early day tomorrow."

"Now just a minute—" Linda began.

"Tell you what, miss," Lamont said, rising, "why don't you stay a while and let your friend here take off. I'll see you get home okay, no strings, no hassle. Give you my word."

"I don't think so," she said slowly.

"Tomorrow then, maybe? We rehearse tomorrow afternoon. Be easier to talk. Either way I gotta go. Don't be strangers now." He flipped Garcia a mock salute and pushed off through the crowd.

"I thought," Linda said, her voice taut, "that part of the reason we came here was so I could get an interview."

"There's something wrong about him," Garcia mused, his eyes still following Lamont. "Can't you feel it?"

"I felt a lot of hostility," she said, "most of it on your part. He's just another ex-con to you, isn't he?"

"No, it's more than that. I meet hard cases every day. Hell, *most* of the people I meet have either killed somebody or are involved somehow. It comes with the territory. This is different. It's like. . . . Look, when you work in places where you can get hurt, in 'Nam or on the streets here, you develop instincts about things, about situations. You look at a shadow and you sense something's waiting for you there, even when you can't see it. Yarborough's like that for me. A shadow."

"And is that his problem? Or yours?"

"Okay, okay," he conceded, "maybe I'm prejudiced, but we don't have to wonder if the guy's dangerous, we *know* he is. He aced his first wife, his lady friend looks like one of Tommy Hearns's sparring partners—"

"She told you he wasn't responsible for that."

"So she did, but she wouldn't be the first battered woman to lie about a beating and you know it."

"You may be right," she admitted. "And as a matter of fact I got the distinct impression he'd be a bad person to cross. But I have the same feelings about you, Garcia, and I'm still here. The

66

point is, he's an assignment. *My* assignment. And you just blew it for me. Maybe you meant well, but . . . I just came out of a relationship where everything was safe. And suffocating. And I'm not interested in going back to that. I'm my own person now, and if that involves taking some risks, I'll just have to chance it."

"One chance with this guy may be all you get."

"If he's such a threat to society, Officer," she said coldly, "why isn't he in custody?"

"He may be before long."

"You know, I never realized what an art policework is. I always thought of it as a science. Too much TV, I guess. Look, it's been a very educational evening, but since you have such an early day tomorrow, I think we'd better go."

"Right." He sighed. "Will you excuse me a minute? I have to visit the little boys' room. Be right back." He rose, not waiting for an answer, and made his way through the crowd toward the bar.

She watched him go for a moment, her lips pursed, drumming her fingertips on the table, and then turned toward the stage. And met Lamont's eyes over the heads of the crowd.

Half of his attention was on her, half on the rolling background he was playing to Sonny's voice, a hill-country love song in a pseudo barn in the urban North. She raised her left wrist over her head and pointed at her watch. He nodded and flashed a quick "one" with his right hand without missing a note, both of them smiling at the ease of the mimed exchange.

At the banquet table facing the stage, Jobeth Lawton also watched the message pass, her eyes flicking between them, empty, expressionless.

"What's your problem, honey," Rhonda Bailey said, touching her arm, "something wrong with your drink?"

Garcia stood near the front door waiting for the song to finish. As the ripple of applause momentarily drowned conversations, he quickly opened the glass display case and slipped the publicity poster for Sonny Earle and the Country Barons out and under his jacket in one fluid motion. He glanced around to be sure no one

67

had noticed, then joined in the applause, barely resisting the urge to take a bow.

"Papa?"

Lamont moved carefully, testing each step before putting his weight on it, sliding his feet along without lifting them at all. The ice was slick with seepage, but there was no rush of water like the day they'd broken through, only a surface sheen of moisture, faintly reflecting the stars and the city lights from the Canadian side of the river. The wind was sharp, and the cold was fierce and deep, welling up from the dark water beneath the surface pack.

His pace slowed as he tired, until finally he stopped, head down, spent, trying not to inhale the frigid air too deeply. No good. Have to go back. He scanned the horizon as he turned. And froze. There was something out there. A smudge, a dark spot against the rim.

"Toby!" The wind swallowed his shout so completely he wasn't sure he'd voiced it at all. "Toby Red! Goddamn it!"

He started toward the figure, picking up the pace of his death row shuffle, moving unsteadily across the broken surface. And he stumbled, and went down, the ice giving a startled squeak when he landed, driving the breath out of him. He scrambled quickly to his knees, chest heaving, and wiped the cold sweat from around his eyes, scanning the horizon. And the figure was closer now. Much closer. And larger.

"Nooooooo!!!"

He tore the clutching hands away from his throat, fighting to breathe, lashing out with both fists at . . . nothing. He sat upright, gulping air, the sweat-dampened sheets bunched around his waist, and realized Jobeth was beside the bed, her back against the wall, naked, clutching her pillow over her heavy breasts, staring at him wide-eyed, terrified.

"You okay?" he managed. His throat felt raw, and abraded, as though he'd been screaming. "Look, I'm sorry. It was a . . . dream, is all. It's over. It's okay now." He lowered himself again to the pillows. He couldn't tell whether she believed him nor not, and it didn't matter.

CHAPTER 10

GARCIA WOKE UP FIVE MINUTES BEFORE HIS ALARM WENT OFF, clearheaded and angry. A bad night. He'd spent most of it thrashing around, mentally replaying the evening, trying to decide where it derailed, what he could have said to change things. But in the end the only thing he was absolutely sure of was that he'd blown it.

He took a cold shower to clear the cobwebs, then phoned in an LEIN request on the names of the musicians on the poster he'd lifted, and asked them to forward the information to the squad room. The phone rang again the moment he replaced the receiver.

"Loop? You up?" Fielder.

"More or less."

"Then you better get on your pony, or you're gonna miss the show. The captain wants you in early this morning."

"Why? What's up?"

"I'm not clear on it myself, but I think he wants you to see a shrink."

The squad room was its usual early morning buzz. Fielder was at his desk trying to cool out a couple of cashmere-overcoated types from Greektown who were shouting for some action on a holdup murder. Wilk and Keller were interviewing an elderly barrel of a black woman in a frayed shawl, witness to a mom and pop shooting. And Joad was sitting on the edge of Garcia's desk, talking to Cordell. Terrific. A bum night and the morning was already on a downhill slide.

Bobby Pilarski was filling the coffee machine, and Garcia paused to grab a cup. If he stalled long enough maybe Joad would evaporate like a bad dream.

"Hey, Loop, how you doin'?"

"Hunky-dory, Bobby," Garcia said, smiling at Pilarski's scowl of concentration as he painstakingly measured the coffee into the filter. Bobby looked like a cartoonist's idea of a cop, clear blue eyes, a thick mane of silver hair, chiseled features, neatly tailored uniform. He'd taken early retirement a few years before, following a stroke that left him slightly lamed and more than slightly confused. But after a few weeks of loafing, he began showing up at the squad room again, to make coffee, run errands and make himself generally useful. And confused or not, on any given day Bobby might be the sanest person Garcia talked to.

"An LEIN report came through for you a couple minutes ago, Loop. I left it on your desk. You catch the Pistons last night?"

"Missed it. Who'd you have, them or the Bucs?"

"I'm not sure." Bobby frowned. "I got it written down, though. If I can find somebody knows the score, I can check and see if I won."

"Try Marv Cream, Bobby. He'll know the score." It wasn't going to work. Joad had glanced up and spotted him, and he was obviously waiting. "Catch you later, Bobby. Keep the faith."

Styrofoam cup in hand, Garcia stalked over to his desk and dropped into his chair. Joad was in midanecdote so Garcia tuned him out for a moment, and began scanning the Law Enforcement Information Network report on Sonny Earle and the

70

Barons. Two of them, Mick Woods the drummer and Gopher
Bailey the steel guitar player, had no record of arrests. Sonny
Earle had a minor bust for possession of controlled substances,
three counts, served thirty days in Saginaw County for it. And
LeeRoy Clayton, aka "Tree," the giant bass guitarist, had done
hard time in Jackson for assault with intent, six years. Garcia
raised his eyebrows at that one. The guy must have . . .

"Don't get too comfortable, Garcia," Joad said abruptly.
"You're leaving."

"Yeah? Where am I going?"

"To the airport. I want you to see a psychiatrist."

Garcia blinked. "A what?"

"Don't panic, I don't mean for a checkup, though that might
not be a bad idea. I chaired a panel at a DRA lunch yesterday.
Detroit Renaissance Alliance? And the guest speaker was Jillian
Easton, a psych professor from UCLA. We talked about a
number of cases in passing and your slasher in particular. She
suggested doing a psychological profile on him. The FBI's done
some pretty impressive stuff with them—"

"Captain, I'm familiar with the technique, but I don't think
this case—"

"If you're concerned about getting some egghead type involved, Garcia, you needn't be. The doctor does a lot of talk
shows, so she's used to dealing with laymen, and I'm sure she'll
be willing to explain anything you don't understand. In any case,
I sent our files on the case to her suite at the Marriott last night
and booked a conference room there for eleven. Sergeant Cream
will be there and the Seventh is sending over a team as well, so
don't be late. The good doctor charges two hundred and fifty per,
and the department's on a tight budget."

"No kidding." Garcia sighed. "I wonder why?"

Easton was a surprise. When Joad said talk shows, Garcia'd
envisioned a blow-dried surfer with a ceramic smile and a
ten-thousand-word psychobabble vocabulary. But the lady was a
square-shouldered, dark-eyed, strikingly handsome woman, early
fortyish, with tousled brown hair and thick horn-rimmed glasses.

71

She was parked casually on the end of one of the gleaming oak conference tables in the Marriott Hotel's fourth-floor conference room, talking to Marv Cream. A contrast in styles. Easton was wearing a brown tweed jacket over a tan turtleneck sweater, Marv, a dark, slubbed-silk suit that positively gleamed under the fluorescent lighting in the room. Rumpled academic meets black TV evangelist.

Two detectives from the Seventh were sitting at the end of the table sipping coffee from Styrofoam cups. Garcia nodded at Dom Tully, a beery, baby-faced blond moose he'd met a few times in passing. He vaguely remembered Dom's partner, a sleepy-eyed hulk in a black leather jacket who looked like a pro fighter with a losing record. Skiba? Sliwa? Something like that.

"Sergeants . . . Bennett and Garcia?" Easton said, glancing up. "Coffee's in the corner, and we'd better get started. My flight leaves at one. Does everybody know everybody?"

"Everybody but you, Doc," Garcia said, pulling up a chair. "And by the way, what are you a doctor of? Medicine?"

"Psychology, Ph.D. But it could be basketweaving, since they don't teach much about the subject at hand in school anyway. I've picked up what I know about it in cells and matchbox offices in prisons all over the U.S. You seem to have some reservations about this conference, Garcia."

"Let's just say I'd rather be doing something more . . . direct about the problem."

"Well, since you're here, you might as well get what you can. And spare me the static, okay? I've already had my ration for the week. I had a parole interview yesterday with a child molester turned Jesus freak who wanted to be placed at Teen Ranch. As a chaplain, yet."

"You gonna recommend him for parole?" Tully asked.

"I don't think so," Easton said, deadpan. "I think he's more likely to turn the teenyboppers onto St. Peter than Jesus."

"That's sick, Doc." Cordell winced. "Maybe you oughta see a shrink."

"Not a chance. They're all quacks. Look, I'm sure you men have some doubts about me, but that's your problem. I think I

72

may be able to tell you a few things about your slasher. Interested?"

"Who are your sources?" Marv asked quietly. "Some of your patients into mass murder, are they?"

"A few. You have seven incarcerated in various institutions here in Michigan, and I've talked to others around the country. Most of them will tell you a lot more than you want to know. Talking about it turns them on."

"And of course they always tell you the truth," Garcia said. "No reason to snow you just because you consult for parole boards, right?"

"Actually," Easton said calmly, "once I get past name, rank, and serial number, I'd estimate that two-thirds of what I'm told every day of my professional life is bullshit, pure and simple. And not just from cons. You should hear a congressman whine about the lack of funds for jails and mental facilities, then promise he'll raise the matter at next month's conference in Honolulu. I also hear a fair amount from cops."

"Yeah?" Cordell said, interested. "What kind you think you hear from cops?"

"Mostly about how rational your motives for being in police work are. 'It's not really a rush to kick in doors at three in the morning, it's just a job.' That kind of crap. The kind you tell civilians. Well, I don't wear a badge or carry a piece, gentlemen, but I spend a helluva lot of time in jails. And I'm not a civilian. Now shall we talk?"

"I like what I'm hearin' so far." Tully grinned. "Go ahead on."

"Good." Easton nodded brusquely. "Suppose I give you what I've worked up, bearing in mind that this is all just paper and it may not be complete, or pertain to this particular case. You've been at the scenes, talked to witnesses, so if anything doesn't ring true, just say so."

"You'll be the first to know," Garcia said.

"Fine. Now what I've done is develop a rough profile of this perp from FBI files, my own clients, the coroner's reports, and your target reports—"

"Target reports?" Cordell interrupted. "What's a target report?"

"Well, your dailies. My assistant's been calling them target reports because of the covers."

Cordell glanced at Garcia. "That ain't a target on the cover, Doc."

"It's not? Well, it—"

"It's a Cheerio."

"A Cheerio?"

"Sure," Cordell said blandly, "the guy's a cereal killer, right?"

Easton stared down at him a moment over the tops of her glasses, then slowly shook her head. "I, ah, haven't been accepting new patients for some time. Schedule's too tight. I might make an exception for you two though. Might be a book in it. A Cheerio. Right. In any case, your Cheerio killer is probably a white male, mid-thirties or older, reasonably intelligent, acceptable appearance. He's probably unacquainted with the victims on a personal basis—"

"Can we slow down a little," Tully interrupted. "Maybe take this a bite at a time? Why a white male for openers?"

"Serials are almost always men. Of the roughly hundred and sixty multiples incarcerated around the country, only ten are women, and four of those used poison. A woman is possible in the present instance, we've come a long way, but as multiple murderers, white males top the stats. Plus, in this town, what do you figure the chances of a black male getting close to four white women late at night would be?"

"Slim," Garcia admitted. "Okay, white male. Why do you think he's older, and doesn't know his victims?"

"Most murderers are in their twenties, most multiples are thirty or more. We don't know why, they just are. And when a multiple knows his victims, the attacks are usually extremely savage, and directed against the sex organs."

"This one slices off heads, or almost, and cuts away brassieres. Doesn't that count as savage?"

"He doesn't carve the victims up," Easton said simply. "They're killed with a single stroke, a vicious one, but only one, and the bras are cut away carefully, without so much as a nick on the skin. We all know killings can be a lot more brutal than that.

Also there's been no apparent molestation, so we're probably not dealing with a sexual deviate in the conventional sense, more likely a schizoid personality acting out a terrible rage against women."

"Why?" Cordell asked. "What's he so mad about? His girlfriend cut him off or what?"

"These disorders are often present at an extremely early point of development, five or six years old. But because children are powerless, they repress it, or at least conceal it. And then an incident triggers it, and it might be something as simple as an argument with a girlfriend, though that doesn't seem likely in this case. The killings are too cool, too calculated. Revenge, perhaps. A dish best eaten cold, as the poets say."

"Or the songwriters," Garcia said. "Why revenge? For what?"

"I don't know. Edmund Kemper used his mom's severed head for a dartboard, so in his case it was fairly obvious who he was mad at. Mr. Cheerio? I'll just have to ask him when you catch him. There's no single syndrome these disorders follow. His wife? His mother? Who knows? It's my considered professional opinion the guy's a wacko."

"You used the word 'calculated,'" Marv observed. "You think he's intelligent?"

"Ah, well. Now I'm only guessing. These types often are, or they simply don't stay free long enough to commit multiple murders. In this case, the perp's been very methodical about picking his spots, the time of night, very . . . businesslike. So we're probably not dealing with someone who's severely retarded. He'd have to be of at least average intelligence, possibly more. Did you notice that the victims have all been in different police precincts? Coincidence perhaps, or maybe the perp was hoping they wouldn't be connected right away, and they weren't. We could be dealing with someone who's familiar with police procedures."

"Like an ex-con, for instance?" Garcia said.

"Maybe, or a cop."

"Why a cop?"

"I didn't say he was a cop, *or* an ex-con. I said someone who's

75

familiar with police procedures, which covers a lot of ground. Don't try to read more into this than it's worth."

"I understand that, but an ex-con *would* fit. Especially one who's already done time for murder?"

"You have a suspect in mind, haven't you? Want to run him past me?"

"Ex-con, white southerner, fortyish, murdered his first wife, presently living with a woman who shows signs of abuse. Makes his living playing guitar, and people around him seem to check out before their time, his stepson, his wife, a woman in the hospital. Sound like a candidate to you?"

"Oddly enough, the only part that doesn't fit is the battered woman. Most schizoids are relatively subdued characters, sometimes even quite personable, until something sets them off and they really blow."

"He claims he's never laid a hand on her. Maybe he's telling the truth."

"Maybe," Easton said, frowning. "You know, his being a performer might explain a couple of things that bother me about this. All of the victims had been drinking heavily, which strikes me as an odd coincidence, and also, how does Cheerio get so close? Nobody picks up hitchhikers in this town, so why do the women stop? But if they'd seen him perform, perhaps arranged to meet him? Is that how you're figuring it?"

"Something like that."

"Well, had they seen him perform?"

"We don't know yet. We're still running it down."

"Interesting possibility. And as likely as any other. The truth is, despite all the research that's been done, we have no consistent mechanism for nailing these guys. This profile may help you narrow your suspect list, and perhaps when it runs in the papers it may bring you a tip that helps—"

"What do you mean, 'in the papers'?" Garcia interrupted. "You can't give this to the press."

"Why not?"

"Because it'll lead to a thousand panicky tips and any solid leads we might get'll be buried in the garbage."

76

"I understand that you're a bit shorthanded—"

"Shorthanded? Jesus, take a look at this room, Easton. You're talking to five guys about a serial killer that would mobilize an army anywhere else. And if you know your stats, you know you can stand on any street corner in Motown, blow somebody away, and your chances of getting caught are six to four against. We're barely coping with the information we have now."

"Look, I sympathize with your situation, Garcia, but when your department engaged me, a press packet was part of the deal. I have to deliver. I suppose I could delay releasing the profile information a few days. Would that help?"

"It might, if Cheerio happens to walk in and confess in the next few days, but if not, you're gonna lengthen our odds, it's as simple as that."

"I'm sorry. I'm afraid that's the best I can do."

"Terrific," Garcia said, crumpling his coffee cup and tossing it in the general direction of the wastebasket. "At least we know how much time we've got to get the job done. Marv, can you give Cordell a lift back?"

"Sure. Where are you goin'?"

"Like I said earlier, I think I'd better try to do something a bit more direct about the situation."

CHAPTER 11

Lamont and the steel guitarist were toying with a song on the dimly lit stage when Linda Kerry walked into the Crossing. She made her way through the darkened dance area to the second-tier table she'd shared with Garcia the night before. After the grayish glare of the winter afternoon, the deserted room had a dank, subterranean feel to it.

Two gaunt, hard-looking brunettes in T-shirts and jeans were the only other customers. They were sharing a pitcher of beer and low-key conversation with Sonny Earle at the first banquet table. The bass player, a tall, curly-bearded giant with hooded eyes, was lounging against his amplifier, his massive arms folded across his chest, waiting for the two guitarists to work out their parts, patient as a tree. The drummer, nearly invisible behind his set, was tapping out the tempo on his high hat with one stick.

Suddenly the music began to take shape, an intricate melody in two parts that seemed to flow together, then separate again, like sunlight through a prism. Both Sonny and the bass player glanced up, interested, nodding approval.

78

"Hey, all right," Sonny called. "That's cookin'."

They ignored him, still working out the last phrase, frowning, exchanging riffs as though the instruments were speaking to each other in a language of their own.

Satisfied, the steel guitarist nodded at Sonny, who uncoiled from his seat and strode to the stage, vaulting up and jerking his microphone free in one fluid move. He finger-popped a quick four and the group swung into a smooth, uptown shuffle that owed nothing to its country roots but the lyrics Sonny belted out. Caucasian blues, about a country boy who builds cars in his dreams.

He put a lot of energy into his delivery, stalking the stage, sharing his mike with the bass player on the chorus, playing to the nearly empty room as though it held a wall-to-wall crowd and a bank of cameras feeding a satellite. Lamont's guitar solo echoed the down-home rural South with a nostalgic country fugue that could have been a hundred years old, but finished with a stinging blues lick that slashed across the past, swinging into the last chorus:

"Workin' twelve hours a day, most of 'em stoned,
Line boss on me, won't leave me alone,
But I keep on keepin' on, dreamin' 'about
    hoooome . . ."

Linda found herself humming along with the chorus. It had an easy lilt to it that felt more like the pop songs she'd grown up with than the hokey, rhinestone wailing she'd expected the night before. Not bad. Not bad at all. She took a narrow stenographer's pad from her purse and began taking notes, the song, the setting, the occasional nods of satisfaction between the men on the stage as the arrangement came together. The song ended and she applauded with the two brunettes at the center table, three pairs of hands clapping in an empty cavern.

Sonny took a deep, melodramatic bow, tipping his gunfighter Stetson to Linda, then to the brunette sisters. "Whaddya think, Gopher, was that tight enough? You guys satisfied?"

"Close enough for jazz," the chubby steel guitarist said. "How about it, Lamont? It's your tune."

"It's comin' around," Lamont said, fitting his guitar into its case. "We'll try it tonight, see if it flies. Meantime I got business."

"The blonde from last night," Sonny said. "Nice stuff. Open season on that or what?"

"She's a reporter, city boy. Maybe she can do us some good, but otherwise she's off-limits."

"Hey, lighten up, Lamont, share the wealth. You oughta do a line, toot up a buzz fine as wine. The chick looks like a double handful and you ain't no kid, you know? Or maybe I should warm her up for ya. I'll send her back after. Always do, right, LeeRoy?"

"I'll make it simple for you," Lamont said. "Her boyfriend's a cop. That clear enough?"

"Whaddya mean a cop?" the bass player said, frowning. "Jesus Christ, Yarborough, are you wiggin' out? If she's mixed up with a cop—"

"Look, I don't mess in your business, LeeRoy, so you'd best stay outa mine. I can handle the lady, but you better tighten the leash on your buddy there before his mouth buys him some serious trouble."

"Hey, c'mon, you guys," Gopher said quickly, stepping between them. "We got a good thing goin' here. We don't need any hassles."

"You're right," LeeRoy said, staring impassively at Lamont. "We don't."

"Glad you could make it," Lamont said, pulling up a chair at Linda's table. "I wasn't sure you'd come."

"All in a day's work," she said. "Shall we get started?"

"Just like that?" Lamont smiled. "You want a beer or anything?"

"I don't drink while I'm working," she said carefully, "and that's what I'm doing here. Working."

"Sure, no problem. How about coffee?"

"Coffee would be fine. On me."

80

"Hey, Curly," he shouted at the elderly bartender working the counter, "two joes, my tab. Okay, honey, it's your show, where do you want to start?"

"Why don't we begin with your band and go on from there. Can you give me a quick rundown, who plays what, that sort of thing?"

Sure. For openers, it's not my band, it's kind of a democracy. Sonny's the front man, I supply the material, and LeeRoy, the big guy on bass guitar, handles the business end of it."

"I can see why you'd want him to."

"He's a little surly, and that's a fact. He and Sonny have been together a while, giggin' around the Midwest. Gopher Bailey, the steel player, joined 'em just before I did, and I've been with 'em a little over a year now."

"Steel player, you said?"

"Pedal steel guitar. It's a double-necked guitar played horizontal. Changes tone with those pedals there on the floor and a steel bar in the player's hand. Used to be called Hawaiian guitars. Most country bands have 'em."

"I've seen them. I never knew what they were."

"They sound like a gut-shot hound if they're not played right, but Gopher makes his sing pretty good."

The bartender placed two steaming mugs of coffee between them and Lamont nodded his thanks.

"Why do you call him Gopher?" Linda asked. "Is there a story there?"

"I . . ." His smile caught her by surprise, erasing years and wariness from his eyes. "You know," he said wryly, "I don't really know." He glanced over at the group sharing the pitcher with the two brunettes. "Maybe it's his sideburns. He looks a little like a gopher, you know? You want me to ask him?"

"Please don't bother."

"'Course it might not have anything to do with his looks," he said, dropping his voice to a whisper. "It might be something weird he does behind closed doors. The one in the blue T-shirt's his wife, maybe we could ask her. Might make a better story."

81

"But not for my department. You know, you really ought to smile more. You have a good one."

"Mmmm, well, seems like I haven't had a helluva lot to smile about lately." He sipped his coffee, not meeting her eyes, the wariness back.

"No," she said carefully. "I suppose not. Sorry, I didn't mean to—"

"It's not your fault. It's my problem. I'm the one who should apologize. That was a nice thing to say. Tell you what, your next question's a free shot. Anything you want to know, the absolute truth. Anything at all."

For a moment the image of the drowned car played in her thoughts, but she shrugged it off. Too soon. "I believe the next question"—she glanced down at her notepad—"is how long have you been playing?"

"About twelve hundred years. Maybe more."

"Really? You don't look a day over seven-fifty."

"I'm serious," he said mildly.

"You're serious. You're telling me you're twelve hundred years old?"

"It's a little more complicated than that. You ever attend a one-room school?"

"I'm afraid not."

"Well, in a schoolhouse like that, the kids in the different grades are all in the same room, and while the teacher works with one bunch, the rest are supposed to study something else. But I didn't study much. I mostly just listened. You ever heard of Taileffer?"

"Who?"

"Taileffer. He was a troubador in the army of William the Conqueror, 1066. I was maybe five years old the first time I heard that story. He led the last charge against the Saxons at the battle of Hastings, twirlin' his sword in the air like a juggler and singing the Song of Roland. He was killed there. And I'm him, or at least I was."

"You were a troubador at the battle of Hastings."

"Nope." He smiled. "I was a five-year-old kid who heard that

82

story, and afterwards, that's who I was, in my mind. And in a way, maybe I still am."

"And were you playing guitar when you were five?"

"No, I was playing a lute, or something like one. But only in my head. My people were hard-shell Baptist, didn't hold with any music outside of church. After I got whupped a few times for singin' songs I made up, I kinda put troubadorin' on hold for a while."

"Then when did you first actually play a guitar?"

"A few years later," he said coolly. "My first day out of isolation block at Brushy Mountain, first day in a cell with other convicts. I was nineteen. This big ol' boy saw I was . . . hurting, and he loaned me his guitar. And saved my goddam life."

"You were only nineteen? Excuse me if this question is out of line, but weren't you in prison for killing your wife?"

"I was married and workin' in a sawmill when I was sixteen. Some things start kinda young down south. I was green as the grass and just about as smart, and I, ah, I killed my woman for cheatin' on me, like some clown in a song on the radio. Maybe you could say I was 'programmed' to do it."

"How can you joke about a thing like that?"

"Lady, you handle it any way you can. What would you do? Cry? Maybe freak? I tried both of those things. Didn't work too well. And I think we've kinda drifted off the subject."

"Yes, I suppose we have," she said thoughtfully, meeting his eyes. "So you learned to play in prison?"

"Sort of. The funny thing was, I could play that guitar almost from the minute I picked it up. Maybe from playing the lute in my head when I was a kid, or maybe I played one somewhere before, I don't know. But it kept me alive in there, and it still does."

"A troubador."

"Something like that." He nodded. "Guess it sounds kinda naive."

"Naive? Not really. Let's just say that you're not exactly what I expected."

"Considering who the source of your information was, that's probably not all bad, is it?"

"No, not all bad."

"Good. Now I've got a question for you," he said, showing the trace of a smile. "If this little history lesson is for your story, shouldn't you be takin' notes?"

Garcia wheeled the Chrysler into a slot in front of the Crossing. A dozen or so cars were parked in the lot, and he almost walked past the BMW without recognizing it. And then it registered. A light-blue three-year-old BMW sedan with a goose-egg-sized ding in the driver's side door. And a press credential sticker in the window. Linda's car. He frowned at it thoughtfully, trying to decide how to handle the situation. Nuts! There was nothing *to* handle. Business was business. Still . . . he walked around the building to the side door.

He stepped to one side of the doorway as soon as he entered, giving his eyes a moment to adjust to the gloom, zeroing in on her like radar. She was sitting at the table they'd shared the night before at the far end of the club, apparently deep in conversation with Lamont, and he felt a sudden chill in his belly, as though he'd just stepped into the cold rather than out of it.

The bar area wasn't busy, the lunch rush was apparently over, and only a half-dozen drinkers remained. The gaunt, bow-tied bartender was on his knees behind the bar, restocking the beer coolers. Garcia walked over, out of view of the dance area, and asked for Grivas.

"He's at the bank," the old man said without looking up. "Be back in a couple hours. You want a beer?"

"No. My name's Garcia. You just tell him I was here, and remind him to call me. Or I'll be back. Got that?"

The old man glanced up at him, unimpressed. "I'll tell him. Officer." He didn't spit after he said it, but looked as though he wanted to. "Now, if you don't mind, mister, some of us gotta work for a livin'."

Garcia shrugged. Nobody wants a cop around until they *want* a cop around. He noticed the door to the men's room was ajar, propped open by a mop bucket. The bartender was pointedly ignoring him and no one else was paying any attention either. He walked casually to the john, slid the bucket inside with his foot, and closed the door softly behind him.

Denny had his back to him, mopping out the farthest of the three toilet stalls, wailing an off-key version of "Amos Moses." Garcia moved up silently behind him and tapped him lightly on the shoulder.

"What—?" Denny whirled in the narrow stall, brandishing the mop handle like a lance.

"Hey, be careful with that thing, okay?" Garcia said, raising both hands, palms outward. "You've got trouble enough without adding assault with a deadly mop."

"Jesus, Garcia, you scared the shit outa me. Whadda you want?"

"I was in the neighborhood, thought I'd pop in and say hello, you know, since I haven't heard from you. Nice little place you've got here, small, but homey. It's definitely you. I'd be careful where you sit though. It looks like somebody puked on your sofa."

"Ahhhh, shit!" Denny said, glancing at the smear on his pants leg where he'd brushed against the bowl. He leaned the mop on the graffiti-scarred wall and tore a wad of toilet paper from the dispenser. "Look, I ain't called ya because I ain't had a chance to get nothing yet." He daubed sorrowfully at the stain on his jeans. "The place was jumpin' last night, and—"

"Denny, Denny." Garcia sighed, squatting on his heels so he and the boy were eye to eye in the narrow stall. "Take a look around you. We're in a toilet. With barf on the floor. It's not as comfy as your cell in Jackson, but then you don't have to give head five times a day just to stay alive in here either. I'll tell you something, there are parts of my job I'm not heavy into, and one of 'em is coming down on a guy where he works, especially when he works in a dump like this."

"So don't come down. Who asked ya to?"

"I wish it was that simple. I'll lay it on you straight, kid, I'm jammed up. I've got bodies in the streets, and I need help.

85

Names, addresses, plate numbers, on Lamont's women or any women who hang around the band. If I can't get it from you, I'll have to find somebody else fast. But first I'll have to send the county mounties over to bust your butt for the weapons violation, just to make sure the next guy I talk to takes me seriously. I hope it doesn't go down that way. I'll feel bad about it, you know? But probably not as bad as you will. So how about it? The clock's running on this."

"Okay, okay already, I'll get it! But, Jesus, you gotta keep away from me. You're gonna get me hurt."

"You don't want me around, fine. Tell you what, you get me what I want by tomorrow and we're dead even. I'll dump your gun and forget I ever heard of you. Fair enough?"

"Yeah, sure it is."

"You don't sound convinced."

"Christ, Garcia, just because I mop out johns don't mean I'm stupid. You ain't gonna forget about me. Not as long as you want somethin'. You'll squeeze me down to nothin' and wipe your ass on what's left."

"Jeez." Garcia winced. "You've got a nasty outlook on life, you know that? Things could be worse you know." He glanced around the filthy stall. "On second thought, maybe not."

CHAPTER 12

GARCIA LEANED AGAINST THE BAY WINDOW FRAME IN HIS LIVING room, staring out into the waning afternoon, waiting. The pallid winter sun had disappeared behind the high-rise across the street half an hour before, but he hadn't bothered to turn on the lights. Ordinarily it was his favorite time of the day, street lamps flickering on in the deep blue dusk, forming silvery light-rings on the snow-dusted sidewalks four stories below, rooftop Christmas trees winking at the stars. Twilight time.

No magic in it tonight though. He was nursing a lukewarm Bud Lite and an uneasy feeling that things were coming unglued, that he was on the edge of a long slide. He tried to ignore Linda's empty slot in the parking lot below, to concentrate on the icy clarity of the winter sky, but instead he kept seeing Denny cringing in that unholy graffiti-scarred stall, and a crimson-spattered pattern on white leather seats.

Linda's blue BMW pulled in at six-thirty, only fifteen minutes later than usual, and she was alone. There was no rational reason for the surge of relief he felt. Still . . . it was the first thing that had gone right all day.

He switched on his electric wok and was scrounging in the refrigerator when the doorbell chimed. He parked his beer, brushed his hair back with his fingertips, and opened the door.

"Hi," she said. "Look, I know I should have called first, but since I was in the neighborhood . . . Can we talk?"

"Absolutely. I was about to call you anyway."

"Were you? Why?"

"About last night. To apologize. You wanna discuss it over dinner?"

"Only if I'm buying. I owe you one."

"Nobody's counting, and if you can handle my cooking twice in a week, I've already got munchables under way. Besides, then you'll owe me two dinners."

"Which nobody's counting. You're sure I'm not imposing?"

"No chance. I'm fixing bread crusts and gruel. You'd be doing me a favor."

"Gee, bread crusts are my favorite. Will they keep a few minutes, do you think? I'd like to change."

"Keeping is what bread crusts do best," he said. "What did you want to talk about?"

"Nothing that won't keep twenty minutes. Or so."

It was closer to a half hour, but worth every second. She'd slipped on designer jeans and a cashmere sweater with a long V-neck that showed a lot of freckles. Funny, he couldn't recall being particularly fond of freckles before. Something Freudian maybe? Her hair, still damp around the edges from the shower, was pinned up in a twist, showing off her surprisingly delicate neck.

She picked up his sportcoat from the back of the couch and carried it off in search of a hanger. He turned, watching her disappear into the bedroom, liking the image so much he seared his thumb on the edge of the wok.

"Ow! Damn!" He popped his thumb in his mouth, trying to ease the sting.

"I've heard of people who really get into cooking," she said, wandering back into the kitchen, "but I think you're overdoing it."

88

"Look, lathy," he mumbled around his scorched thumb, "to a thrue artitht, pade medes nothing. I wath juth making thure it wath hot enough, thath all."

"Can I kiss and make better?" She took his hand in both of hers and kissed it lightly on the back, then leaned against him, resting her head on his shoulder as he stirred the brown rice. He felt some of the uncertainty that had been gnawing at him all afternoon begin to dissolve. Maybe it was going to work out after all.

"Look, about last night—" she began.

"I know, you want my apology notarized."

"It's not that. I've been thinking about it, and maybe it was partly my fault."

"Which part?"

"Maybe I set up what happened at the club by pushing you too hard on the way there. About your past, I mean."

"Asking questions is part of your job."

"That's not why I did it and you know it."

"Look, suppose we call it a draw and start over? Fair enough?"

"Fair enough. What sort of gruel are we concocting tonight?"

"Tonight, madame, we're dining on viands of the Orient, garnished with delicate spices from the land of the Khans."

"No kidding? Gosh, and I thought you were cooking Chinese. Whatever it is, it smells delicious."

"It's authentic too. Learned to make it in the back of my mama's yurt."

"You know, Yarborough was right about one thing. You *are* the weirdest cop I've ever met. You don't really have a fetish about socks, do you?"

"Nope, but I do have some Muppet feety pajamas I'm pretty fond of. Play your cards right and maybe I'll model 'em for you."

"I can hardly wait."

"Did he give you anything interesting today?"

"I didn't say I talked to him today."

"Roy's Country Crossing, about one-thirty, ring a bell?"

"You followed me?" she said, stepping away from him, looking into his face with wonder.

"Zay do not call me ze bloodhound of ze Sureté for nozzing."

"You bastard," she said, the color draining from her face, "you had no right to do that."

"Hey, wait a minute," he said, stunned by the depth of her anger, "I didn't follow you."

"You just said you did."

"I was *kidding*. I'm the guy with the Muppet pajamas, remember? I was only kidding."

"Then how did you know I'd talked to Yarborough today?"

"I was at the Crossing this afternoon, but—"

"By coincidence, I suppose. I'll just bet it was."

"I was there on business, dammit, and that's the truth. Look, what is all this? I don't understand."

She stared hard into his face, reading him like a stranger. "Maybe you don't," she said at last, "but I'm not sure it matters. I'm afraid this just isn't going to work out, Lupe. Not dinner, not anything. I'm sorry. I really am."

"Hey, wait a minute," he said, grabbing her wrist as she turned away. "Please. This isn't fair."

"I know it's not, but please let go of my arm."

"Okay, okay, sorry," he said, stepping back, wanting to hold her, afraid to try.

She paused at the door, her hand on the knob, then turned to face him. "My husband had me followed," she said abruptly. "Rex is a surgeon, very successful, but a very traditional sort of man in many ways. I gave up my job at the VA hospital after we were married to avoid any appearance of impropriety. But I wasn't satisfied just staying at home, so I decided to try a career change, and went back to school. Rex was . . . unhappy with my decision, but I thought he'd accepted it. And then I began noticing this man around the campus, a tall man with his hair combed sideways over his bald spot. He tried to dress like a student but there was something . . . Anyway, one day he just marched up and announced he'd been following me, that he was a *detective*." She spat the word out.

"I can see—"

"Let me finish. This lemon proceeded to haul out his note-

90

book and tell me everywhere I'd been for the previous two weeks. Everywhere. And then he pointed out that there were times I wouldn't be able to account for, times when I could have been meeting a lover, for instance. Of course if I could see my way clear to be *nice* to him, he'd give me a clean bill of health and I'd have a lock on Rex and the six-figure income forever."

"Hey," he said softly, "I'm sorry it happened, but I didn't—"

"You don't understand," she said, avoiding his eyes. "The thing is, I, um, I thought about it."

"Thought about what?"

"About going to bed with him. For a moment the idea of losing everything, my home, Rex, of being on my own, was so frightening that I actually considered it."

"But you didn't."

"No, I didn't. Quite the contrary. That night I had a cool, rational discussion with my husband, and filed for divorce the next day. It seemed like the end of the world at the time, but I don't think I regret it. Much."

"And you think I'm like that detective? I'm not, you know."

"No, I don't think that at all. As a matter of fact, I think you're a reasonably terrific guy, Garcia. And in a way, that's the problem."

"Hey, if you can't handle terrific I've been told I do pretty good rudimentary."

"True enough," she said, smiling in spite of herself. "And what's more you make me laugh, even when nothing's funny. Especially then."

"And this is a problem? Am I missing something here?"

"In a way it is. Straight out, Lupe, it would be very easy for me to get all girlish and enthusiastic about you. Maybe even try for a serious relationship. But if I do that now, I'll never know if I can . . . survive on my own. And I need to know. It's very important to me. Am I making any sense at all?"

"Yes, I think so, though to be honest, I think you may be overreacting a bit. It's no sin to be afraid. Everyone's afraid sometimes."

"You're not," she said positively, "or at least not like that."

91

"You're wrong. I get as spooked as anyone else. On a daily basis."

"But if it happens, at least you know you can handle it. And that's something I have to find out."

"And while you're finding out, where does that leave us?"

"Friends, I hope. Good friends for now. After a . . . suitable cooling-off period."

"I see," he said slowly.

"From your tone, I'm not sure you do."

"Well, let's just say I hope I do. I like you a lot, Linda, well enough to try to help you get whatever you want. And if space is what you want from me now, well, I guess I'll just have to give you some. I think I'd rather give you my car, though. Or maybe my record collection."

"I'll settle for a little time for now. And not too much, I hope."

"I hope so too. And since we're good friends who aren't going to see each other for a while, shouldn't we kiss good-bye? Or something?"

"No." She smiled, meeting his eyes. "Not a chance, friend. But for what it's worth, I have the distinct feeling that I may be making one of the bigger mistakes of my life here."

"Yep, I agree. But just so you don't feel like the Lone Ranger, let me make one. Don't spend any more time with Yarborough. Please."

"You're right," she said, her smile fading. "That was a mistake."

"Yeah, well, sometimes that's part of being a friend, offering good advice whether it's welcome or not."

"Perhaps so. Still, I wish you hadn't said that. But since we're talking friend to friend here, as a reasonably neutral observer, I think you're the one who may be overreacting. Whatever happened in Lamont's past, the loss of his stepson must have been a devastating experience—"

"Is that how he struck you? Devastated?"

"My personal reaction to him isn't important. I'm not a policeman. People who rub me the wrong way don't wind up in jail."

"There's a lot more involved here than my being rubbed the wrong way."

"I'm sure you think that's true," she said coolly, opening the door. "Still, as a friend, I wish you'd . . . think about it."

"Okay, I'll think about it. And I'll be seeing you around, right?"

"I hope so," she said.

"Yeah, me too."

She didn't slam the door when she left. He would have felt better if she had.

Maish felt a gentle touch on his shoulder. He shrugged it off and huddled further down under his tattered cardboard sheets. Rats, maybe. Cold nights, little bastards hunted him down, tried to share the warmth of the warehouse wall he slept against, get into his clothes, bite him if he moved too sudden. Carried fleas too, even in wintertime, make life a misery. Always around, maybe after his bottle. They—

He felt the nudge again, firmer this time, shaking his shoulder. Beamon? The old man sat up slowly, blinking blearily, trying to focus. The newspapers stuffed inside his overcoat and wrapped around his legs rustled in the darkness.

"Beamon? That you?" Couldn't tell. Guy was outlined against the streetlight, not sayin' nothin'. Not Beamon though, too tall. Maybe one of the little punk-ass gang bastards that hassled him sometimes. "Go away. Git on away from me! This's my place. Ain't botherin' nobody here. Hey! Lemme alone!"

Maish clutched at his jacket as the guy began tugging at the newspapers stuffed in his coat. The guy was stealing his papers!

"Hey, you lemme be—" He felt the breath of the icy night wind around his collar as the guy grabbed his hair, jerking his head back. And then the sharper, deeper bite of cold steel at his throat, a chill that seemed to penetrate to his soul, trickling down his shoulders like icewater, soaking his coat, seizing his thudding heart. He tried to call for help, for Beamon, but his voice couldn't carry above the roaring in his head, as the darkness collapsed on him like a black avalanche, hammering him down to nothing.

93

CHAPTER 13

GARCIA'D BEEN CATCHING THE PHONE ON THE FIRST RING ALL morning, hoping. The weekday bustle in the squad room was at its peak, with half of the unit trying to catch up on paperwork before another weekend of party killings and mom and pop murders rolled over them. Cordell was over in Greektown trying to get a line on a suspect who was supposedly working as a cook. It was Garcia's turn to bring their reports up-to-date and he was having at it with a vengeance, hammering away at his Selectric like it was an Olympic event, using the racket from the machine and the background noise of the office to shut out the quiet click of Linda closing his apartment door. The program was working well. Sometimes he'd go for fifteen minute without hearing the click, without thinking of her at all. The phone beside him buzzed and he snatched it up.

"Homicide, Sergeant Garcia." No one answered, but he could hear traffic noises in the background. "Hello?"

"You, ah, you said I could call you anytime."

It took a moment for the voice to register. "Jobeth? Are you in trouble? Do you need help?"

"Yeah. I'm in trouble, but . . ." Traffic noises again. Phone booth?

"Is there something I can do to help?" Garcia asked quietly. "Has Lamont been roughing you around again?"

"No, it's nothing like that, he . . . ain't coming home much now. And he doesn't sleep much when he does."

"Where do you think he's been going?"

"I don't know. And I'm afraid to ask."

"Does he seem upset when he comes in? You know, angry or excited?"

"No. He's just, I don't know. Burned out. Really tired."

"Do you suppose he might have a new girlfriend or something? Could that be it?" He felt a sudden cold knot in the pit of his stomach. Irrational? Damn right. "If it's another woman—"

"If that's what it was I wouldn't worry so much. I could handle that, he's done it before. But it's not. It's more'n that." She was speaking more brusquely now, as though she'd made a decision. "Look, maybe talkin' to you isn't right, and he'd sure as hell kill me if he knew, but you said you'd help me, right?"

"If I can."

"Can you find out things from Tennesse?"

"Tenn—? I don't understand. What kind of things?"

"I'm not sure. But I think something happened in Tennessee. A long time ago, maybe, but it's like it's started eatin' at him again since Toby drowned. Maybe if I knew what it was . . ."

"Has he threatened you?"

"No, it's not like that. I don't think he'd hurt me, it's . . . I'm afraid if I don't do somethin' he's gonna blow. Kill somebody, or maybe himself."

"Look, you know he's done time, don't you? And why?"

"I know about his wife, if that's what you mean. But that's not what this is about. Least I don't think so. So can you help or not?"

"I will if I can, but I need to know more, Jobeth. Tennessee's a big place."

"Merrimac. Merrimac is the place."

95

"So what about Merrimac? Did he say something about it that—?"

"He hasn't said nothin' about it. Look, I already told you everything I know, which ain't much. Finding stuff out is what you do, right? So why don't you give it a try? Look, I got to go now. If he finds out I talked to you—"

"He won't, I promise, but wait a minute, please. If he hasn't said anything about Merrimac, what makes you think—?"

"He sings about it sometimes," she said dully. "He sings about it in his sleep. I got to go."

He listened to the dial tone a long time before hanging up.

"County Sheriff's office. This's Sheriff Lowe."

"Hi, my name is Garcia, Detective Sergeant Lupe Garcia. I work out of Metro Homicide in Detroit. I have a problem and I hope you can help me out."

"*Que pasa, compadre? Nosotros ensayo ayudar.*"

"I'm afraid I don't speak much Spanish, Sheriff."

"Hell, I don't either, but I'm tryin' to pick it up. Like to trot it out when I can. What can we do for you?"

"I'm working on a multiple homicide investigation up here, and we've received a tip that it may be linked to your area."

"Linked how? Another homicide, you mean?"

"I honestly don't know, Sheriff. Does the name Lamont Stacy Yarborough mean anything to you?"

"Not offhand. This something recent?"

"No, sir, I'd guess a few years ago at least, maybe more. I really don't know."

"Has to be longer than that. I've been here six years now, got elected after I retired from the force at McMinn, and I don't recognize the name. We got a computer, though. Lemme punch it in, see what we get. You mind holding?"

"No problem."

Lowe came back on the line in less than a minute. "Look, Sergeant Garcia, is it?"

"That's right."

"You know, I don't believe I got your badge number. Why

96

don't you give it to me, and your squad commander's name, and let me call you back."

"My badge is twenty-eight forty-one," Garcia said, puzzled. "The squad commander is Lt. Al Fielder, and our phone number—"

"That's all right," Lowe said coolly. "I'll get it from the directory if it's all the same. I'll get back to you."

The call came in a few minutes later. Fielder took it and relayed it back to Garcia.

"Sorry about the holdup, Sergeant," Lowe said. "These days a man can't always be sure who he's talkin' to."

"No problem, Sheriff. What did you turn up?"

"Not much, I'm afraid. There was a killing here all right, two of 'em, in fact, but I don't see how it can have much to do with anything now. It was nearly ten years ago."

"Look, Sheriff, I've got a string of homicides up here, a slasher, four female victims so far, and I'll take any help I can get. Anything at all."

"Well, it was a cutting all right," Lowe said cautiously, "but there were no women involved. Happened in the county jail here, and it was a black-white fracas, which is why I wanted to be double sure I wasn't talking to some reporter. The last thing we need is publicity on a thing like this."

"I understand. What happened exactly?"

"Well, your man Yarborough and two other cons were shipped down to Merrimac from the Brushy Mountain pen. They had less than six months to go before parole, and their records were good. This is farm country around here, and we got a work-release program where we put men like that to work in the fields. It helps out the local farmers some, lets the cons put somethin' aside before they're released, and eases the overcrowding at the Mountain a little. I don't know what your prison situation is like up there, but—"

"We're jammed to the walls too. Please go on."

"Well, you see, we don't keep these men in cells. We got an open-bay barracks for 'em, and not all the men in it are from

97

Brushy Mountain. Some of 'em are local. Anyway, what happened, apparently somebody smuggled in a jug of shine. They all got tanked up and . . . there was an incident of homosexual assault. A gang rape. Then two of the men involved were stabbed to death by the man who'd been raped. So you can see it probably doesn't—"

"Maybe it does. What was the outcome? Parole revoked?"

"Uh, actually, it didn't work out that way. You see, the incident of rape, and the racial aspects of it—and mind you, this happened long before I took over down here, but I don't know that I'd've handled it any different. Anyway, they decided to keep a lid on it. They held a closed inquest to determine the facts of the matter. Everybody involved had been drunk. There was clinical evidence of the rape, and the testimony of the other prisoners indicated that what happened was self-defense or close to it, so the story they released was that the two cons had killed each other in a scuffle. Case closed. No trial, no publicity, and I'm afraid no help for what you've got going now."

"You said it was a stabbing. What weapon? A shank?"

"That's right, but they never did determine who it belonged to. A lot of cons carry 'em."

"Still, maybe it helps a little. It proves that Yarborough knows how to handle a blade, at least. Maybe he acquired a taste for it."

"Pardon me?"

"I said it shows—"

"Son, I heard what you said, but we got us a little communications problem here. Are you saying you've got Lamont Yarborough in mind as a suspect?"

"That's right."

"That'd be a pretty good trick, Garcia. See, Lamont wasn't the boy did the cutting. He was one of the boys that got killed. He's been dead nearly ten years now."

Garcia could hear the buzz of office noise in the background, typewriters, a muted conversation. "I guess we have some kind of a mix-up," he said at last.

"I'd say so."

"Sheriff, could there have been some mistake in identifying the body? I mean, you said they were trying to keep a lid on things."

"Nobody was trying to cover anything up, if that's what you mean. They may have fudged the record a little because of the circumstances but, well— Hold on a minute."

Lowe covered the mouthpiece at his end for what seemed like a very long time. "Look, I just checked with my desk sergeant to be sure. He's from Merrimac here, and he knew Lamont. There's no doubt he was one of the boys killed in the scuffle. He's buried out behind the Baptist Church."

"I see," Garcia said softly.

"Well, if you do, your eyes are better than mine. How certain are you of the ID on your man?"

"Sheriff, until they pulled him out of the river a few days ago, I'd never heard of him."

"What river was that? The Styx?"

"Maybe it was. You know what? I think I'll ask him."

CHAPTER 14

CORDELL SWUNG THE CHRYSLER INTO HARRY'S RIVERVIEW COURT A little before noon. He kept the car at a crawl as they rolled past the row of seedy mobile homes, made a U-turn at the end of the lane, and parked facing the last trailer in line. Jobeth's. The metallic brown pickup was parked in front.

"Wasn't there a Chevette parked in front when we was here before?" Cordell said.

"It belongs to the woman." Garcia nodded. "The truck's Yarborough's, which means he's alone, I hope. I'll take the front door and I can cover the rear door from there. Why don't you bop around to the back and make sure he doesn't take a header out a window."

"Jesus, Lupe, the snow's ass-deep to a giraffe back there."

"So we definitely don't want to chase him through it, right? I'll take the back if you want."

"I'll take it," Cordell grumbled, easing out of the car. "You just remember whose turn it is next time."

Garcia shifted his Airweight Smith from his waistband to the

100

outside pocket of his leather trenchcoat while Cordell lumbered through the snow toward the rear of the trailer. He winced as the big man stumbled to his knees in a drift, feeling a pang as he remembered a much younger Cordell sprinting after a long pass in a touch football game outside their hooch in Da Nang. God, what happened to that guy? Too many years and maybe forty pounds. He hoped Yarborough wouldn't make a run for it. He wouldn't have to be very fast.

Cordell set himself at the rear corner of the trailer and gave him a nod.

Garcia peeled off his left-hand glove and moved quietly to the front door. He listened for a moment, then rested his left palm flat against the door and knocked sharply with his right. And felt the subtle vibration of someone moving inside. He stepped back and drew his weapon, holding it in plain view as the door opened. Lamont Yarborough squinted at him, blinking into the pale winter morning. He was unshaven, bleary-eyed and bare-chested, wearing only a pair of faded jeans, and looking slim and hard as a railroad tie.

"Howdy, pard," Garcia said. "Time to roll outa the ol' saddle blanket. You're busted."

"What do you mean, busted? You got a warrant?"

"You're wanted for questioning. It's a little complicated to talk about here, but if you come along nice maybe I won't lose your paperwork and leave you in a holding cell overnight. How's that sound?"

"It's sounds like a roust. And I don't think I'm in the mood."

"Actually"—Garcia smiled—"I was kind of hoping you'd feel that way." Their eyes met and held through the doorway.

"Yeah," Lamont said softly, "I can see that. Jesus, I must be livin' right. Federalés before breakfast. What the hell, lemme get some clothes on."

Chas Mullery took a massive bite from a cardboard-flavored Danish as he lounged in the doorway of Joad's office. The squad room was busy. Wilk and Keller were worming a statement out of a balding, ratty little guy wearing a Garden City East letterman's jacket. They were playing him like a violin, wearing him down with marshmallow questions, each answer giving them a little more information. Good cops those two, yuppies, educated, motivated, regulation haircuts. The department could use more like 'em. The little guy would fold soon. He was already sobbing, wiping his nose on his sleeve, smearing his mustache. Chas decided to postpone interviewing Mr. Garden City until after lunch.

Al Fielder was talking in the corner with two young blacks and their equally black lawyer, court-appointed from the looks of his off-the-rack Sears suit. Neither boy looked more than sixteen, barely old enough to shave, but already wearing the scars and colors of the Young Pharoahs. Chas quickly flipped through his mental catalog of story lines. Broken homes? Deprived environment? It was getting tough to write about the gangs with any sympathy at all, but taking a hard line meant the few sources open to him would dry up. Maybe there'd be an angle on the lawyer.

Marv Cream's collar looked more promising. The soft-spoken detective was filling out paperwork on a guy wearing some kind of uniform. Army? Mullery wasn't sure. Service uniforms had all changed lately and . . . Garcia stepped into the squad room and took a key for the interrogation room off the board. Mullery caught a glimpse of a man wearing faded denims standing in the hallway with Bennett. Familiar, but he couldn't place the face. He frowned and took another bite of his Danish.

"Wendell, save an old man some legwork and give me a quick rundown on today's villains. Any of them good copy?"

Joad glanced around the front of the tall armoire in the corner of the office. "It'll have to be quick," he said, loosening his tie. "I've got a meeting in twenty minutes. What do you want to know?"

"The fella in the letterman's jacket?"

"Mom and pop shooting. Argument that got out of hand. Nothing interesting about it but the weapon, one of those John Wayne Winchesters with the oversize lever action."

"And the fella in the army uniform?"

"Not an army uniform, Chas, just a uniform. His name's Harold Hobart, family's Hobart Developments, shopping mall in Birmingham, two golf courses. Harold's got substantial holdings of his own, but he's mental. He's into uniforms, which wouldn't be a problem except that he completes his ensemble with an army .45. He shot up one of his own apartment houses last year because he thought he smelled marijuana in the hall. Flunked his mental evaluation, but his family managed to get him released anyway. Very influential people, the Hobarts. You might want to bear that in mind."

"Noted." Mullery said. "What did he do this time?"

"Flipped out in a restaurant, a Hardee's over on Eight Mile. Took offense at some dried egg on his fork and started waving his gun around. I let Sergeant Cream roll on it because he knows Harold. He's arrested him a couple of times before. He talked him out of the restaurant by borrowing a uniform cap from a patrolman and giving him a direct order to holster his piece. If half my men followed orders as well as Harold we'd up our conviction rate fifty percent. And that'll have to cover it, Chas. I'm due at the Ponchartrain for lunch."

"With Dr. Klevenger to kick off a MADD membership drive for the Detroit Renaissance Alliance board, correct?"

"Does anything ever happen in this town that you miss?" Joad asked wryly, slipping off his sportcoat.

"Nothing important, I hope, and this could be damned important for you. I take it your little talk the other day made a favorable impression on the DRA membership?"

"It seemed to go over well."

"It must have, if they're bringing you in on this. Mothers Against Drunk Drivers is Dr. K's favorite cause. Which may mean he and the DRA board are considering you for bigger things. And speak of the devil, here comes the good doctor now. Wearing his plastic paw, I see. Should be an interesting lunch."

"Plastic paw?"

"The flesh-colored prosthesis he wears for public occasions. Yanks it off in the middle of his 'carnage on the highways' speech.

103

Very effective theater. 'Morning, Doctor," Chas said, stepping aside to let Klevenger by. "How's the body shop business?"

"Dead." Klevenger grunted. "How else? Are you ready to go, Captain? We're on in twenty minutes."

"Be right with you," Joad said. "Just changing my tie."

"So, Doctor," Chas said, "are you going to flash your rubber surprise again this year?"

"Perhaps I'll have a body wheeled in instead, Mullery. Why don't you come down and find out? We could use the coverage."

"I've assigned a new man to cover the drive," Chas said. "Maybe he'll faint."

"A heart attack would be better," Klevenger said. "It might even get us on the six o'clock news. You really should do a story on us yourself though, Chas. Drunk drivers do more damage in a week than this slasher you've been puffing up will do in his entire career."

"Exactly the problem, Doc. Drunks are so common they make dull copy."

"And that's the bottom line for you?" Klevenger said, flushing. "Pushing a few lousy newspapers?"

"Easy, Doc, we're in the same business, you and I. We're both ghouls, so to speak. I write about bodies and you whack 'em up."

"The difference is that for me the job's a necessity," Klevenger said, "but with you I think it's a vocation. I'll wait for you in the hallway, Captain. I spend enough time with corpses, without lounging about with a vulture." He brushed past Mullery and stalked out of the squad room without a backward glance.

"I'll be right with you," Joad called after him. "Dammit, Chas, that wasn't too bright. Dr. Klevenger's—"

"A charter member of the old-boy network, I know," Mullery said. "Don't worry about it, Wendell, the Doc and I understand each other. But take a word or two of advice from an old hack. When Klevenger whips off his rubber stump, try not to smile. He lost his wife and his left hand when his car was rammed by a drunk years ago and he takes this drunk driving business very seriously."

"I can see where he might," Joad said.

"And secondly, if perchance the good doctor approaches you about membership in the Renaissance Alliance, act surprised, hesitate five seconds, then accept gracefully. It could be the best career move you ever make. There's a lot of money in that crowd, Wendell, and they spend it on more than just playgrounds and that oversized bird cage they're building downtown. Whatever you may think of Klevenger as a coroner, you have to admit he's one canny political animal."

"I'll keep that in mind, Chas. Is my tie all right?"

"You look positively dashing. Just one last thing before you go—that fella Cisco and Bennett just brought in? He seemed familiar to me."

"He should. His picture was on your front page a few days ago. Yarborough. The swimmer."

"The one they pulled out of the Detroit? Is he a slasher suspect then?"

"He's . . . at the moment we have a problem with his identification, nothing more. I'd appreciate your discretion on this one, Chas."

"Noted. If Cisco's handling it, it probably won't amount to much anyway. Break a leg, as they say, and remember, don't smile."

Garcia unlocked the gunmetal door to the interrogation room and motioned Lamont in ahead of him. Cordell followed them in, closed the door, and leaned against the jamb, blocking the only exit.

Lamont glanced around the room, a barren green cubicle with a battered card table, a couple of wooden folding chairs, a coffee urn in the corner, a large mirror on one wall. He swung around and faced Garcia. "All right, how we gonna play this? Good cop, bad cop? Silent treatment? Or what?"

In the corridor outside, Chas Mullery paused a moment, glanced around casually, then stepped into the darkened observation office next to the interrogation room and closed the door. He lowered his bulk into a folding chair facing the one-way

105

mirror, tilted it back, and relaxed, methodically munching his stale Danish.

"Let's take it from the top," Garcia said. "Do you have any identification on you?"

"All kinds of it." Lamont fumbled in his wallet and began flipping cards on the table. "Driver's license, Social Security, Visa, Sears charge. That enough?"

Garcia examined each card carefully, then passed them to Cordell. "Run 'em." Cordell nodded and left the room.

Garcia hung his leather trenchcoat on a hook by the door and loosened his necktie. He ran himself a cup of coffee from the urn. Lamont didn't ask for one, Garcia didn't offer. "So," Garcia said, "how's the music biz?"

"Jesus, you're fuckin' this up already."

"How do you mean?"

"If you're playin' good cop, you shoulda offered me some coffee and I don't figure you're bad enough to be the bad cop."

"We don't play that game much anymore. Too many people've seen it on TV."

"No? So how do we play it?"

"Straight up. I never was much on games. You born in Tennessee, Lamont?"

"That's right. Hill country. Pineywoods, no smog, sawmill work, Grand Ole' Opry on the radio Saturday nights. Good people. No spicks, and the blacks all call you mister."

Garcia let it pass. "And you did time in Brushy Mountain for murder? How much time?"

"Eight years and change."

"And how much time in the Merrimac County slammer?" A hit. Maybe this wasn't going to be so tough. Lamont's shoulders had hunched unconsciously, and he seemed suddenly wary. Garcia felt a tingle of anticipation in his diaphragm. "How long did you say?"

"I didn't say."

"But you were there, right?"

"Yes."

"So how long?"

106

"I, ah, I don't know. A few nights." Lamont pulled out a chair and sat down, avoiding eye contact. "Not very long."

"I understand you had some trouble there." Garcia slid into the chair facing Lamont across the card table. "In fact, the sheriff down at Merrimac tells me Lamont Yarborough was killed there."

"He . . . was. Throat got cut."

"He's dead then?"

Lamont nodded.

"Then who are you?"

Lamont looked up slowly and met Garcia's stare, his pale gray eyes as empty as river ice. "You know who I am," he said softly. "I'm Lamont Yarborough."

In the darkened observation office Chas Mullery eased the front legs of his chair quietly to the floor, his cud of Danish forgotten.

"I don't understand," Garcia said.

Lamont closed his eyes a moment, frowning in concentration, his forehead beading with perspiration. And then he looked up, and the vulnerability was gone. "I imagine there's a fair amounta stuff you don't understand," he said calmly. "Anything else you want to know about?"

"Anything else? We haven't even started yet! Who the hell are you?"

"You know who I am. Your buddy's runnin' my ID and it's gonna check out. Why don't we get to what this roust is really about? Ask me how my nooner with your lady reporter friend went. You a little nervous about that?"

"Not really, but if you want to talk about women, how about Louise Barrett? Or Sister Mary Senchuk. Carol Loomis maybe? Those names mean anything to you?"

"Sure, they mean something. I read the papers. I read a lot of things. Old habit. Used to have more time for it."

"Maybe I can fix it so you can catch up. Where did you meet Louise Barrett? At the Crossing?"

"I don't know." Lamont shrugged. "I might have."

"You're admitting you knew her?"

"I'm not admittin' a damn thing, but to tell you the truth I can't swear I never met Louise whatsername. Or any of 'em. I meet a lot of women in the clubs, even reporters sometimes. I can't remember 'em all. But I sure as hell didn't kill any of 'em. I think I'd remember that."

"You sure about that? Christ, I'm not even sure what your fucking *name* is!"

"You oughta be. I told you what it was. And I don't know how things work down in Tijuana or wherever the fuck you're from, but I know you can't hold me for long without a charge, so if you wanna ask me anything else you better get to it. I've about had it with this dump." He stood up and thrust the chair aside, and Garcia rose too, with only the card table between them.

Cordell stepped into the room, eyed the two men, and pointedly closed the door behind him. "Anything goin' on?" he said.

"No," Garcia said. "Nothing."

"ID checks out," Cordell said, tossing the cards on the table. "Numbers match, picture hasn't been altered."

"That doesn't mean much, he—"

"Pack it in, Mex," Lamont interrupted. "Computers don't lie. And you got to show your birth certificate to get a driver's license here, or didn't you know that?"

"How about a death certificate, Lamont? You show them that too?"

"You're comin' unglued, Mex, you know that? I figure it's really the woman that's buggin' you, but that's your problem. I'm leavin'."

"Mr. Yarborough," Garcia said evenly, "at the moment you're being detained for failing to properly identify yourself in a felony investigation. You can call a lawyer if you like, but as far as questioning goes, we're just getting started, so sit your ass down!"

Mullery eased out of the observation office, closed the door softly behind him, and padded to the bank of pay phones at the end of the hall. He used his credit card to place the call.

"Tempo section. Kerry speaking."

"Would this be the Linda Kerry whose glance sets men's souls ablaze?"

"Who is this?"

"A colleague, calling from durance vile."

"Chas?"

"The very same. Look, you know that fella they pulled out of the river last Sunday, Yarborough? Are you involved with him, personally, I mean?"

"Involved? I'm . . . we're doing a story on him. Why?"

"Oh, just a mite curious. You see, your friend Cisco has him here at Metro Homicide for questioning, and your name keeps coming up. Why would that be? Would Garcia roust him out of jealousy, do you think?"

"I don't think so. What's happening, exactly?"

"Not much so far. There seems to be some confusion about Yarborough's identification, or even whether he's alive or not, though he looks healthy enough to me. He may not stay that way for long though, now that the Kid has him in a back room. Hot-blooded types, these Latins."

"Chas, I can't believe Garcia would arrest Yarborough because of me, I really can't."

"Are you sure enough to bet Yarborough's life on it? Because if you're wrong; that's what you'll be doing. And how well do you really know the Kid? Do you even know what he really looks like? His old face, I mean, not the one he's wearing now."

"I don't see how that's relevant."

"My point is that you really *don't* know Garcia all that well, but I do. And if you want Yarborough to stay healthy, I'd suggest you get him a lawyer. Try the ACLU and ask for Isobel Cabb."

"What's this got to do with the ACLU?"

"Nothing, but I guarantee Miz Cabb will be interested in anything involving Garcia. He blew up one of her clients once, probably before he'd paid her fee. She'll help. Call her."

"If you're so concerned, why don't you call her yourself?"

"Sorry, but helping out a suspect under detention could be very bad for my business. On the other hand, if you help him,

Yarborough is rescued, Cabb gets a client, and my column will write itself for weeks."

"The Cisco Kid rides again, you mean? Why? It's something personal with you and Garcia, isn't it?"

"Not at all. I don't dislike the boy, and if he was a bartender I'd let him serve me lunch. But as a cop—I don't trust him. I think he's as much a renegade as the poor bastards he hunts. And Yarborough may be in danger from him because of you."

"I can't believe that."

"Whether you do or not's a moot point. He's over the line on this and you know it, Linda. Besides, you owe me."

"I owe you? For what?"

"Did you think the chance to do the story on Yarborough just fell out of the trees? I got it for you. You said you wanted a shot. Well, you have it. And now I'd like this small favor in return." He brushed a fleck of icing from his lower lip. "Linda? Are you there?"

"Damn it to hell," she said softly. "I don't suppose you have the number for the ACLU handy?"

"As a matter of fact, I have."

"Yeah." She sighed. "Somehow I thought you would."

CHAPTER 15

ALL FIELDER RAPPED ONCE ON THE DOOR AND OPENED IT. LAMONT was leaning back in his chair, boots resting on the card table, pointedly ignoring Bennett and Garcia.

"Loop," Fielder said, "I'm afraid your guest has a visitor." He stepped aside, held the door for a tall, slender, cafe-au-lait woman wearing gold-rimmed glasses and a beige suit that would have pleased an English tailor. Her dark hair worn short, a tight cap of curls, but there was nothing mannish about her, she was an absolute stunner. And well aware of it.

"Gentlemen, and I use the term loosely," she said, nodding at Bennett and Garcia, "you'll never learn, will you? Mr. Yarborough, my name is Isobel Cabb. I've been asked to confer with you by a friend who's concerned that your civil rights are being violated by these officers. If you require an attorney, I'm willing to represent you for a retainer of one dollar, payable in installments if necessary. Gentlemen, if you don't mind, I'd like a word with my client."

"Hold on, lady," Lamont said quietly. "Nobody said you were hired."

"Mr. Yarborough, are you here voluntarily?"

"You've got to be kidding."

"And have these officers prevented you from contacting an attorney by use of threats or intimidation?"

"Tell you the truth, lady, you scare me more'n they do. And who's this friend we're supposed to have in common?"

Cabb lowered her head to Lamont's and murmured something. "Is that a fact?" He nodded, a faint smile raising the corners of his mouth. "Well, in that case, it's your call. Ma'am."

"Gentlemen," Cabb said, straightening, "my client will not answer any further questions. The party's over."

"Or maybe not," Garcia said. "Lieutenant, can we talk?" He grasped Fielder by the bicep, led him out into the hall, and closed the door. "All right, what the hell's going on here, Al? The guy didn't ask for a lawyer or make a call."

"You offer him a call?"

"Come on, Fielder, you know damn well I did, and he's only been here a couple of hours. What kind of crap is this?"

"The kind you'd better get used to, since it looks like Isobel's his lawyer now."

"Bullshit. He never heard of her and he didn't call anybody, so what's going on?"

Fielder stared at him impassively. "Maybe you should tell me. Do you know a Linda Kerry?"

"Linda—?" Garcia said, shaking his head in disbelief. "Jesus H. Christ."

"I take it that's an affirmative answer, right? Terrific. Okay, I'll lay it out for you, Loop. Isobel's been in the captain's office for the last ten minutes screaming false arrest, abuse of process, and vendetta, because you and your suspect are supposedly sharing a girlfriend, and our fearless leader did everything but drop trou and say be gentle with me. Now have you got a legit bust on this guy or not?"

"We picked him up for failure to properly identify. Joad okayed it. Cordell ran his ID through, and so far it all checks out, but

I . . . we've got bits and pieces that indicate he may be a slasher candidate. Dammit, I need more time with him."

"You getting anyplace? I mean, he wasn't exactly running off at the mouth when I came in."

"He's talking a little," Garcia said, "but mostly just to pass the time. I can't say I'm getting anywhere, no."

"Then he might as well walk, right? Look, Loop, the way Isobel's rolling we'll be lucky to keep Internal Affairs out of this. You've gotta cut the guy loose. Now."

Linda was talking with Joad at the end of the hallway as Garcia followed the others out of the interrogation room. Cordell stalked angrily off to recheck Lamont's ID in the vain hope that they'd missed something, pointedly ignoring Linda as he passed. Garcia tried to catch her eye, but Lamont said something to her and she turned away, smiling. Garcia shrugged and trailed the group into the squad room. Bobby Pilarski, immaculate as usual in a freshly pressed uniform, gave him a vacant smile and a Styrofoam cup of coffee at the urn by the door. Garcia nodded his thanks, watching Joad usher Linda, Lamont, and Isobel Cabb into his office like a B-movie headwaiter. Garcia winced. Even Bobby's coffee tasted lousy today.

"Offhand I'd say you've got a problem, Loop," Fielder said, accepting a cup from Pilarski, eyeing the conference in Joad's glass-paneled office.

"No kidding."

"I'm not just talking about your case, or even your girlfriend there. You notice the captain suckin' up to Isobel? Give you a clue, it's not because he's got a warm spot for minorities. She's been named co-chairperson of the mayor's reelection committee."

"So?"

"So the bottom line is, the mayor's got coattails and I don't think Joad sees himself serving out his thirty in this dump. Isobel could help him a lot. And if you don't watch it you might end up being a campaign contribution, you know?"

"If Joad wants out he'll get my vote, but right now I'm more

113

worried about keeping Yarborough off the street. Where do you stand on this, Al? If IAD gets into it, are you gonna back me up?"

"Could be," Fielder said, sipping his coffee. "I'll give you a definite 'maybe' on that."

"Terrific. That's something I've always liked about this place, decisive leadership."

"At least you know where you stand, Loop."

"Yeah," Garcia said, catching a flicker of Linda's quick smile at some remark in Joad's office. "I'm afraid I do."

"Sergeant Cream? Permission to speak, sir."

Marv Cream paused in midsentence, his hands poised above his typewriter. Harold Hobart was staring past him at the captain's office. "Sure, Harold, go ahead."

"Those people in the office, sir."

Marv glanced over his shoulder at Joad's office. Isobel Cabb, the captain, two others he didn't know. "What about 'em, Harold?" Hobart didn't seem to hear. His eyes looked glassier than usual and a sheen of perspiration on his forehead reflected the overhead fluorescents, giving him a waxen look. At Joad's request, Marv had put off booking Hobart. Instead, he'd called the guy's office, his parents, his shrink, his lawyer, everybody but his tailor. No luck so far, everybody was out. Wilk and Keller had already booked their man then split for lunch and Joad had been to a damn banquet and back, while Marv was stuck babysitting some rich wacko. Well enough was enough. The guy was getting booked, period. Marv cleared his throat. "Was there something about the people, Harold?" Nothing. The guy probably forgot he asked.

Hobart was sitting at attention, back rigid, spit-shined jump boots at a 45-degree angle, eyes empty as an abandoned bunker. With his skinhead haircut and iron-pumper's build, he could've modeled for recruiting posters. For the Waffen SS maybe, or the Foreign Legion. Marv shrugged and resumed typing. This was the third time he'd busted this clown and the guy was getting stranger every time. Maybe this one would do it, if they could make armed robbery stick.

"Sergeant Cream? Permiss—"

"Cool out, Harold. The sooner I get your forms typed, the—"

"I'd like to make my phone call now."

"Harold, I've already talked to your secretary and somebody's supposed to get right back to me. Do you want me to call your doctor again maybe?"

"Sergeant Cream, according to the regulations you have to let me make one call. I know the rules."

"I'm sure you do." Marv shrugged, shoving his desk phone across. "Do you need a book?"

"I don't think so." Hobart frowned, mulling it over, "No, just the phone. Can you take off my handcuffs?"

"Sorry, Harold, but that's against the rules. You understand."

"Yessir. Regulations." Hobart reached across the desk and picked up the phone with both hands. He paused, listening for a moment, then nodded and slammed the receiver into Marv Cream's forehead.

Marv reeled back, stunned. Hobart swarmed over the desk, carrying the detective and his chair over backwards, hammering him to the floor with his cuffed fists, teeth bared, grunting with each blow, the chains coming back bloody from a streaming gash over Marv's right eye. Dazed, Marv tried vainly to ward off the blows, but Hobart was just too quick, too strong. He finished him with an elbow to the throat.

Hobart clawed frantically at the detective's coat, groping for the pistol in his shoulder holster. He jerked it free and backhanded Marv across the temple with the butt. Then up, wheeling to face Garcia and Fielder charging at him from the doorway. He fired a shot between them that sent them diving to the floor, the handgun roaring like a cannon in the enclosed space. He fired a second shot that tore into the desk above Garcia's head, blowing paperwork into the air like confetti.

Garcia risked a glance around the corner of the desk. Hobart was half concealed behind Marv's desk, and Joad's office was directly behind him. No chance for a shot.

"Bobby!" Fielder yelled. "Get down!"

Garcia glanced back. Pilarski was still standing by the coffee urn in plain sight, bewildered by Hobart's attack on Marv.

"Bobby, goddammit!" Fielder shouted, too late. Hobart snapped off two quick shots. The first caught Pilarski in the chest, spinning him around, crumpling him to his knees; the second blew a hole in the coffee urn, spraying the walls and the wounded man with boiling water.

Garcia fired a shot into the ceiling as Fielder scrambled back toward Pilarski on his hands and knees. And then Hobart was up, sprinting to Joad's office, covering the distance in three strides, slamming into the door with his shoulder, exploding through it in a shower of glass and splintered wood.

"All right, hold it! Everybody!" Hobart dropped into a combat crouch, swinging his weapon in a tight arc, covering the group on the floor of the office. Joad tossed his pistol aside without being told. *"That's better."* Hobart said, "much better."

For a moment the only sound was the gurgling of the smashed coffee urn, and a soft moan from Bobby Pilarski as Fielder dragged him to cover behind a desk. Cordell peered around the door from the hallway and Garcia mimed a palm sweep and a two-handed hold at him. Keep everyone back. And get a rifle. Cordell nodded and disappeared.

"Okay," Hobart said, "everybody on your feet and fall in."

Cabb and Joad exchanged glances, but no one moved.

"I said fall in, goddammit! Don't you people speak *English?* Line up! Form a rank in front of the desk. *Move! Move! Move!"*

Lamont nudged Linda gently with his elbow. They rose slowly and moved carefully over to the desk. Cabb and Joad followed them reluctantly, taking positions on either side of them. Hobart risked a quick glance over his shoulder to check the squad room.

"You out there! Don't come any closer, you hear? Just stay put!"

"Okay, Harold, whatever you say," Fielder said tautly, "but—"

"Shut Up! You just remember it's whatever I say! Whatever!"

"Look, Harold," Isobel began cautiously, "if you—"

"No talking in ranks!" Hobart screamed. "Christ, don't you dipshits know anything?" He wiped his nose with his left wrist,

116

smearing blood across the lower half of his face. His left arm and shoulder were bleeding from a dozen wounds where he'd crashed through the door, staining his tan uniform into tiger stripes.

"You," he said, pointing the .38 at Joad, "you're the officer in charge here, right?"

Joad stared at him, his eyes glazed with panic. He managed a nod.

"You keep money here?"

"We, ah," He swallowed. "We have some money here, yes. Not much, but—"

"How about a mess hall? Is there a mess hall in this building?"

"A mess—? We have a snack bar downstairs. I'm afraid that's all."

"All right. Tell 'em to bring me all the money, and some hot food. But I wanna look at their plates first. I won't eat off dirty plates."

"I'm not sure I—"

"I *said I want all your money and all your goddamn plates!*" Harold roared. "You tell those guys out there to get 'em."

"Of, of course," Joad stammered. "Lieutenant Fielder, did you get that? Fielder?"

"Yes, sir, all the money and the, ah, the plates. It may take a little time to arrange it though."

"It better not," Hobart said. "You haven't got much time."

"Mr. Hobart," Joad said carefully, "there's no reason to be hasty. We can—"

"There's no reason to be hasty, *Sir!*"

"All right, sir, then, but—"

"There's no excuse for that! You're a fucking captain, you should know proper military procedures."

"I probably should, yes, but—"

"I probably should, *sir*, you asshole! Christ, no wonder the gooks are rubbin' our noses in it all over the place, you— Is something funny?"

Lamont looked down, examining the pattern of the carpet.

"Something the matter with you?" Hobart asked, his eyes

117

narrowing. He moved the pistol to within an inch of Lamont's chin. "You were smiling. I saw you."

"I don't think so. Sir."

"Yes, you were, and— Wait a minute. I know you," Hobart said, frowning. "I thought so before. I know you from somewhere."

"Not likely," Lamont said. "I don't hang around many funny farms."

"What's that supposed to mean? I don't—?"

"For God's sake, Lamont," Linda broke in. "Harold, you've probably seen his picture in the paper. He's been—"

"*Nobody asked you!*"

"I'm sorry, but—"

"Women! Bitches always butting in, telling me what to do! Time to get up! Straighten your room, take your pills, mouths at both ends telling people about me and now they're in the army and we never lost any wars and stuff before and *I don't wanna hear it anymore!* And I don't hafta take it, either. You can keep it." He eared back the hammer on the .38 with an audible click. "You can keep it, bitch. I don't need it." His eyes were emptying like fluid down a drain.

"Wait a minute now," Joad said, instinctively backing away from what he saw in the gunman's face. "Just hold on." He stumbled against the desk.

The noise distracted Harold for an instant and Lamont lunged for him, sweeping the pistol up with his left forearm, his momentum slamming them into the smashed door, going down in the wreckage and broken glass.

Lamont clawed frantically for the weapon but couldn't get a grip on Hobart's bloody wrists. Hobart writhed beneath him, dumping him off with a hip thrust. The gun went off as he jerked his hands free, blowing out a glass wall panel, showering the room with splinters. Lamont hammered his right fist into Hobart's face but the gun was coming up—and then Garcia grabbed the handcuff chain, forcing Hobart's wrists to the floor, holding them there with his foot. He pressed his two-inch Smith against the tip of Hobart's nose.

118

"All right, that's it! Don't move a goddamn muscle. Al! Gimme a little help!"

Lamont reached across and took the pistol from Hobart's splayed fingers, and found himself staring down the barrel of Garcia's weapon.

"Hand it over. Slow."

"Lupe!" Linda said sharply. "For godsake, he just saved our lives."

"So now you can save his. Tell him to hand me the piece. Now."

Without taking his eyes off Garcia's, Lamont pressed the gun against Hobart's chin and squeezed the trigger. The hammer clicked harmlessly on a spent cartridge. Hobart went absolutely rigid, eyes wide, blood draining from his face.

"Bang," Lamont said, with a grin that never reached his eyes. "Christ, Mex, didn't they teach you guys to count?"

Fielder squeezed through the doorway, moving cautiously to avoid the broken glass. Lamont passed the pistol to him butt first, and stood up slowly, brushing bits of glass from his denim shirt.

Fielder knelt beside Harold, checked his pulse, and rose again. "He's all right. Somebody call an ambulance."

"How's Bobby?" Garcia asked.

"Bruised," Fielder said, smiling weakly. "Maybe a busted rib, but that's all. He was wearing a Kelvar vest under his uniform. Crazy bastard."

"Not so crazy," Garcia said, shaking his head. "Sometimes I think he's the only guy around here who knows what he's doing."

Hobart groaned and sat up slowly, still trembling. "Come on, Harold," Garcia said, gripping him under the arms, hauling him to his feet, "let's get outa this mess."

"Where are you taking him, Sergeant?" Isobel Cabb asked.

"Upstairs to a cell, where the sonovabitch belongs, why?"

"Maybe I'll walk along with you," she said coolly, "to make sure he doesn't . . . fall down along the way."

"What about Marv Cream or Bobby Pilarski?" Garcia said. "You're not worried about them?"

"They seem to be all right, and at least they're among friends. Mr. Hobart isn't."

"No argument about that, Isobel. You want me to give him his damn gun back so he doesn't feel insecure?"

"There's no need to be abusive, Garcia," Joad snapped. "We've all been under a lot of strain, and—"

"And some of us don't cope all that well, do we, Captain!"

"Meaning what?"

"Just speaking for myself." Garcia sighed. "Come on, Harold, and watch your step. You stub your toes and I'll probably be the one who ends up in the cell."

"Garcia," Joad said stiffly, "that's excellent advice. About watching your step, I mean."

CHAPTER 16

"**Y**OU KNOW, YOU OUGHTA GET YOUR COP FRIEND ONE OF those books," Lamont said, sitting on the edge of Joad's desk, picking shards of glass out of his denim shirt. He and Linda were alone for the moment in the trashed office as the others helped the paramedics with Marv Cream. "*How to Win Friends and Influence People* maybe? Doesn't seem to have much talent for it, does he?"

"Perhaps not," Linda said. "Look, I, ah, I'm a little short on speeches for the occasion but, well, thank you for what you did. It was a very brave— What's so funny."

"Nothing," Lamont said, shaking his head.

"Come on," she said, smiling with him, "this is serious stuff."

"I know. I'm supposed to scuff my toe in the dirt and say 'twarn't nothin', ma'am, take this silver bullet.' But the truth is, if I tried to scuff my toe right now, I think my knees'd fold."

"Shaky knees or not, it was a brave thing to do."

"Guitar players are supposed to be crazy." He shrugged.

"Besides, the guy's a stone psycho. He probably would've whacked us all anyway."

"Maybe, but he wasn't threatening you when you tackled him."

"If he had been, maybe I wouldn't have. I just wish I'd had somethin' to conk him with," he said, wincing as he flexed his right hand. "A two-by-four woulda been nice."

"Let me see that." She took his hand in both of hers, examining it carefully. "Open and close your fist."

"You a nurse too?"

"I've been a nurse's aide, yes. Any sharp pain when you do that?"

"Not really. It aches a little, but I'll live."

"You have some contusions around your knuckles and they're beginning to swell a little. Nothing appears to be broken, but you really should have it X-rayed to be sure, and you ought to get some ice on it for the swelling."

"Sounds reasonable. You, ah, know where a fella could come by some ice?"

"Most party stores sell it in bags," she said, without releasing his hand, "or you can find it in the average refrigerator. Doesn't your ladyfriend have a refrigerator?"

"I'm not so sure she's a friend anymore. When your buddy rousted me this morning Jo was gone, and she's usually around mornings. And he asked me some odd questions, things only Jo coulda told him. I think maybe he's turned that girl's head."

"Why did Garcia arrest you? Exactly."

"He didn't. He picked me up to check my ID. He was trying to think up a reason to hold me when your eight-foot lady lawyer showed up, for which I thank you, by the way."

"That was all? He brought you in for questioning? I, ah, was told my name came up. Did it?"

"I believe you were mentioned once or twice. Nothing to talk about though, is there?"

"No. Damn, I didn't believe he'd do something like that."

"I wouldn't be too rough on him. Mighta done the same thing

122

myself if I was him. Look, I guess he's told you a few things about me."

"A few."

"Thought he might have." He gently withdrew his hand. "Well, for what it's worth, it was probably all true and then some, so I guess I'll see you around. I'd better hunt up some ice. I have to play tonight."

"We still have an interview to finish," Linda said carefully, "and we have a lot more to talk about now. Like it or not, you're about to become a celebrity."

"Yeah, well, I've had about all the celebrityin' I can take lately. Unless maybe you'd want to handle it? Exclusive? What do you think? You know a place where we can talk? Maybe a place with some ice?"

She hesitated a moment, reading his face, then nodded. "Yes, I suppose I do."

LeeRoy Clayton took a deep toke of Black Sheba, holding the smoke in his lungs, feeling the rush shiver through his shoulders. He held the joint slightly above his head near the exhaust fan in the ceiling. It was a shame to waste the smoke, but it was too damn cold to burn one outside and Grivas was a prick about smokin' dope in the club. It was good weed, but not worth getting his ass fired. He started to take another hit, then paused, holding the joint an inch from his lips. He could hear a voice above the buzz of the fan. Somebody else was in the john. Damn! Grivas? No. Denny maybe. It sounded like Denny's voice. But who was he talking to? Frowning, LeeRoy eased the toilet stall door open a crack.

Denny's mop bucket was propped against the restroom door, holding it closed. He was talking on the pay phone. Seemed to be reading something off a slip of paper. Numbers? From the rear stall he couldn't quite make out what the kid was saying. And then LeeRoy heard his own name. And his address. The little bastard. The dirty little snitch motherfucker!

He silently closed the stall door and took a last, fierce drag on the joint, then ground it out in his palm, wincing at the flash of

123

pain, but welcoming it, using it to get a handle on his anger. He slipped the roach into the front pocket of his chambray vest and leaned against the wall, idly scanning the obscene graffiti without really seeing it, thinking, waiting for Denny to leave.

CHAPTER 17

"SIT," SHE SAID. "I'LL GET AN ICE PACK FOR YOUR HAND."

Linda glanced back as she filled a Zip-loc bag with ice cubes from the refrigerator dispenser. Lamont was wandering around her living room, and she felt a sudden twinge of concern. Not about what he might do, but at what he might think. The apartment was the first place of her own she'd had in years, and in the months following her move to Detroit she'd filled a lot of hours making it a declaration of her independence. Scandinavian modern, off-white carpeting, alabaster walls, gracefully curved wood-and-canvas furniture, black-and-white photographs on the walls. She was pleased with her efforts, but as it happened, Lamont was the first stranger to view her handiwork. And he'd probably think a wagon wheel over the mantelpiece would add a little pizzazz.

"One ice pack," she said, handing it to him.

"Thanks." He absently placed the bag over his hand, still absorbing the room. Mirabel sauntered out of the bedroom with elaborate nonchalance. She eyed Lamont with feline suspicion, circling him warily, her back arched, tail up.

"A black cat?" Lamont said. "I thought the witches union had a lock on those."

"Do cats bother you?"

"No, not much bothers me. But I'm surprised they allow pets in a place like this."

"She's not a pet. She just lives here. Is anything wrong?"

"Sorry, didn't mean to gawk. This is quite a setup. You must've spent a lot of time on it?"

"I . . . as a matter of fact, I did. So?" She heard a trace of uncertainty in her voice and felt a flash of resentment at it.

"And you live here? All the time, I mean?"

"Of course. Why? Is something the matter with it?"

"Not a thing. It's really nice. It just doesn't look like anyone lives here."

"Maybe you'd feel more at home if it had bars on the windows."

"Nope," he said evenly, "but I don't exactly mesh with the decor, do I?"

"Mesh with the decor?"

"What's the matter? Didn't I say that right?"

"The phrase just . . . surprised me, that's all."

"Coming from me, you mean? Look, I'm not well-spoken, lady, but I'm not an illiterate. I read a lot. A social worker in the joint told me I was the product of a deprived environment."

"Somehow I have the feeling you did as much damage to your environment as it did to you."

"Well, I promise not to damage yours," he said. "Where should I sit?"

"Anywhere you like. Coffee?"

"No, thanks. This ice'll do fine." He peeled off his denim jacket and eased down on the cream-colored sofa. She sat on the arm of an easy chair, facing him, and took her notepad from the inner pocket of her blazer.

"Well, shall we get started?"

"You know, for a minute there we were just talking, like

friends. It was nice. Then out comes the notebook. You use that thing like your boyfriend uses his badge, you know that?"

"In the first place, he's not my boyfriend, exactly, and in the second, I'm a reporter, Lamont, and you're my assignment. It's as simple and as complicated as that."

"Is that how you really figure it? Or is it a way to keep people at a distance?"

"In your case, both. Look, I'm grateful for what you did at the station, very grateful. And I'm sorry you hurt your hand, but let's not confuse the situation, okay? This is still business."

"Fair enough. Then maybe I can save you some trouble. Ask me about the women."

"The women?"

"The ones Garcia figures I snuffed. Look, I know you aren't just interested in the music biz, or even what happened at the cop shop. So let's clear the air, okay? You wanna ask about the women?"

"If I thought there was any chance you were involved in that, you obviously wouldn't be here now."

What makes you so sure I'm not?"

"I worked in a VA hospital for four years. I've seen mentals, schizophrenics, battle fatigue, even a few who were homicidal, like the man in the squad room today. You're not like that."

"Or maybe I just hide it better. Still, if you got any doubts, I'd rather you put it to me straight than slide it in sideways. We both know the game here. You want a story that'll sell papers, and maybe help you up the ladder. And me, well, I'm in a hard place in my life right now, real hard. And I figure either I make somethin' out of all this or, or let it break me. And I'm not ready to fall yet. Not yet. Motown's a big market for music and publicity can't hurt. As long as you spell my name right."

"You may not like all of the questions."

"You may not like the answers either. Why don't we find out?"

Linda glanced at her watch when the phone rang, surprised that more than an hour had passed so quickly.

127

"Excuse me," she said. "Can I get you something while I'm up? Coffee?"

"No, thanks," Lamont said. "I'm okay."

But he didn't look okay. She glanced back as she stepped into the kitchen to take the call. He looked exhausted, running on empty. She switched on the coffee maker and picked up the phone. "Hello?"

"Linda? Chas. What the hell are you doing at home? I've been trying— Look, we have to talk. I ran the essentials on the Metro Homicide shootout in the afternoon edition, but I want some first-person interviews for the morning run. Any idea where the man of the hour's got to?"

"He's here, Chas, with me."

"There? At your apartment, you mean? Look, can he hear your end of the conversation?"

"I think so, yes."

"Then listen. Don't talk. I don't think having him there is such a good idea, story or no story."

"Chas, there's no problem—"

"*Listen* to me, dammit! There *is* a problem. I've done some digging on Yarborough, and you know what I've found? Zip. A prison record for murdering his wife, and that's it. The man has no history. I followed up a lead I got this morning about a jail he'd been transferred to in Tennessee and got absolutely stonewalled. They're obviously covering something up, and there's no trace of him afterwards for nearly ten years."

"But there must be. His son—"

"Was only recently adopted, and we can't very well interview him, can we? Look, I've had a trifle more experience with this sort of thing—"

"But at the moment you're stalled, correct? Well, I'm not. I'll have everything you need for the morning edition, Chas. Meanwhile why don't you see what you can do about getting me transferred out of Tempo to something more substantial? Metro desk, say? Maybe the police beat?"

"Linda, you're not listening."

"Of course I am. And I value your judgment. But at the

128

moment I'm in a slightly better position to evaluate the situation, Chas, and I can handle it. I'll get back to you."

"Linda—"

"Bye, Chas."

She thoughtfully replaced the receiver, mulling over what he'd said. She poured two cups of coffee and carried them back into the living room. Lamont was sitting with his arms folded across his chest, head down, sound asleep on the sofa. She felt a twinge of annoyance, then dismissed it. She already had more than enough for a morning edition sidebar and it'd been a very rough day. She could use a breather herself.

He stirred momentarily when she replaced the ice pack on his hand, but didn't awaken. Dead to the world. She stood over him a moment, gazing down at his face. A man with no past, Chas said. A dangerous man. In sleep he looked quite different, gentler somehow, and much younger. He must have been a heartbreaker as a boy, and in his rough way was still very attractive. No denying it. How would she describe him to a friend? An Urban cowboy? Rural Romeo? She winced. A ladykiller. Literally. And yet this afternoon, in the station, he'd saved her life. Or had he?

She decided to mull that one over later. Time for a break. He obviously needed some rest and she felt like she'd been sleeping in her clothes for a week. She carried her coffee into her bedroom, and carefully locked the door.

The wind had a nasty chemical bite to it, a bitter blend of auto paint and industrial fumes. It had trailed him out from the Detroit side of the river, dogging his steps with the malignant tenacity of a wolf pack, whining, circling hungrily in the darkness, tugging savagely at his jacket, snapping at his numbed legs. It didn't matter. He would escape it soon.

Ahead, gleaming in the moonlight, was open water, a pool, with jagged, clearly defined edges, a broken window into the darkness below the pack. Agony waited in the water, and he knew it well. It would sear his nostrils and surge into his lungs as it had before. But maybe if he could endure the pain this time, if he could bear it for just a few moments longer, and hold tight to the rope . . . He shuffled ahead toward the open water, leaning into the wind, shifting the sled's towrope from one numbed hand to the other.

And then it snagged. He tugged at the rope, trying to break it free. He was only a few feet from the edge of the water now, a yard away from his chance. And the pain. And he wanted it. He wouldn't give in this time. He'd hold on, or die. And he didn't care which. Better dead than . . . But the sled held firm. And suddenly he knew why.

And he turned, slowly, on lifeless legs, with the icy water swirling about his ankles. And Toby was there, looking up at him, trusting. Not in the dark pool ahead. Behind him. Still on the sled. But not alone. The black man was standing beside him, watching, waiting with his infinite, terrible patience. And he was smiling, gently, sadly. And placed his foot reluctantly on the sled, resting his great weight on it, and began pushing it slowly down through the ice.

"Wait!"

But he didn't, of course. There was no forgiveness, no exceptions, only the law. Even. Things come out dead even. The water was rising above the sled runners now. And Toby was still staring at him, waiting, clinging to the rails.

"Papa?"

"Nooooo!"

And the nameless one reached down and cupped Toby's chin with one dark hand, raising it, exposing it to the bitter wind. And the sliver of steel slid from his wrist into his free hand, glittering in the icy moonlight. And the blade swept down, and Lamont leaped toward it, knowing that he was too late.

And the water closed over them, and exploded into flame, setting him alight, searing his skin with unendurable agony, ripping at his very heart.

"Nnooooo!!"

"Nnooo."

Linda cocked her head, trying to hear above the hiss of the

130

shower. She pushed the chrome lever down, turning off the water, her ears ringing in the sudden silence.

"*Nnooo!! God!*"

The anguish in the cry froze her to immobility for a moment, then reflex snapped in, galvanizing her as it had in the corridors of the VA hospital. Pausing only long enough to slip on her robe, she fumbled the locked door open and hurried toward the sound of the pain.

Lamont was writhing on the sofa, drenched with sweat, his eyes squeezed shut in torment, tearing blindly at his shredded shirt, the skin beneath oozing crimson from a dozen welts.

She seized his shoulders, shaking him roughly, her hands slipping in the blood smears.

"Lamont! Wake up! Dammit!"

No effect. She grabbed at his wrists, but they were sweat-slicked and she couldn't hold them.

"*Nnooo!*"

She threw herself across him, trying to immobilize him with her weight, grasping for his wrists, cursing as they slipped away, her robe falling open as he twisted beneath her. Suddenly his shoulder slammed into her forehead as he arched upward in a spasm of agony, tumbling them off the sofa to the floor.

She lay beneath him, stunned, ribbons of darkness dancing before her eyes, the taste of blood from his torn shoulder in her mouth. She shook her head, trying to clear it. Then felt his hands on her shoulders, gently pulling her robe open to the waist.

"Stop it!"

He didn't seem to hear. His palms slid over her breasts, peeling the robe down."

"*Stop it!*" She swung a fist at his head, but her shoulders were tangled in the robe and the blow landed with no real force. Still, he stopped. He stared down at her, dazed, unseeing. And then his gaze seemed to clear, and their eyes met, and held for a dozen heartbeats. And there was only the sound of their breathing. And then he gently pulled her robe back into place.

He eased himself away from her and stood up, swaying. He

walked unsteadily to the window, brushed the curtains aside, and stood with his back to her, staring out into the dusk.

Linda slowly sat up, readjusted her robe, then leaned back against the sofa, waiting for her breathing to moderate. Mirabel peered cautiously out of the bedroom, then stalked stiffly to Linda's side, arching her back to be petted. Her low drone of contentment underlined the silence for what seemed a very long time.

"I'm . . . sorry," Lamont said quietly. "Are you okay?"

"I'm all right," she said, surprised at the steadiness of her tone. "Thank you for your concern."

He didn't reply. She rested her chin on her knees, gently stroking the cat.

"What, ah"—she cleared her throat—"why did you call out? What was happening to you?"

"I was on fire," he said softly. "I was dying."

"Has this happened to you before?" She felt detached, an observer again. And her sense of her own strength begin to return, to regenerate.

"It's happened a couple of times since . . . we went through the ice. Into the river. But not the same way. It's always different." He shook his head slowly. "I die differently every time. And it seems so *real*, I'm surprised to be alive when it's over."

"Do you feel guilt over what happened on the river?"

He glanced over his shoulder at her for a moment, but she didn't look up. "I am guilty," he said simply. "Of letting go of the rope. And more. A lot more."

"Were you in the water when you let go?"

"I was under the water. Under the ice."

"And if you hadn't let go? What would have happened if you'd held on?"

"I don't know. I would've died, I guess. Maybe I should have. Look, I don't want to talk about this."

"Probably not. But you have to. To someone. I've seen this before, at the vets facility. You were in agony. In hell. And unless you break the cycle, it'll get worse. And one of these times you won't wake up. You won't make it back."

132

"So I don't make it back. That's my problem. What about you? You got any problems? Like almost bein' raped a few minutes ago?"

"I'm not sure yet. I haven't decided."

"Jesus Christ. You haven't *decided*?"

"Things happened too fast. But you didn't hurt me, Lamont, or at least, not intentionally. So I'll define what happened in my own terms. And I'll decide. But I think you'd better go."

"I, ah, yeah, I guess you're right." He hesitated as he picked up his denim jacket from the sofa, searching for the right thing to say, but nothing came. Mirabel disengaged herself from Linda and followed him to the door, stalking him, rubbing against his ankles as he paused in the doorway to slip on the jacket.

"Look, I don't want things to end like this," he said quietly. "I want to see you again. Not here, necessarily, or at the club. Neutral ground if you like. Anyplace at all."

"I don't think so. I think you may be a little more than I can handle. Or care to. And I'm not sure you're worth the trouble."

"Probably not. But it's a little early to say, isn't it? And maybe you owe me one."

"I don't know. I'll think about it."

"You do that. And let me know. I'll be around."

CHAPTER 18

T HE MUSIC WAS PUMPING HARD, "LODI," THE OLD CREEDENCE JAM
done as a tough shuffle, flat out, with balls to the walls energy.
Sonny bopped across the stage, swivel-hipped, finger-popping the
beat, feeling a righteous tightness in his chest, a solid buzz from
the music and a fine as wine line he'd tooted on his last break.
The Crossing had been jumping all night. A heavier than usual
crowd, high on holiday spirits, had packed the smoky club early,
whooping and applauding after every song, keeping the dance
floor so jammed you could barely boogie. The air was hazy gray
and thick enough to feel, dense with the blended scents of
hairspray and perspiration and perfume. The musk of action.
And there was primo stuff in the mix tonight.

Sonny'd moved in on a Chicano chick during the second set,
a stone fox in a red silk blouse and skintight jeans, coal-black
hair, a beauty mark on her upper lip, and tits to the max. Little
heavy in the ass maybe, but she looked solid, round and firm,
and fully packed. And young, seventeen, eighteen tops, and he
was in the mood for some young stuff. One piece of ass is pretty

134

much like another in the dark, but sometimes hustlin' the Geritol trade got old, business or no business. None of his regular ladies in sight, so tonight, a little taco bender for breakfast. Taco flour? Flower? Might even get a lyric out of it.

He shot the chick a quick wink and checked his watch. Time for one more song, unless Lamont kept cooking this one, and he probably would. The redneck was smoking tonight, ripping off chorus after chorus of dynamite leads, jamming every tune, slick as a lizard, never missing a lick, so hot he had the rest of the band on a tear, pushing them, keeping everybody on the edge of the best they could do. The fucker was a bitch to work with sometimes, but when he was hot . . .

Sonny grinned across the stage at LeeRoy, met his stare, and instantly came crashing down from his high, cold turkey in under a second. Tree had the look on. The giant bass player was swaying with the song, grinning at the crowd, but his eyes were hard, and bright as rhinestones. Which meant deep, deep shit for somebody. Sonny just hoped to God it was somebody else. He scanned his memory for a panicky second, but couldn't come up with anything he'd done that might've ticked LeeRoy off. Still, with Tree, it didn't pay to take chances. He boogied over beside the big man, and leaned against him, clowning it up for the crowd.

"Yo, Tree, what's up?"

"Business," LeeRoy said, still grinning. "You stick around after the gig. Guar-on-tee it'll be interestin'."

"Whatever." Sonny nodded. He bopped back to his mike to make his closing pitch. The Chicano flower did a little shimmy, shaking her rack at him, but he barely noticed. She'd have to wait. Interesting, the man said. Sonny felt a shiver of anticipation across his shoulderblades. Interesting.

"So where the fuck's he headed?" Sonny asked. "A couple more blocks and we'll be in coontown." He twitched the wheel of his black Camaro, dodging a broken bottle in the street. They'd followed Denny Weitz's rust-bucket '71 Vega all the way into Detroit after the Crossing closed, a straight shot down 94, then

135

north on the Corridor and off into the maze of side streets around U of D. LeeRoy hadn't said shit the whole time and he didn't answer now, or even look as if he'd heard. He was zoned out, his eyes glued on the Vega's tail lights. And Sonny was getting antsy.

Sonny'd been hooked up with the Tree for a few years, and he was used to his moods, black, blue, and otherwise, but he never got used to the freeze, when the giant would just drop out, silent, staring, sometimes for hours. He hated it. Sonny was naturally wired. He liked *action*, talk, sex, coke, something happening all the time, and around the Tree it usually was, but when he got like this—

Ahead, the Vega swung over to the curb and parked.

"Slow down," LeeRoy snapped, "but don't stop." He swiveled in his seat as they crawled past, watching Denny climb out of his car and saunter down an alley.

"Pull up around the corner and park it."

"Why?" Sonny said, easing the Camaro over. "What's down there?"

"Blind pig. TicTac, KitKat, somethin' like that. You ready to party?"

"I was born ready, you know that, but you wanna tell me what's happenin'? I mean, I'll back you—"

"You're gonna back me? Against Denny? Jesus, that's a comfort. Look, you stay close to me, roll with the flow, and keep your mouth shut. Understand?"

"Yeah, right. Whatever."

"Listen, boy, I ain't fuckin' around here, you dig? So you do like I tell ya," LeeRoy said, unfolding his massive frame from the car seat. "Besides, you'll get off on this place. Guar-on-tee."

Sonny could hear the faint sound of music as they stalked down the alley, their breath clouding the icy air. He shivered, hugging himself. His short embroidered leather jacket was useless against the chill. He followed LeeRoy down a narrow flight of steps to a basement apartment.

The guy who answered the door was nearly as big as LeeRoy,

but soft, a lard sculpture in a cheap suit, sunglasses at three in the morning, a Louisville Slugger close at hand.

"Ten bucks a head, five for anything at the bar. And no trouble."

LeeRoy forked over a twenty without a word, and moved past the doorman, with Sonny right behind.

The music was from a massive stereo against one wall, but the room was so dim it took Sonny several moments to spot it. The room wasn't large, forty by forty or so, and it was packed, nearly as full as the Crossing had been. A dozen or so couples were swaying on the postage stamp dance floor, and several of the men were shirtless, their bodies gleaming with oil in the smoky gloom. And Sonny realized that most of the couples were men. In fact, with the exception of a pair of women dancing together, and a stacked-to-the-max barmaid in pink leotards and an outrageous beehive hairdo, there were no women in the room, only men, laughing, whispering, nuzzling each other. And he sensed the sensual electricity in the ambience, the tang of males in heat.

He glanced the question at LeeRoy, but the big man was already shouldering through the crowd toward the bar. He ordered two beers, passed one to Sonny, and glanced around, checking out the action.

"Jesus H. Christ," Sonny whispered, "wild, really wild."

"Thought you'd like it." LeeRoy nodded. "Just remember to stay close. Wouldn't want to lose you in here. Dig the table in the corner."

Sonny followed his gaze. Denny was sitting with a pudgy, balding type in a business suit, frowning, shaking his head at whatever the guy was saying. LeeRoy sauntered over, bent down, and whispered something in business-suit's ear. The guy paled, gave up his seat, and moved quickly off into the crowd. LeeRoy eased down into the empty chair.

"Denny." He smiled. "So how's it goin'? Guy givin' you some trouble?"

"I, ah, no, no problem," Weitz said, glancing from LeeRoy to Sonny, who'd taken the other seat. "What—?"

"Are we doin' here?" LeeRoy finished. "Actually, I could ask you the same. I come here now and again, don't recall seein' you in here either."

"No, I haven't been here, ah, before. Just came to check out the action, you know, watch the fags?"

"I can dig it," LeeRoy said easily. "You know, it's kinda lucky we run into each other. I been wantin' to talk to you anyway."

"Me? About what?"

"Business. Might have a little proposition for you."

"Nah, I don't think I'd—"

"Hey, don't be sayin' no so quick. You don't even know what I want yet. Do you?"

"Ah, no, I guess not."

"So why don't we use one of the rooms? Too noisy in here to talk."

"The rooms?"

"Yeah, the rooms," LeeRoy said, standing up, towering over the kid, his smile fading. "Like I said, I been here before. Through that door over there next to the blue light."

Denny glanced around nervously, then shrugged and pushed off through the crowd with LeeRoy and Sonny close behind. The door opened into a narrow, dimly lit corridor, thickly carpeted, with a series of doors that opened off both sides. Denny moved quietly down the hallway past several doors until he found one open, then went in.

At LeeRoy's nod, Sonny stepped in and closed the door. A single red bulb gleamed overhead, giving the room a dusky scarlet glow. There was a cot with a bare mattress against one wall, a bright yellow nightstand with a can of Crisco and a roll of paper towels on it, a metal condom dispenser beside the door. The pulse from the stereo hammered through the paisley-papered walls like a heartbeat. Sonny felt himself growing hard. He licked his lips, savoring the tension. Action. Just a breath away.

Denny turned to face them, his back to the bed. "So, ah, what you got in mind?"

"Business," LeeRoy said. "I'm surprised we haven't got to it before. We got a lot in common, you and me."

138

"Like what?"

"Three thousand Cooper Street, Jackson. You did time there, right? Well, so did I. Six years hard time, assault with intent."

"All six? That's a pretty heavy stroke for assault."

"Well, I had me a few problems in the joint there. Needs, you know? A man has needs."

Denny's ferret glance flicked back and forth between Sonny and LeeRoy, his eyes widening. "I shoulda known," he said softly. "I shoulda guessed about you two."

"Maybe so," LeeRoy said, "but then everybody's got a secret or two. Even you."

"I don't—"

"You were on the telephone this afternoon. In the john at the club. I want you to tell me about that. Straight out, the first time, you dig? Or I'm gonna rip off your fuckin' arms and legs one at a time."

"Jesus, I can explain about the call, I—"

"Good. Only don't *explain* nothin', just give it to me. Now who were you talkin' to?"

"Garcia. It was Garcia."

"That cop that's been hasslin' Lamont? What'd he want?"

"Names, license numbers, of the women Lamont's been hangin' with, or hangin' around with the band, that's all."

"I heard you mention my name, motherfucker."

"Well, he, ah, wanted, like names of everybody connected with Lamont. I think it's because Lamont's hustlin' his woman, the one from the paper?"

"So you just rolled over and give him the names? You were inside, you know about talkin' to the man."

"I didn't have any choice! He's got me on a weapons violation and I'm on parole. I don't wanna go back."

"That's hard, real hard. Shit, maybe I wouldna done no different, I was you. What names did you give him?"

"Ah, Gopher's wife, Rhonda, and her sister, Shelley. Jobeth, and that Naomi Sonny hangs out with sometimes—"

"Jesus Christ," Sonny breathed, "you told him about her?"

139

"I didn't want to give him nothin'." Denny pleaded, "You don't know this guy, he's—"

"What about Sonny's other women?" LeeRoy interrupted. "You give him any others?"

"No, those are the only ones who been around."

"So far, you mean?"

"Look, I didn't know there was a problem. I mean, it wasn't like he was askin' me to fink on nobody. He wants a few names, what the shit? No harm, right? But if you don't want me talkin' to him, then that's it. I won't."

"He gonna let you slide, is he? Way I see it he's got you by the nuts, boy, why shouldn't he squeeze?"

"Yeah, but it's Lamont he wants, not you guys. I can—"

He was cut off as LeeRoy's massive paw shot out and seized him by the throat, lifting him off the floor, slamming his scrawny frame into the wall and pinning him there. LeeRoy ripped open Denny's shirt, baring him to the waist, then he clawed at his own belt buckle. It came off in his hand, with a short, flat three-inch blade attached to it. The blade slashed across Denny's torso, once, twice, carving a streaming X into his chest. The kid writhed and squirmed, flailing helplessly like a rabbit in a snare, his face suffusing with blood as he keened for air.

Without easing his hold, LeeRoy turned and offered the dripping belt knife to Sonny. His yellowed teeth were clenched in a wolf grin, his nostrils flared above his beard. "Take it!" His eyes were alight, urgent, as though sharing a mystery. "Take it!"

And Sonny was ready, hard, only a second from climax. He closed his fist around the buckle, and plunged it in, twisting it, as Denny's heels thudded a shuddering tattoo on the paisley wall.

CHAPTER 19

THE SQUAD ROOM WAS IN A STATE OF TOTAL CONFUSION WHEN Garcia made it in the next morning. Two white-coveralled workmen with temp personnel tags dangling from their collars were demolishing the remains of Joad's office door with wrecking bars. Harry Fein, called in off vacation to pick up Marv Cream's caseload, was yelling at a maintenance supervisor that he didn't *want* a different desk, bullet hole or no goddam bullet hole, the maintenance guy saying his men hadn't hauled a desk all the way up from the friggin' basement for the friggin' exercise and read the friggin' work order! The only people who looked organized were Cordell and Fielder. They were waiting next to Garcia's desk, neckties squared away and suitcoats buttoned. A bad omen. Cordell'd quit buttoning his jacket when his waistline hit 40.

"You guys look like the doormen at a mausoleum. What's up?"

Fielder held up the morning edition of the *Free Press*. "You seen this?"

"Nope, I eat breakfast with Jane Pauley. Good news?"

Fielder tossed the paper to him. "Check the front page, left side. 'Tragedy Victim Rescues Hostages.' Sound like anybody you know?"

Garcia quickly scanned the article. And the one beside it, "The Wrong Man," by Linda Kerry. Both pieces covered the shoot-out, but from different perspectives. Mullery's was full of sound and fury, liberally laced with quotes from Isobel Cabb. Linda's piece took a human-interest slant, making Lamont sound like a cross between Jean Valjean and John Wayne.

"Jeez, if my mom reads this she'll probably want her Christmas cookies back."

"Spare me your so-called wit, okay, Loop?" Fielder said. "We got an appointment with the captain *and* the deputy commissioner in five minutes, and I don't figure it's for congratulations on a job well done. Look, I don't like asking this but, dammit, this thing with the woman, Kerry? Straight out, did you bend any procedures to get at Yarborough? Any at all?"

"Not a one. The guy's a suspect. Joad gave him to us, we were checking him out. That's it. And I don't much care for the question."

"Too bad. I got a feeling it's just the first of a bunch you're not gonna like. The difference is, *I* believe you. I think. Let's go upstairs."

They walked into the deputy commissioner's outer office at 9:25, five minutes early, and waited another half hour. Commissioner Powell's receptionist, a photogenic uniform named Angel Luna, waved them toward the overstuffed sofa but otherwise ignored them. Another bad omen.

Cordell ran his fingers over the material as he sat down. Leather. Real leather. And thick green carpeting, long enough to need mowing. "Nice," he murmured, "very nice."

"You've never been up here before?" Fielder asked.

"Just once, when Holmes was still commissioner. Got a citation for disarmin' a wacko on a bus. It was just an office then, nothin' like this. Looks like the parlor for a yuppy whorehouse now."

"Maybe it is," Fielder said glumly. "At least there's a real good chance we're here to get screwed."

142

Powell's inner office made the waiting room look positively austere, hand-rubbed walnut paneling, overstuffed leather chairs, an ebony desk the size of a compact car. The pungent stench of cigar smoke hung heavy in the air, mingled with the scent of old leather. The aroma of power.

A larger-than-life photograph of Mayor Young beamed down on the man seated at the desk, who was almost larger-than-life himself. A heavyset, fair-skinned black with close-cropped, rust-colored hair and a liberal dusting of freckles across his broad cheekbones, Nathaniel Turner Powell had been a token patrolman on the almost lily-white Detroit force before the riots. He'd persevered, despite pressure from his liberal, well-educated family, and now he wore tailored conservative suits, a diamond-studded American Legion flag in his lapel, and chaired functions for the Detroit Symphony and the DRA, sharing the dais with nationally prominent politicians and celebrities. On the force he was considered fair, but hard, a man who never forgave a slight, real or imagined.

Joad was standing slightly behind Powell, hands clasped at parade rest, ill at ease, but thankful to be out of the direct line of fire.

"Lieutenant Fielder, gentlemen, I suppose I should feel grateful that celebrities of your stature can spare me a few minutes this morning," Powell said acidly, tapping copies of the morning papers with a blunt forefinger. "Front-page coverage in the *News* and *Free Press* both, Channel Two, Channel Seven. Even departments with their own PR office don't get ink like this. Not that they'd want to." He picked up one of the papers, scanned it for a moment, then tossed it aside in disgust.

"All right, I've heard their side of it. Now I want yours. Lieutenant, how the hell did that maniac get hold of a gun in the middle of a goddam police station?"

"He, ah, took the weapon from Sergeant Cream, sir," Fielder said. "It was—"

"The Freep said he hit him with a telephone?" Powell interrupted.

143

"Yes, sir, he did, but Hobart wasn't a murder suspect. He's mental, but he's never been particularly violent—"

"I know who Harold Hobart is, Fielder, and why your man was processing him, and I gather Cream underestimated him. Which still doesn't explain how an armed officer allowed himself to be overpowered by an unarmed suspect wearing cuffs!"

"I honestly can't say at this time, sir. Maybe Sergeant Cream can, but at the moment he's sedated and we can't talk to him."

"He's still hospitalized? How's he doing? And how's Officer Pilarski?"

"Bobby was treated and released last night. Badly bruised ribs but otherwise he's fine."

"I understand he was wearing his vest."

"Yes, sir, it probably saved his life."

"I think Bobby's probably a helluva lot brighter than most of us give him credit for," Powell said. "What about Cream?"

"Concussion, and a nasty laceration on his forehead. He should be out in a few days."

"There's no rush. As of today Sergeant Cream is on two-weeks suspension, two-weeks reduced pay."

"Sir, I don't think that's quite fair—"

"I wasn't aware I needed your concurrence, Lieutenant. Or would you prefer that I bust him to patrolman? I could, you know."

"No, sir," Fielder said, a flush climbing slowly above his collar. "I, ah, two and two, yes, sir."

"Let's move on, then. We have a hostage incident in one of our own squad rooms, perpetrated by a man who shouldn't have been able to, and then resolved by a man who shouldn't have been there. Is that a fair summary, Garcia?"

"No, sir, it's not. Yarborough's a homicide suspect. He was being held for questioning."

"I see. But he was released immediately after the incident?"

"Yes, sir. We didn't have sufficient grounds to hold him at that time."

"What grounds did you have, Sergeant?"

"We had reason to believe he hadn't properly identified himself."

144

"Garcia, half the perps we pick up use phony ID, or try to. You ran him through LEIN?"

"Yes, sir," Cordell put in, "no wants or warrants on him. Driver's license went back three years. Charge cards and Social Security were legit."

"So what's the identification problem?"

"I talked with the sheriff of Merrimac County, Tennessee," Garcia said, "running down a tip. He told me that Lamont Yarborough was dead, killed in a jailhouse brawl down there more than ten years ago."

"He seemed pretty lively yesterday for a dead man. And since his ID checks, I'd say you got a bum tip."

"The sheriff was quite positive, sir, he—"

"I don't give a damn what some cracker county sheriff's got posted on his outhouse wall—"

"They have a computer. Sir."

"So it's a *computer* foul-up, and goddammit, don't interrupt me. I don't care about problems in goddam Tennessee, we've got a shitstorm right here! Now listen up, Garcia, I'm not going to ask you about your girlfriend and this suspect because I dislike prying into a man's personal life and because I assume there's at least some truth to—"

"Sir, I didn't roust—"

"What I want to know *is*," Powell raised his voice, cutting Garcia off, "do you have any solid physical evidence or testimony linking this man to the slasher killings? Any at all?"

"We have bits and pieces that indicate—"

"I said solid physical evidence or testimony, Sergeant, and I don't like repeating myself. Do you have it? Yes or no?"

"We, ah, no, sir, we have nothing solid now, but—"

"That's what I thought."

"Dammit, Powell, can I finish, please? We're talking about murder here—"

"Sergeant Garcia," Joad snapped, "that's enough. You're—"

"Let him finish, Wendell," Powell said coldly. "I believe in giving a man as much time as he needs. And as much rope."

"Sir, I've been in Homicide six years, and I've got a good

resolution record. Now I admit that we don't have much on this guy yet, but he's wrong. You were a street cop, you know what I'm talking about. The guy's wrong."

"Wrong." Joad snorted.

"Maybe," Powell said mildly, "maybe he is. I've played hunches in my time, Garcia. And sometimes they turn out to be dogshit. Correct?"

"Yes, sir, sometimes they do."

"All right, I'll put it to you straight. I should pull you off this investigation right now and jerk your shield for the connection with the woman, if nothing else. But I'm not going to. Yet. Not because of anything you've said, but because I don't want it to even *appear* that the press can influence a departmental decision. And that's the only thing that's saving your ass at the moment, Garcia. *But* I don't want to see this guy's name in the papers again. We can't afford it. When I have to fight for our cut of the budget at council meetings, I don't want to waste my time explaining crap like this! So you'll stay on the investigation, but you'll use proper procedure every step of the way. If Yarborough comes up again, you clear any moves with your captain before acting, clear? And Yarborough is *not* to be the focus of your investigation. You stay the hell away from him. If he's the man, you'll eventually turn up solid evidence that ties him in if you do your damn job, correct?"

"Yes, sir, but—"

"Garcia, I've cut you all the slack I'm going to. Now can you continue this investigation under the conditions I've just outlined or not?"

"Yes, sir. If I have to."

"Then do it. By the book. Or you're out. And I don't mean just off this case. I mean out. Understood?"

"I understand what out means, yes, sir."

"Garcia, I've checked your record." Powell sighed, massaging his knuckles. "And I can't decide whether you're an independent thinker, or just a fuck-up. It's a fine line, a tough call to make sometimes. You know how I make it?"

"No, sir."

"I don't. When an officer of apparent ability screws up, I don't try to figure out the whys and wherefores. I just fire him. It's like hunting squirrels with a shotgun: it may not be pretty, but it gets the job done. Now get the hell out of my office."

"I think maybe we dodged the bullet," Cordell said, slumping heavily into his battered desk chair.

"For now, maybe." Garcia, perching on the edge of the desk, watched Fielder grab his coat and stalk out of the squad room. "Thing is, I'm not sure whose side Al's gonna be on next time."

"The man just saw his career pass before his eyes. He'll be okay."

"How about you? You see your career passing?"

"Maybe I wouldn't give much of a shit if it did," Cordell said bluntly. "It ain't exactly the high life, cost me my family . . ."

"You figure that's what it was? The job?"

"I'd like to think so. Beats tryna figure where else I fucked up."

"Being a little tough on yourself, aren't you?"

"Drop it," Cordell snapped. "We've got some phone messages here. Grivas called, wants a call back. I guess under the circumstances, I better handle that. Denny Weitz called in some names, addresses, license plate numbers yesterday."

"Great sense of timing. Hell, file 'em for now. Maybe we'll figure a way to use 'em later."

"And this one's all yours." Cordell flipped a memo card at Garcia, who caught it in midair.

"Carl Lorch?" Garcia scanned the card. "Who's he?"

"Victim number four's brother, from Seattle. Flew in to ID the body and claim it. And it's your turn to do the morgue tour."

"You know, this is not turning out to be a day to relive during my golden years."

"I talked to Lorch when I notified next of kin. He took it pretty cool. Said they'd been out of touch."

"He'll wig out on me. The cool ones always wig out."

"Yeah." Cordell grinned. "Seems like they do, don't they?"

"Sergeant Garcia?"

Garcia paused, with one hand on the door of his Chrysler. A

147

blocky patrol cop was waving him down from across the department parking lot. He tried to place the face as the cop trotted
over. Bee—Beamon, one of the patrolmen who'd taken the
squeal on the Caddy in the river.

"Got a minute, Sarge?"

"Sure, what's up?"

"Probably nothin', but you remember that wino we talked to
the other night at the river? Maish?"

"Sure. The old man who thought he saw flashers."

"That's him. Look here, it, ah, probably doesn't mean nothin'
but he got hisself killed. I found him last night, but he coulda
been dead a day or two. Wintertime it's not so easy to say."

"What happened?"

"Torched," Beamon said, his face expressionless as an ebony
mask. "Somebody torched him good. Used gasoline. Almost
nothin' left."

"Are you sure it was—?"

"It was him. Recognized his shoes. They, ah, they used to be
mine. My old army brogans."

"I . . . see. Any idea who did him?"

"Nah, coulda been anybody. That area down there's no-man's-
land, two or three different gangs claim it. I musta told the old
bastard a thousan' times to— Anyway, I thought maybe you
oughta know about it."

"You think it had anything to do with the car in the river?"

"No, nothin' like that. I, ah, I guess I just thought I oughta tell
somebody he was dead, and at least you'd know who he was.
Wouldn't anybody else even know who he was, you know?"

"Yeah, I think I do. We probably won't handle the case
though. It'll go to the Sixth."

"I know. I just thought— Never mind. Dumb idea. I'll see you
around, Garcia."

"Beamon," Garcia called after him. "Look, I'm sorry about the
old man."

"Yeah. Sometimes I hate this fuckin' town, you know that? I
just fuckin' hate it."

CHAPTER 20

Garcia picked up carl lorch at the ramada inn near metro Airport. Lorch was a chubby, dapper butterball of a man, fiftyish, with watery blue eyes and a neatly trimmed blond mustache. His tweed overcoat and loden alpine cap gave him an avuncular, affable look; Walter Cronkite's little brother.

He complained mildly about his flight (delayed), the weather (you fly two thousand miles, it should be a little warmer), and his room at the motel.

Garcia let him ramble, nodding at appropriate intervals. The man had flown to a strange city to collect his sister's body, cut him some slack. Still, there was a pettiness to Lorch's complaints that grated after a while. Beamon had shown more real pain for a derelict wino than Lorch apparently felt for his sister.

"Mr. Lorch," Garcia broke in, "maybe I'd better give you a quick rundown on the identification procedure. We try to make it—"

"I got a fairly good idea of what happens, Sergeant. Believe it or not, we have TV in Seattle too. It's not the back of the moon, you know."

"Still—"

"Look, don't worry about me. I can handle it. Maybe you oughta spend your time worrying about who killed her."

"All right then, let's do that. Could you give me a quick rundown on your sister's recent activities?"

"I already told the officer who called, Bennett, was it? I haven't seen Louise in years, not since before her marriage. She wrote now and again, but I didn't answer."

"What did she write to you about?"

"Nothing. What do women write? How are you, I'm fine, that sort of thing. I'm not much on writing anyway, and she knew how I felt."

"How you felt?"

"About Barrett. I suppose it's more common here, where blacks are the majority, but—"

"Your sister's husband was black?"

"You mean you didn't know?"

"No, sir, we didn't. Maybe you'd better tell me about her husband."

"He's been dead for years. What difference could it make now?"

"Maybe none. Tell me anyway."

"Well, he wasn't . . . very black, probably only a little darker than you are, but of course who knows what their children might've looked like? Buncha pickaninnies at a family reunion wouldn't go over so good, you know? Louise had been married once before, to a construction worker. A dumbshit. Alcoholic, I think. They were divorced in California, and a year or so later she wrote and said she was engaged to this *exceptional* man, and sent us a picture. He was exceptional all right. My parents did their best to talk sense to her, but she married him anyway. And like I said, after that we didn't stay in touch. We were close as children, real close, but there are limits to what a man can take. Even from his sister."

"Were there any children?"

150

"No, thank God. They married late, and with all the moving around—"

"Moving around?"

"Have you people done any work on this at all? Barrett was a marine officer, they were always on the move. He brought Louise here to be near his parents when he went to Vietnam. He was killed in action there, but at least he didn't come back nuts or a junkie like the rest of 'em."

"You want to run that by me again?"

"Don't go hypersensitive on me," Lorch said coolly. "You know it's true. And I can even sympathize. I did a hitch myself. Korean war. Eight months on a destroyer in the Yellow Sea back in fifty-six."

"I thought that one ended in fifty-four."

"For the army, maybe, but the truce didn't make much difference to us. No shelling, of course, but we would've been right in the middle of it if things'd started up again."

"I guess you would have at that."

"Anyway, after Barrett was killed she could've come home. We were tight when we were kids, and the folks would've come around eventually. But she didn't. Maybe she was ashamed, I don't know. Hard to figure."

"Yeah," Garcia said drily, "hard to figure. Look, do you know if your sister ever went to bars, you know, to have a drink, maybe listen to some music, that sort of thing?"

Lorch stared at him, not bothering to conceal his disbelief. "I wouldn't know," he said finally. "Like I said, we've been out of touch. But I doubt it. Except for maybe a little wine at dinner, Louise didn't drink."

"She'd apparently been drinking the night she died. The coroner's report showed a blood alcohol level of one point eight."

"Really?" Lorch said doubtfully. "Well, maybe she changed after she married Barrett. She probably let a lot of things slide, you know? It'd be . . . inevitable, I guess."

"Right," Garcia said. "Inevitable."

Lorch hesitated just inside the main entrance at the Wayne County Morgue.

151

"Something wrong?" Garcia asked.

"Wrong? No, it . . . just doesn't look the way I'd expected, that's all. It sort of looks like . . . a bank."

"I guess it is a bank, in a way," Garcia said, leading Lorch across the lobby to the polished oak counter. He checked with the clerk, then escorted Lorch into the viewing room, a quiet, carpeted cubicle with a half-dozen office chairs and a wall-mounted TV set. A white-smocked attendant, carrying a clipboard, followed them in. He looked much too young for the job. He should have been slinging fries at McDonald's.

"Identification of Louise Lorch Barrett," Garcia said quietly.

"Should be coming up now," the kid said, checking his clipboard. "Please observe the monitor."

The set flickered to life as he spoke, showing what appeared to be a photograph in black and white. A close-up of a woman's face, a sheet pulled up tightly to her chin. Makeup in place, no signs of violence. Her lips and jaw were slightly averted, as though she were holding a hard-boiled egg in her mouth. Lorch stared at the screen a moment, then turned away.

"Mr. Lorch, is this your sister, Louise Barrett?"

Lorch looked back at the screen again, frowning. "The . . . her face doesn't look right. The mouth . . ."

Garcia glanced at the attendant. "There was some, ah, damage to the tendons of the throat, sir," the kid said. "There may be some distortion of her features as a result."

"I don't think so," Lorch said.

"Mr. Lorch—" Garcia began.

"No, that's definitely not Louise," Lorch said with growing certainty. "You people have botched this somehow. For one thing, this woman's much too old."

"Mr. Lorch, when did you last see your sister?"

"That doesn't matter. We were very close as children and I'd sure as hell recognize my own sister. I don't know what you're trying to pull here, Garcia, but that's not Louise."

"Right," Garcia said, grasping Lorch by the upper arm. "Let's take a closer look, just to be sure."

"Wait a minute, can't you show me another picture?"

"Afraid not, and if it's not Louise, what's the difference? Come on, you can handle it. After Korea this'll be duck soup."

The attendant stepped aside, shaking his head doubtfully, as Garcia led Lorch through the inner door.

The banks of overhead fluorescents were painfully bright after the dimness of the viewing room. A bitter, sour-earth odor of decay hung heavy on the air, mingled with the sharp tang of antiseptic. A dozen, perhaps fifteen cadavers, most of them nude, on stainless steel gurneys were scattered randomly around the long, low-ceilinged lab.

At first the bodies didn't seem real, there were just too many. Some bore the marks of recent violence, torn flesh, a severed limb lying beside a torso. Some were agonizingly contorted, and some lay like department store mannequins waiting to be dressed, paper bags containing their belongings parked casually between their knees.

Lorch didn't hold back. He seemed to take it all in, his head swiveling like a radar screen as Garcia let him through the carnage to the gurney positioned beneath a ceiling-mounted TV camera. A sheet was draped over the woman's upper body to hide the wound to her throat, but it only reached to her navel. She was nude below it, wide-hipped, a dark thatch of pubic hair, heavy marble thighs dimpled with pads of cellulite. Lorch stared at the body, swallowing rapidly. Garcia casually tugged the sheet down, covering her torso.

"Well, Mr. Lorch? How about it?"

"I . . . I don't know." He coughed, and wiped his nose on the sleeve of his tweed overcoat.

"Take your time, it's been a while. Not since she got married, you said."

Across the room, Dr. Klevenger reached up and switched off the microphone and the high-intensity lamp above the black teenaged corpse he was dissecting. He tossed his scalpel onto the instrument tray, and ambled over to the identification station. He was dressed for surgery, a pastel green smock and cap, elbow-

153

length rubber gloves, and a transparent plastic apron spattered with a bouillabaisse of blood and body fluids.

"What seems to be the problem, Garcia?"

"A little trouble with an ID, Doc. Mr. Lorch here hasn't seen the victim in some time."

"Does the victim have any identifying marks you can recall, Mr. Lorch?" Klevenger asked. "Moles, birthmarks, surgical scars?"

"She had her appendix out when she was fourteen. There was a scar."

Klevenger raised the sheet to expose the abdomen. "Like this one?" he said, indicating the faint line on alabaster skin. "Anything else?"

"I . . . it just doesn't look like Louise," Lorch said unsteadily. "Her face—"

"Mr. Lorch, the woman's had her throat cut," Klevenger said brusquely, yanking the sheet down to expose the wound. "And when muscles and tendons are severed it changes the shape of the face. We have a positive print match, so unless you're absolutely convinced there's an error . . ."

Lorch gagged and doubled over, stumbling blindly toward the door, careening through the gurneys like a drunken halfback.

"Asa?" Klevenger clacked the two digits of his prosthetic steel hand together at the attendant who was prepping the next corpse for viewing, and pointed at Lorch. The boy nodded, set his makeup tray aside, and trotted after him.

"Quite a bedside manner you've got, Doc," Garcia said. "Very sensitive."

"My patients don't seem to mind," Klevenger said wryly, "or at least they never complain about it. Your man'll sign the ID form now. Just give Asa a couple of minutes with him. Now if you'll excuse me, I'm in the middle of a mugging victim. Hate to keep a customer waiting."

"Right," Garcia called after him, "and thanks, Doc."

"No problem."

Garcia glanced around the room, wondering how much time Asa would need. He didn't like this place, not so much because

154

of the carnage, or even the stench. It was the . . . businesslike atmosphere. Grocery bags on the tables, tags on toes, cadavers scattered about like a cosmic rummage sale. No sense of reverence for life or the remains. Meat. Like the back room of a butcher shop. Maybe it was the honesty of the room that bothered him.

Or maybe it was more than that. Something felt . . . out of place here. Klevenger was back at his surgical station, doing a play-by-play into the mike as he worked, and the only other vertical person in the room was Charlie Skowron, the assistant medical examiner, who was checking over a body in the far corner. Not the living, then.

Garcia made his way slowly through the corpses, looking into their faces, coldly repressing the surge of horror and outrage, the urge to flee that skittered about his subconscious like a cockroach on a hot griddle.

Nothing. Young, old, intact, or torn, they were only empty husks now, with no message for him. No one at home. Nothing . . . He stopped.

In an alcove directly across the room was a corpse he couldn't see clearly. The gurney was facing away from him. He could only see the top of a head. Frizzy, dishwater blond hair, like the overripe tassel of a dandelion. It could have been anybody of course, black, white, anybody. But it wasn't. As he walked slowly toward the alcove, somehow he already knew who it was.

He was lying on his side, nude, his bony knees drawn up into a fetal position, his hands clasped over his genitals, sleeping. An X had been carved across his chest, with a deeper, darker wound just below the nexus.

Garcia stared down at the body, waiting to feel a reaction, anything, but there was nothing. Hell, how well had he known the kid? Still, you ought to feel something at a time like this. Or say something. You see a guy in a toilet one day, and then in the morgue a day or so later, there ought to be something worth saying. We can't go on meeting like this. Something.

"So, Denny," Garcia said softly, "other'n this, what else is new?" A trickle of snot had congealed on the kid's upper lip.

Garcia reached down to wipe it away, and realized his hand was trembling. He stared at it, surprised, as though it belonged to someone else, then he thrust his clenched fists into the pockets of his leather coat. For a moment the room seemed to waver, shifting into red, and then it stabilized again. He took a deep breath, and leaned out of the alcove.

"Hey, Skow, got a minute?"

Charlie Skowron glanced at him over his steel-rimmed bifocals. "In a sec. Can you ID that one?"

"Yeah," Garcia said. "Alas, I knew him well, and get your ass over here. Now."

Skowron's eyes raised, then he shrugged and walked over, jotting a few quick notes on his clipboard as he came. He was a tall, bird-faced man with deep acne scars and thick glasses, central casting's idea of a diffident bookkeeper, except for the unlit White Owl cigar he kept permanently clamped in the corner of his jaw. Garcia'd never seen him light it. Maybe it was the same cigar every time. Hell, maybe it was rubber.

"Okay," Skowron said, flipping up a new sheet on his clipboard, "shoot. Name."

"His name's Weitz, Dennis. I don't know his stats offhand, but they'll be easy enough to get. He's a Jackson grad, still on parole. How soon can I have the autopsy results?"

"You can have 'em right now. Cause of death, multiple stab wounds to the chest, one piercing the aorta, secondary trauma to the upper body contributory, probably inflicted prior to death with an edged weapon of undetermined type. Off the record I'd guess it's a double-edged knife, heavy blade, a paratroop dagger or an Arkansas toothpick."

"Could it've been the same weapon used on Louise Barrett and the other serial killing victims?"

Skowron removed his cigar, frowned at the saliva-smeared end of it for a moment, then slid it carefully back into the corner of his jaw. "I don't think so, no. The wounds aren't really similar."

"What about the gashes on his chest? Maybe he tried for the throat and missed."

"Unlikely. The lacerations aren't the proper depth or direction for that. I'd guess we're dealing with a different weapon here."

"But you're not positive?"

"Without actually examining the weapon we can't be certain, but dammit, I'm fairly sure—"

"Garcia, what's the problem now?" Klevenger interrupted, stepping into the alcove, "or isn't our little enterprise far enough behind schedule for you?"

"Doc, I think there's a good chance this victim was killed by the same man who greased Louise Barrett and three others. Is there any way you can verify it?"

"Possibly," Klevenger snapped, "but if we run every possible test on every cadaver, we'd have 'em stacked to the ceiling. Hell, they damn near are now. So what makes this one so important?"

"He may be the connection we need, the first killing that isn't random. If we can tie him to the others—"

"This victim wouldn't be part of a certain soap opera I happened to read about in the Freep this morning, would he?" Skowron interjected. "Is that why he's so special?"

"He might be," Garcia said evenly, meeting Klevenger's gaze. "How about you, Doc? Do you believe everything you read in the papers?"

"Usually," Klevenger nodded, "but maybe not this time. We'll do your tests, Garcia. You should have the results late this afternoon."

"But, Les—"

"Dammit, Charlie, don't tell me how to run my lab! And don't worry about the workload, I'll run the damn tests myself. Now if you gentlemen can spare me, I've got an impatient patient and I'm a little shorthanded today. And every other day, for that matter."

"He won't find anything I didn't, you know," Skowron said sourly, as Klevenger stalked back to his surgical station. "The wounds weren't made by the same weapon."

"Maybe not, but at least he's willing to look." Garcia shrugged. "Sorry if I jammed you up, Charlie, but it's important."

"You'd better remind yourself how important it was every time you open your shower door, Loop, because one of these times you're liable to find half of a ripe cadaver using your tub."

"Anybody ever tell you you've been working here too long, Charlie?"

"Just about everybody. See you around campus, Loop. And remember. It'll be in your bathtub."

CHAPTER 21

GARCIA MADE IT BACK TO THE SQUAD ROOM A LITTLE BEFORE FIVE, after dropping off a very subdued Carl Lorch at the Ramada Inn. The place was deserted except for Harry Fein, Marv Cream's partner. Garcia checked the board for messages, then ambled over to Fein's littered desk.

"Hey, Harry, welcome home. Having a nice vacation?"

Fein gave him a death-ray glare, and continued typing. Blocky, balding, with permanent fluid-filled pouches under his eyes, Fein was the squad's perfect shadow, the quintessential anonymous man. He could pass for anyone, and often did, a garbage collector, a stockbroker. People met him at their own family reunions and never doubted he belonged. Unless they happened to notice his USMC, SEMPER FI tattoos. But not many people had seen them. Joad had ordered him to wear long sleeves while on duty.

"Cordell gone for the day?" Garcia asked.

"He said he'd be at Tufic's till six, so—" Fein checked his watch. "Jesus, is it five already? I'm never gonna get outa here."

He surveyed his desk glumly. It looked like a mock-up of the city dump, a shambles of open files, paper cups, a half-eaten sandwich.

"How's Marv doing?"

"He's doing great, just great," Harry snarled. "Some fruitcake conks him with his own fuckin' phone, and then another fruitcake dicks him over with two and two. He's doing about as terrific as I am."

"Anything I can do to help?"

"Yeah, you can call Kelly Girl and rent me a fuckin' orangutan to help with this damn paperwork. He couldn't screw it up worse'n Marv has already."

"You want to borrow my desk lamp?"

"Your lamp? What for?"

"You could pretend you're getting some sun. Enjoy your vacation, Harry."

"Right." Fein sighed. "Enjoy your dinner. I hope you get fucking botulism, Garcia."

Tufic's Green Line Grill was busy as usual, miniskirted waitresses scurrying between green felt-draped tables, the clatter of dishes and conversational buzz overpowering the background Muzak. The food was barely adequate, the service so-so, but modular phones were available on request, and the place was the only restaurant with a liquor license within easy walking distance of the Metro Central station. And Tufic sent more money home to Lebanon than the World Bank.

Garcia spotted Cordell sitting alone in a rear booth. He was hunched over, brow furrowed, speaking carefully into a red modular phone, which meant he was probably talking to Su Hua. He always spoke with exaggerated precision when talking to his Vietnamese ex-wife, though the need for it had long since passed. Maybe it was one of the reasons she was his ex.

Garcia made his way through the crush, slid into the booth, and pretended to scan the menu while he waited for Cordell to finish. Some men handle divorce badly and turn to women or booze for solace, some take it well and consider women and booze the reward. Cordell simply didn't accept his divorce. He hung on like a pit bull, taking the emotional bruising, helping with the kids, the rent, and every way he could short of chauffeuring Su and her dates around, continuing to treat his ex as though the three-year-old divorce was just a minor detour on their journey through life together. Irrational? Or admirable? Garcia couldn't decide which. Maybe both.

"Look, I've gotta go," Cordell said. "You want me to stop by tonight'n talk to him? Maybe we could . . . Okay, the weekend then. I'll be there, and don't worry, okay?" He replaced the receiver reluctantly, with near reverence that would have been pathetic in someone else. "Terry's in trouble at school," he said grimly. "Jesus, that's all I need. How'd it go with Lorch?"

"He ID'd her, barely," Garcia began, when a waitress wearing rhinestone glasses and a mouthful of braces materialized beside the booth.

"Hi, y'all ready to order?"

"Corned beef on rye, fries and gravy, coffee," Garcia said.

"Just coffee for me," Cordell said.

"Back in a jiff." She scooped up their menus and bustled off.

"Just coffee?"

"I'm goin' on a diet," Cordell said defensively, "and you oughta watch it yourself. That crap you just ordered is loaded with cholesterol. So what's with Lorch?"

"He said he'd been out of touch, but said she'd never been a drinker, never even touched the stuff."

"She'd apparently been touchin' it pretty good the night she bought it. One point eight blood alcohol level, wasn't it?"

"Something like that. Was there any booze at her apartment when you checked it?"

"Nope, but don't be surprised if the lady did her drinking in bars. My Greektown cook turned out to be nothin', but I got a home run and two base hits anyway."

"On what?"

"The cowboy connection. Number one, Carol Loomis, the secretary? Bar hopped two or three nights a week accordin' to her roommate. Didn't know which bars for sure, but she did listen to country music at home. Roomie said she'd check her stuff for matchbook covers or whatever and get back to me. Penny Arvin, number two? Home run. Her ex-husband sounds like he just fell off a turnip truck from Tupelo, said she definitely used to hang out at the Crossing now and again. Said he quit partyin' there after he ran into her a few times. And how come I got the feeling you ain't too impressed?"

"You said two base hits."

"Right. The nun."

"The nun? I thought her family—?"

"Wouldn't talk to me, right. But the head nurse at the hospital where she worked helped out some. The Sis has a younger brother, works at Ford Rouge and drinks his paychecks, which is a pretty good trick considering what those guys make. And it seems the good Sister Mary Margaret spent a fair amount of time in and out of pubs, supposedly looking for her brother, which might explain why she was buzzed the night she bought it. The brother works swing shift, gets off at eleven, maybe he can nail down the places she mighta been. And I still get the impression you don't give a shit and this is the good stuff."

"Does that mean there's bad stuff?"

"Well, there's . . . shaky stuff, maybe. Part of our problem here is that we don't have any solid background on Yarborough, right? Could be I know somebody who could help us out."

"Like who?"

"Verdell Booker."

"Right," Garcia said, slapping his forehead with the heel of his palm. "Verdell Booker. Why didn't I think of him? Who the hell is Verdell Booker?"

"A hugger-mugger, hangs out on the Corridor, really gets into his work. Beats people up sometimes when he rips 'em off, usually women. Came across his name in the files early on but didn't bother with him 'cause he's got this great alibi."

"Like what?"

"He's in the slammer. Got him over at DeHoCo for assault. He spends a lotta time in jails, probably 'cause he's easy to pick out

162

of a lineup. Big dude, with a shaved head and only one eye. Hard man to forget."

"So what's he got to do with this?"

"Maybe nothin'. But he isn't local talent. He came up here four, five years ago from Knoxville. Tennessee. After gettin' outa jail. Out of Brushy Mountain, to be exact. And he was there twice before, six to a dime for assault, both times."

"Pretty thin. The Mountain's a big place."

"Sure it is. I said maybe it was nothin'. But there's another reason Verdell spends so much time in jail. He's easy to find. He's a street singer, you know, stands around on corners singin' for change? And playin' his guitar."

"He plays guitar?"

"Sure does. Not bad, either. I've seen him a couple times around Hart Plaza durin' the summer festivals. Wintertime he mugs people. Guess it's too cold to sing."

"And he was at Brushy Mountain."

"Twice."

"Could be." Garcia nodded. "Might be worth a look. Thing is, I'm not sure we need background anymore. I bumped into Denny Weitz this afternoon."

"So? He give you something?"

"Not exactly, no."

"Then what? You mean you ran into him at the morgue?"

"That's right, and he wasn't there on a pass. Prowl car found him in an alley off West Lafayette. Cut."

"Cheerio?"

"They aren't sure. The wounds are different. Dr. K's checking to determine if a similar weapon was used, said he'd call me if he gets anything."

"But weapon or not, you like the redneck for it, right?"

"Hell, yes. Don't you?"

Miss Rhinestone Glasses came hustling out of the crush, parked their orders on the table with a flourish and a steely grin, and was off like a shot.

"It could be Denny's number just came up," Cordell mused, eyeing Garcia's plate wistfully. "The kid was a doper."

"You believe that?"

"Sure," Cordell said. "That and the tooth fairy. No, I think the redneck probably made Denny and wasted him. The little fuck-up wasn't any better at snitchin' than he was at anything else."

"I guess not. I should've known he wouldn't be. He knew it."

"Hey, he reserved a slab down there the day he bought his first nickel bag. It was only a matter of when."

"Maybe. But not this week. Not when he was working for me."

"Look, he was goin' down the tube anyway. You know it and I know it, and he even fuckin' knew it, so let's tip a beer to him sometime, but meanwhile let's figure how to nail that cracker to the wall. We got us a major problem there. Even if we can tie Denny to Cheerio, we can't necessarily tie it to Yarborough. If we haul the guy in, he'll just dummy up again and Powell will have us walkin' street beat in Inkster. Question. Why would he waste Denny now, with all this heat on? The dude's crazy, but not stupid."

"Maybe he just likes jerking our chain."

"Could be, but I think it had to be more than that. What was the kid giving us?"

"Names and info on women who hung around with Yarborough or the band. Not much."

"Offhand I'd say the redneck thought it was," Cordell said, sipping his coffee. "Suppose he's got a hit list or something. If he's working out a compulsion, maybe he can't change the list, needs to know 'em close up and personal, somethin' like that."

"What's your point?"

"Suppose we pass on him, concentrate on the women, and nail him when he shows up."

"Same problem. Catch-twenty-two. We can't ask for Major Crimes Mobile surveillance on the club without explaining why, and if we do that we're history."

"I don't figure we give it to Mobile. We'll have to handle it ourselves."

"Us and what army? Denny gave me half a dozen names."

Garcia noticed Miss Rhinestone waving at him from the bar,

holding an imaginary telephone to her ear. He picked up the receiver of the modular on the table. "Garcia . . . Hold on, Doc, lemme get a pencil. Okay, shoot."

Cordell used the interlude to do some wrist isometrics, locking his hands together, straining, raising a few beads of perspiration along his hairline. He sighed, eyeing Garcia's dinner, then reached across and copped a couple of fries.

"So how will it be filed? But, dammit, if it's . . . Okay, okay, please, I'm eating. I appreciate your help on this, Doc. It was above and beyond the call. I owe you one." He carefully hung up the receiver. "That was Klevenger. His tests weren't conclusive, but his best guess is that Denny was killed with the same weapon used in the other four murders."

"Then we've got our connection."

"Not necessarily. He's going to file it as unconfirmed. Joad won't okay mobile surveillance without hard evidence and I don't think a best guess'll qualify, even if it's Dr. K's."

"Probably not," Cordell agreed. "Which takes us back to Denny's list. What do ya think?"

"I don't see where we've got much choice. We can stake out the Crossing and take the ladies as they come, targets of opportunity. The roll Yarborough's on, we may not have long to wait." Garcia slid out of the booth and tossed a ten on the table. "Catch the bill, okay? I gotta go."

"What's the rush? Nothin'll be doin' at the Crossing for a couple hours."

"Which oughta be just enough time to catch supper at DeHoCo. And maybe talk to whatsisname Booker. See you at the Crossing around, what? Eight?"

"Eight's fine. But we still got us a problem," Cordell said carefully. "Your little friend, Linda."

"What about her?"

"It looks like she's got somethin' goin' with Yarborough, but I don't see how we can tag her. She knows us both, and if she makes us and blows the whistle, the game's over. So how do we handle her?"

"I guess we don't," Garcia said slowly, meeting Cordell's gaze.

165

"You're right, she'd spot us and we can't risk it. I guess she's on her own."

Cordell reached across and lifted a fry from Garcia's plate. "Smarts a little, don't it," he said casually, "wantin' a woman who don't want you." There was an edge in his tone, hard and unfriendly. Maybe it was showing in his eyes but the light was poor and Garcia couldn't be sure. Maybe it had always been there.

"I'll see you later," Lupe said. "Don't forget your cowboy hat."

"Right. And tell the boys at the jail to save us a cell. Way things are goin' we may be needin' one."

CHAPTER 22

THE KEY WOULDN'T FIT INTO THE LOCK. AND AFTER A MOMENT'S fumbling, Linda Kerry realized why. The key slot was in the wrong position. Her apartment door wasn't locked. And she always locked it. Always.

Her first thought was to walk away, to call security, but she hesitated. She only knew one person with burglary skills, and she wasn't afraid of him. Or at least, not exactly. The truth was, she wasn't sure how she felt about him. And maybe it was time to find out. Still, she turned the knob and very quietly, then gently eased the door open and stepped back, ready to run or—

The living room was bathed in the flickering glow of candles placed on either end of the coffee table, their reflections dancing on the lid of her sterling serving tray, with plates, silver, and napkins for two arranged neatly beside it. She could hear the sound of music from within, a medieval air played on a guitar.

She stepped in cautiously, keeping the door open, her hand on the knob.

Lamont was sitting on the carpet with his back against the sofa,

167

wearing his usual dark T-shirt and jeans, his fingers whispering softly on the neck of the small acoustic guitar cradled in his lap. Mirabel was perched on the arm of the sofa like a familiar, her dark head nearly touching his, the candle flames glittering in her golden eyes. She acknowledged Linda's presence with a cat's greeting. Awareness. No greeting at all.

"I hope I'm not intruding," Linda said coolly.

"Nope. In fact, we were kinda hoping you'd drop by. Make yourself at home."

"How did you get in here?"

"The same way you did, through the front door. Only it didn't take me quite as long."

"Apparently I'd better speak to the management about security. This building is supposed to be burglarproof."

"It probably is," Lamont said equably, "but I don't imagine your lease says much about pickers." He flexed his right hand without missing a note. "Locks and guitars aren't so different."

"Lamont—"

"Look, I know you're probably ticked about me being in here without an invitation. I would've waited outside but I figured the dinner might get cold. You've been . . . decent to me. I just wanted to do something nice for you. A surprise. Candlelight, some music, 'have a hard day at the office, dear?' Like that."

She didn't say anything.

"So what's it gonna be? You gonna roust me out in the cold or do we have dinner?"

"That's what we're talking about?" she said carefully. "Dinner, and then you go?"

"Absolutely. I have to play tonight anyway. And we already know I can take 'no' for an answer, don't we?"

"Yes, I suppose we do."

"Leave the door open if you like, or call a friend to chaperon. But I only brought dinner for two and it's not gonna stay warm forever. What do you say?"

"All right." She slowly closed the door behind her. "But I'm warning you, at the first sign of a problem I'll shout this building down."

"You'll have no cause to. I give you my word."

"Very reassuring. Why the two bottles of wine?"

"Heck, I'm just a country boy. I wasn't sure which color goes with what."

"Why don't you spare me the hayseed act?" she said, unzipping her parka and tossing it on the sofa. "Just for tonight. Maybe you were a country boy once, but it was a long time ago. What you are now . . . well, I'm not altogether sure about that. But you're no hick."

"Wull thankee mayum, that's shorely a kindly thing to say, and we appreciate it."

"You're welcome." She sighed. "What's for dinner?"

"Big Macs."

"Big Macs? Hamburgers?"

"Well, technically I think they're cheeseburgers. 'Course we got fries too. And two Mcpies, one cherry, one apple, and you can have first choice. I do sorta favor the apple ones myself, but don't let that influence you."

"I won't." She took a throw pillow from the sofa and eased down on it beside the coffee table. "If you've really got Big Macs under there, why all the silverware?"

"I wasn't sure a quality lady like yourself would want to eat with her fingers. Declassé."

"You know what you are, Yarborough?" she said, choosing the red and filling both goblets halfway. "You're a snob. A blue-collar snob. The Stanley Kowalski of country music. Aren't you afraid you'll get lopsided from that chip on your shoulder?"

"Maybe I'm just defensive about my roots."

"Sure you are. That's why you dress like Roy Rogers. Well, are you eating too, or just providing dinner music on your guitar?"

"Eating," he said, "and it's not my guitar. It's Toby's." He stopped playing, but the music continued, and for a disorienting moment she thought the dead boy's guitar was magically playing itself. Then she realized the sound was coming from her stereo. Lamont had been playing seamless counterpoint to it. She picked up her goblet to cover her confusion. The candlelight shimmered on the surface, dancing in the glass.

169

"What is that music?" she asked quietly. "It sounds . . . antique."

"It is. It's a collection of airs and ballads from the eleventh century by a lutist, Julian Bream. Like it?"

"Very much. I noticed you weren't having any trouble playing it, but then I suppose you remember most of the songs from your troubador days."

"Nope." He smiled. "I had to learn 'em. Or maybe relearn 'em. The ole memory gets a little shaky after six or seven hundred years." He turned and placed the guitar gently on the sofa. The black eagle tattooed on his bicep seemed to shiver and flex its wings. For an instant she recalled Rex padding barefoot into the master bedroom of their suburban home, two towels draped over his arm, his pajama top flagrantly unbuttoned, the elastic waistband digging into his doughy midsection. She shook her head, dismissing the thought. And met Lamont's eyes.

"Penny for your thoughts?"

"None of your business," she said. "Shall we eat?"

"Why not?" He lifted the lid on the serving tray, releasing a fog of hickory-scented steam.

"Big Macs?" she said.

"Mama Magnolia's Biloxi Barbecue. Short ribs, grits 'n greens, 'n rhubarb pie. Guaranteed best BQ north of Mobile."

"You lied to me."

"I know. I do from time to time. But mostly in good causes. Risk a taste?" He lifted a rib from the platter and held it out to her, the thick red sauce oozing around his fingers.

She hesitated, then took a small bite. It was hot, and tart, and smoky, and exquisitely delicious.

CHAPTER 23

T HE WEST-QUARTER CELL BLOCK AT THE DETROIT HOUSE OF Corrections was in semichaos, Christmas carols over the PA system competing with a half-dozen ghetto blasters tuned to different stations, every third cell door standing open for the dinner/exercise break, dungaree-clad inmates pacing the corridor, exchanging obscenities and conversation with men still in lockdown, or playing cards on the scarred picnic tables bolted to the floor in the twenty-by-fifteen recreation area at the end of the block.

Garcia moved casually down the aisle, scanning the cell numbers, pointedly ignoring the inmates' thousand-yard stares. The bleary-eyed black floor captain had okayed the unscheduled interview reluctantly, agreeing to keep Booker in his cell and let him eat with another shift, "but talkin' to him better be all you got in mind, Sarge," he warned. "You piss the sonofabitch off and you're on your own. I ain't sure we got enough personnel in the building to cool him down."

Garcia could hear groaning as he approached Booker's cell,

then realized someone was singing. The voice sounded muffled and metallic, a melody mumbled through a megaphone.

The cell was a four-man eight-by-ten, empty bunks stacked on both sides of a narrow aisle, with a sink and toilet in one corner, and Verdell Booker sitting on a low stool in the other. Or at least Garcia assumed it was Booker, judging from the sheer size of the man. He couldn't be certain because the guy had a bucket over his head.

He was wearing the galvanized metal pail like an oversized, eyeless helmet. And singing inside it. "Stormy Monday Blues." The old T-Bone Walker song echoed off the peeling walls, filled with a world of pain, but sung with more anger than anguish. Energy pulsed through the lyrics like a heartbeat, accented by Booker's sausage-sized fingertips tapping time on the bucket's rim.

Too much. It was just too much for one day. Garcia eased down on the edge of the rumpled bunk facing Booker and gave up, letting the blues wash over him. Too much. He half-expected a white rabbit to jog through the cellblock squeaking, "I'm late, I'm late." But no rabbit came, only a jumble of images flickering across his eyelids, Denny pleading with him in the alley, Yarborough watching him from the stage over the heads of the dancers, Skow coolly examining Denny's scrawny wrist, letting it drop . . .

The song wound slowly down as Booker belted out the final lines. Resisting an urge to just topple back on the bunk, Garcia tapped the dungaree-clad giant on the shoulder before he could begin another song—and nearly got his arm torn out of its socket.

Booker seized his wrist with a huge paw that clamped on like a vise, jerking him from the bunk to his knees on the cell floor. Garcia clawed frantically for the gun he'd checked at the admin office, too surprised to call for help. He struggled against Booker's grasp for a moment, then gave it up. His forearm was already going numb, as though he'd been hammered with a baseball bat.

Booker slowly lifted the bucket off his head and set it aside, eyeing the man kneeling at his feet. Garcia tried to meet his gaze but found himself staring into an empty eye socket. A puckered, bruised eyelid sagged above the open wound, and a purplish keloid scar seemed to flow down the massive cheekbone like a smear of chocolate pudding. Please, God, he prayed, don't let him unzip his fly.

"So," Garcia said, "how you been doin'?"

Booker's wounded eye socket twitched angrily. "Who the fuck are you?"

"I'm Garcia, the guy who wants to talk? Didn't they—"

"You busted up my song. Piss me off if somebody do that."

"Sorry about that. Can't say I like being here on the floor much either."

"So why don't you do somethin' about it?"

"Maybe I will."

"Like what?"

"Scream for help," Garcia said, surprised. "What else?"

"Nothin' else," Booker said grimly, releasing his grip. "Not one fuckin' thing. Tell you flat out, I don't like pigs. Put me where I don't wanna be, think guns and shit make 'em badass. You some kinda badass too?"

"Sure." Garcia sighed, brushing off his pants legs. "I'm awesome. Lucky for you I promised to go easy." He resumed his seat on the edge of the bunk, wincing as he massaged his wrist, resisting the urge to bolt for the door.

"So what you want?"

"To talk. About old times."

"I don't talk to no pigs. I do my time. I stand up. That's it."

"Look, I'm not asking you to dump on anybody. When I said old times, I meant *old* times. Brushy Mountain, ten years back, maybe more."

"Why should I? What you got for me?"

"If you've got something to trade, we can work it out."

"Damn straight we can, if you figure on gettin' outa here in one piece. Tell you what, I'll give you somethin' up front. Don't lean back on that bunk."

"Why not?"

"It's DeJohn's. He be carryin' on before, prob'ly havin' a wet dream. How much is that worth?"

"Suppose we total it in at the end," Garcia said, sliding as close to the edge of the bunk as he could.

"I keep a tab on it. What else you wanta know about?"

"Lamont Stacy Yarborough. Name mean anything to you?"

"Lamont?" Booker echoed doubtfully. "What you wanta talk 'bout him for?"

"You know him then?"

"Daddy Y? Sure I know him. Everybody know him down at the Mountain. Even played in a band with him. The Mountainhawks. Cookin'est damn band ever was, inside the walls or out."

"You played together in a prison combo?"

"Wasn't no combo, man, not like the usual jerkoffs you hear in the joint. We was a *band*. We was special. Lamont made it special."

"How do you mean?"

"Hard to say, if you din't know him, but . . ." Booker massaged his empty eye socket with his fingertips, frowning. "It wasn't just we played together, it was . . . bein' together, to talk and like that. He knew about all kinda things, books, an' old-time stories, and . . . life. I don't think he'd been to no school, but he was a educated man, readin' stuff all the time. And he was a boss con too. Ran D-block like a seventh son. Lamont say frog, people jump, you know? But the band, the Mountainhawks? Bein' in that band was probly the best time I ever had in my life. We even played with the King once."

"The King?"

"Sure," Booker said, his face contorting into a facsimile of a smile. "Here, man, I show you." He knelt beside his bunk and retrieved a tattered cardboard box from beneath it, tearing off one of the flaps as he opened it. "Got a pitcher here someplace," he muttered, pawing through a cheap pasteboard photo album. "There, see? That's us with the King hisself."

He passed the open album to Garcia. A faded yellow newspaper clipping was scotch-taped to the page. The picture was a live action shot of B. B. King performing on a crude stage with a band of inmates clad in prison dungarees. The photograph was grainy and poorly focused, but Garcia had no trouble recognizing

174

Booker, even though he still had both of his eyes at the time. Lamont was even easier to spot. His was the only white face on the crowded stage.

It was a good picture. King, younger and slimmer then, his face gleaming with perspiration, a guitar hanging at his side, was sharing a microphone with a black inmate, the two of them belting out the blues with energy that almost leapt from the page. The caption read: B. B. King Appears at Brushy Mountain. The article, apparently clipped from a local paper, said little more than that.

"Quite a picture," Garcia said.

"It was quite a band," Booker said, caressing the edge of the photo with his oversized thumb. "We had us some times. And Lamont? He was special, you know?"

"You haven't seen him lately, then?"

"Lately? Nah, ain't nobody seen him lately, man. He's dead, been dead a long while. Why you ask if I seen him?"

"Because," Garcia said softly, "he's not dead. At least, not anymore. I've seen him."

Booker leaned back, searching Garcia's face with his good eye. "You wrong," he said at last. "Lamont's dead. Happened not long after this pitcher was took. Got killed on the work farm down to Merrimac."

"Did you go to the funeral? Actually *see* him dead?"

"No, man, I didn't see him. I was still up at the Mountain with a nickel to go. But I heard, and I know it was true."

"Well, apparently it wasn't true. Don't you get any newspapers in here? His picture's been in the papers a couple of times."

"I don't read no papers, man, and I don't need to read no papers. Hell, if I could read I wouldn't be in here now. So what you tellin' me? How he be alive?"

"I don't know how, maybe a foul-up at the jail, but he's alive all right. I've even heard him play."

"No shit now, you ain't jivin' me?" Booker's face looked almost wistful. King Kong gazing at Fay Wray. "Where you hear him? He still good?"

"At a redneck joint out in Romulus, and he sounded pretty good to me. I think he's even playing the same guitar."

175

"Same guitar? What guitar?"

"The one in the picture, the Gretsch. It looks like the same one anyway."

"A Gretsch?" Booker said slowly. His bologna-size finger slid over the photograph, seeking it out. "This one, you mean? A red one? Country Gentleman or somethin'?"

"I think so. I'm not sure about the guitar, but it's the same man all right. He's older now, but—"

"Pigs," Booker said, shaking his head slowly, staring at the floor. "Shit." His shoulders were shaking and a low growl was rumbling deep in his chest. Wet dream or not, Garcia edged a little further back on the bed. When Verdell looked up again, the grimace that passed for a smile was back. Maybe.

"You know, I almost forgot you was a pig. We got to talkin' about them times and I almost forgot. I shoulda known."

"Should have known what?"

"You know, my second stretch at the Mountain? I was bum-rapped."

"No kidding?" Garcia said. "Sorry to hear it."

"You oughta be. Don't get me wrong, I ain't sayin' I didn't mug nobody. I mugged lotsa people. It's what I *do*, man. But the cops didn't nail me for them other times, and the one I was sent up for, I never done."

"I don't follow you."

"Fuck no you don't. That's 'cause you're a pig, and pigs don't get nothin' right. That ain't Lamont playin' guitar in the picture. That's Lamont singin' with the King."

Garcia stared at the faded clipping. "Singing with— Then who's this guy playing guitar?"

"Bucky Paley." Booker spat the name out. "Daddy Y's white punk. He the one cut Lamont's head off down to Merrimac."

"I didn't know him when he first come in," Booker said. "He was just a green kid outa the pineywoods, two weeks in isolation block, then into regular cell. Got gang-banged and beat half to death his first night. Lamont seen him in the yard, walkin' around like a zombie, feel sorry for him. Showed him a few licks on his guitar there in the yard. Funny about that. Bucky took to it right off, like he'd been born with a ax in his hand. So Lamont used a little juice, got the kid transferred to his cell."

"Didn't they keep the, ah, races separate then?"

"Pretty much. Still do, but Lamont was a boss con, see? Man, he knew everybody, run everything in his block, not just because he was bad, but 'cause he was *smart*, man, special. If he need to be bad, he got people like me to take care of business. Never in no trouble hisself. Screws, they use people like him, keep things cool, you know? The kid's gonna get killed in the cell he's in, so they give him to Lamont. Maybe he still get punked, but at least he stay alive."

"Somehow I have trouble picturing this . . . Paley, as a kid."

"He changed a lot," Booker said. "Lamont changed him. Showed him how to take care of hisself, pump iron, use a shank. I got paroled, maybe a year after Paley come in, and when I got sent up again a couple years later he was different. Bad mother-fucker. Hard. Damn near a boss con his own self. He was still in Lamont's cell, but I don't think he was punkin' for him no more. It's more like they was . . . friends. Or like a father and son, maybe. Bucky took heat from the white cons 'bout bein' with us, but he could flat take care of his own shit by then. And he could smoke a guitar too, man, I mean really *cook* it. And then after all Lamont done for him, the punk-ass motherfucker done him." Booker slowly shook his massive head.

"What happened down at Merrimac?"

"I don't know for sure. They got this work farm there for trustees and guys due for parole. Bucky'n Lamont was both due to get out so Lamont fixed it so they go down there together. Like a vacation almost. You get to work outside, get some air. But them county places be pretty bad sometimes. They get people in there oughta be in a psycho block, you know? What I heard was, somebody got aholt of some white lightnin'. Bunch of 'em got crazy drunk and they try to gang-bang Bucky. Only he ain't takin' that shit no more. He get a shank, cut some people up. Two of 'em died. Lamont was one. Damn near cut his head off, I heard."

"But why would he kill Lamont? I mean, if he'd been his punk?"

"Who knows? It was dark, they was all drunk. Maybe it was a accident. Maybe not."

"And somewhere down the line, Paley took Lamont's name?"

"I don't know nothin' about that. But it ain't hard to get your name changed, man. You just need a half-ass reason and twenny-five bucks. Or the welfare people'll do it for nothin', you work it right."

"But usually a guy changes his name to lose his record. What was Paley in for?"

"Same thing Lamont was. Killed his wife. Only Bucky got parole first 'cause he's white. Always like that."

"So why would he take over Lamont's name?"

"I don't know, man. Maybe he feel bad about what happened. Maybe he's crazy. Shit happens in here, messes up your head. You don't know what it's like inside. You look like you been around, maybe you think you pretty bad, but how bad you be in here, man?" Booker rose slowly to his feet, blocking the aisle. "You think you could fight me for your cherry? Maybe three more like me? How long you think you last in here?"

"I don't know," Garcia said honestly, glancing around the cramped cage with its peeling walls and feral stench, trying to imagine what it would be like to spend years in a cell like this. With men like Booker. "Maybe not very long."

"I think we 'bout through talkin', man. You ready to settle up?"

"I guess. You got something in mind?"

"Look here, you must want Bucky for somethin' or you wouldn't be askin' me this shit, so I tell you what. If you bust him, you see he gets up in this buildin'. You wanna know why he done Lamont? You send him to me. Lemme ask him. I'll find out. I'll find out anything you want. Whaddya think? Deal?"

"Maybe," Garcia said. "I'll see what I can do."

"You do that. Give you somethin' else for free, Mr. Pig. If you try to take Bucky, you best watch yo' ass. He had a good teacher. The best."

"You worried about me, Verdell?"

"I don't give a shit 'bout you one way or the other." Booker shrugged. "But if Bucky kills you, they might send him somewhere's else. And that'd piss me off."

"Yeah," Garcia said, "me too."

CHAPTER 24

T HE PARKING LOT AT THE COUNTRY CROSSING WAS A THIRD FULL when Garcia pulled in a little after eight. He cruised through the lot slowly, checking license numbers against Denny's list, but only two cars matched, Grivas's silver Continental and a gray Olds Ciera that belonged to a woman, Naomi Sims. He parked the Chrysler near the center of the lot and left it. Clutching his trenchcoat collar closed against the freezing wind, he jogged over to Cordell's salt-spattered maroon Mustang and climbed in.

"Sheesh, it smells like a pizzeria in here."

"Picked up a heavy Domino on the way over," Cordell said. "Might be a couple crusts left."

"I'll pass. What about your new diet?"

"What about it?"

"Right, sorry I asked. I made it over to DeHoCo," Garcia said, sliding a pair of minibinoculars out of his leather coat and zeroing in on a red Dodge van as it crawled past. "Had a cozy chat with Booker. Nice fella, just misunderstood."

"So? You understand him?"

"Sure, and he gave me some interesting stuff. For instance, he told me that Lamont Yarborough the First *was* killed in that jail down in Tennessee, and that our redneck is the guy who killed him. By cutting his head off, he said. Our guy's name is Paley, or at least it used to be. He's apparently been using Yarborough's name for some time, maybe out of oedipal guilt. Or something."

"Verdell talk a lot about oedipal guilt, did he?"

"I'm not sure those were his exact words, no."

"Didn't figure they were," Cordell said. "Any wants or warrants on Paley?"

"Nope. He's clean under both names."

"Mmmmm. Well, maybe if we get lucky, we can do somethin' about that."

At 8:20 they watched one of the hard brunettes Garcia'd seen at the band table go into the club. Shelley Kinsel, according to the license number on Denny's list. At 8:35 Gopher Bailey, his wife, and two other couples pulled up in a customized Ford van. They sat in it a while passing a bottle around before they stumbled through the snow to the club, hunched against the cold. Ten minutes later Lamont's brown pickup pulled in, followed closely by Linda Kerry's blue BMW. Cordell glanced at Garcia, then pointedly found something else to watch through the side window. Lamont opened Linda's door for her with a flourish, then they walked to the club together, shoulders brushing, breath misting in the parking lot lights as they shared laughter. Neither man in the Mustang said a word. Moments later, Sonny and LeeRoy drove past in a black Nova.

"Aren't those the guys in the publicity picture you copped?"

"The tall one with the beard plays bass," Garcia said. "LeeRoy Clayton, aka 'Tree.' The younger one's Sonny Earle, the lead singer."

"That bass player's one big dude. Bet he has to turn sideways to make it through the door. He double as the bouncer?"

"Most of the guys in that place look like bouncers. The women too, for that matter."

"Maybe that's Cheerio's thing. Offin' ugly women."

180

"I thought one and three were above average, which is all the more reason to want the guy. Nice ones are in short supply."

"At least one nice one's doin' her best to spread it around. Gotta give her credit."

"Up yours," Garcia said.

"Way things are goin'," Cordell said evenly, "you might be gettin' down to that."

The lot was completely filled by ten, with latecomers parking on the shoulder of the road and trudging in through the frozen slush. For a parking lot, there was plenty of action. Jacketless men sauntered out the front door to urinate in the shadow of the building, small groups of both sexes hurried out to their cars to burn a joint, the reefer smoke mixing with the exhaust clouds rising through the mercury-lit glare into the night sky.

A little after eleven a coatless couple scampered arm-in-arm to a pickup parked a row ahead of Cordell's Mustang. The truck roared to life, then sat there idling as the couple's embrace, clearly visible through the pickup's rear window, turned into an X-rated wrestling match, a struggle with their clothing and each other on a bench seat arena.

"Damn, these are fairly basic folks, you know that," Cordell said softly, watching the pickup rocking gently on its springs to its own private rhythm. "If he'd had trouble gettin' the door open they'd be makin' it in the snow."

"We've got a customer," Garcia said, checking his list. "The woman getting into that gray Olds by the bar. Naomi Sims. You better take her, she's already pulling out. Tail her home, put her to bed. If I'm not here when you get back, try to pick up another one." He slid quickly out of the Mustang. "I'll see you tomorrow if not before."

Cordell caught a momentary glimpse of the woman as she drove past, mid-thirtyish, square face, closely cropped dark hair, then she was gone. He fired up his Mustang, gave her a couple of car lengths' lead, and then trailed her out, gunning past the parked cars on the shoulder and into traffic on the four-lane.

Headlights flashed across his rear-view mirror as a car pulled away from the shoulder of the road directly behind him.

The woman turned left onto Ecorse and he followed, checking his mirror as he turned. The second car was still behind him. He mulled it over, frowning, his eyes flicking between the Olds ahead and the headlights in his rear-view mirror. The car had been parked on the shoulder, but nobody'd walked past them to get to it, which meant the driver had been sitting there. Waiting?

As they approached the next interchange, Cordell slowed, flipped on his turn signal, and moved into the right lane. A green Pontiac cruised by on his left, a young guy at the wheel, Latin, gaunt, ferret-faced, long hair slicked back and tied off in a short ponytail. The car was bare-bones basic, and wearing rental plates. Cordell let him get half a block ahead, then turned his signal off and eased back into traffic behind him.

The Pontiac pulled to within a car length of the gray Olds, then backed off a little, content to be her shadow. It didn't fit. The guy was too young for her, and too nasty lookin' anyway. He looked like a low-rider, one step out of the barrio. He should have been driving a '58 Chevy with pimp sidewalls and a body an inch off the pavement, maybe a couple of fuzzy dice hanging from his mirror. No way he meshed with the lady in the Olds. She looked like the president of the Roseville PTA.

The Olds made two more turns, heading northeast in the general direction of Grosse Pointe, but going through the commercial district instead of using the freeway. The low-rider tagged along, but not too obviously, occasionally letting cars get between them, then catching up again. Neatly done. Professional, maybe. After the second time, Cordell backed off a little, keeping at least two cars between his Mustang and the Pontiac. They were almost downtown now, and except for an occasional delivery truck, the area was as deserted as the back of the moon this time of night. He was getting a very hinky feeling about the guy in the Pontiac. Too smooth. He was way too smooth.

They caught a stoplight. Cordell unbuttoned his topcoat, made sure the butt of his weapon was clear, then reached down and turned off the heater. It seemed to be working overtime. The car felt like an oven and he was beginning to sweat.

A cube van cut in front of him, heading for the left turn lane, blocking the Pontiac from view. He touched his brakes to give the truck room, then gunned around it on the right, looking for the Pontiac, realizing too late that he'd already passed it. Passed them both.

Both cars had pulled over to the curb in a shadowed area beside a warehouse. Nothing else there, no reason to stop. The Latin was already out of his car, walking up to the Olds carrying a red-coned flashlight. He'd waved her over with a damn flashlight!

Cordell stomped the Mustang's brakes, sending it into a powerslide, losing it on the slush-slick pavement and skidding backwards in a slow spin before its rear wheels banged over the curb. He scrambled out of the car, pounding back toward the Olds, his street shoes slipping on the icy sidewalk. He couldn't see the low-rider at first, then spotted him beside the woman's car, staring at him wide-eyed, watching him come.

"Hold it! Police!" Cordell shouted.

The guy dropped his flashlight, and then Cordell's feet shot out from under him and he went down hard on his right shoulder, rolling into a cluster of snow-covered garbage cans ten yards from the Olds, sending a barrel spinning into the street.

He lay there a moment, chest heaving, the wind driven out of him by the fall. "Police," he croaked again, struggling to his knees. He held his shield up in his left hand, groping under his coat for his piece, his right hand too numb to feel it.

The Latin was grinning now, shaking his head. He pulled a fist-sized automatic from under his suede overcoat, rested his forearms on the roof of the Olds, and fired twice. A hammer blow slammed Cordell in the belly, spinning him half around in the welter of garbage and snow, stunned, surprised. The little gun looked too small to—

The low-rider fired again. The slug whined off the sidewalk and thwacked into the warehouse wall. And then the gray Olds was peeling out, engine roaring, rear end fishtailing in the slush.

The low-rider scrambled back out of the way to avoid being run down.

Cordell clawed desperately for his weapon with his left hand. The Latin was coming for him now, cool, collected, his pistol held loosely at his side, scanning the street for witnesses, still wearing that faint smile. Pushing himself along the sidewalk like a crippled insect, Cordell tried vainly to find cover behind an overturned trash can. It was no use. The low-rider stopped about ten feet away and dropped into a combat crouch, holding his automatic in both hands now, the smile gone, all business.

Cordell's fingers closed over the butt of his weapon, and he fumbled it clear of his coat, knowing he'd lost, that he was too late. He jerked the trigger without aiming. The .38 roared, bucking in his hand, slamming a slug into the garbage can beside him, kicking it away, leaving him exposed.

But it spooked the low-rider, blowing his cool. The Latin ripped off two hasty shots that went wide, then wheeled and sprinted for his car. Clenching his teeth against the agony in his belly, Cordell tried to steady his numbed arm, praying for just one decent shot, just one, but his sights seemed to be blurring, fading. He pumped three futile rounds in the general direction of the Pontiac as it went tearing off, tires shrieking, howling like a wounded animal into the night.

Cordell sat up slowly in the snow. He took a ragged breath, then forced himself to look down at the massive crimson smear on the front of his coat. It couldn't be. The guy only had a dink automatic. It couldn't make a mess like . . . Gut shot. Jesus, I'm gut shot. He flashed to a guy in his platoon who took one in the belly near Hue, remembered holding him, zonking him with morphine syrettes to keep him from screaming and blowing their position. Seeing him later at the base hospital, doped, eyes glazed, his body wastes draining into a plastic bag. Gut shot. God.

He carefully pushed his weapon into its holster, then stumbled to his feet, both hands clamped tightly over his midsection. He took a hesitant step and nausea surged through him like a dark wave as the sidewalk began to writhe beneath his feet. His car seemed to be shrinking at the end of a long wavering tunnel a mile or so away. He began shuffling slowly toward it, fighting against the agony that wrenched him with each movement, trying to focus on the snowflakes tumbling softly out of the night sky, caressing his face, swirling silently in the streetlights. And the light in the tunnel began to dim as the darkness closed in, and the Mustang seemed to be shimmering, drifting farther and farther away.

Garcia eyed the body in the snow through his binocs, considering the variables. The guy had staggered out of the Crossing, coatless, weaving, obviously bombed out of his skull. He blew nearly five minutes trying to find his car, which was parked directly across the drive from Garcia's. Another three minutes to fish his car keys out of his jeans, three more to fit the key into the slot and jerk his car door open. Then he doubled over, puked into his front seat, stumbled backward, and sat down hard in the snow. He hadn't moved since. He was just sitting there, his head between his knees.

It was a problem in elementary physics. Garcia mulled it over, dividing his attention between the guy in the snow and the front door of the club. Which way had the guy been facing when he spewed? Was he sitting in it now? Would it be dripping on him from the side of his car? These were facets of a serious problem, because the amount of puke the guy was wearing could determine whether Garcia climbed out to help him, or left the stupid bastard to freeze to death.

He was trying to scope out the situation with his mini-binocs when he caught the plate number of a be-on-the-lookout call on his radio. Gray Oldsmobile Ciera. He checked Denny's list. Naomi Sims, the car Cordell had tailed out forty minutes ago. And the call before that had been officer down somewhere downtown. He snatched the mike from the dash console.

"Central, this is Delta One-six-seven. What's the situation on the BOL?" But he was already cranking the Chrysler and gunning into the drive before the answer came back. Then he hit his brakes, cursing. He charged out of the car, leaving his door open, and sprinted over to the guy in the snow.

"Get up!" He grabbed him by the collar and hauled him to his feet. "Come on, get the fuck up, you sonovabitch!" The guy mumbled something and tried to push him away. Garcia backhanded him across the face, hard, then shoved him in the general direction of the club and ran back to his car.

He caught a glimpse of the guy in his rear-view mirror as he roared out of the parking lot. He was crawling toward the bar on his hand and knees, making pretty good time.

CHAPTER 25

S AMARITAN HEALTH CENTER. BIG SAM. A FOUR-STORY STATE-
of-the-art medical facility built by the Sisters of Mercy across the
street from Parkside, the heart of the ghetto. A noble gesture, or
a huge mistake, still too soon to tell. Garcia hated the place, the
brilliantly lit parking area, the shush of the automatic doors, the
fresh paint smell of the halls. He hated Big Sam and every other
hospital. Nothing good had ever happened to him in one.

He checked in at emergency admitting. The duty nurse,
young, black, and bored, told him Cordell was in surgery on two,
didn't know his condition, they'd know more on two. Follow the
green line on the floor to the elevators and push the button. God,
he hated hospitals.

The second floor was chaos, a mix of green-smocked staff
bustling about with harried efficiency and dazed, overwhelmed
civilians, waiting for news. Due to its prime location, Big Sam
does a lot of business after midnight.

The head of station was a tall, heavy-busted black RN wearing
a cheery red reindeer-patterned sweater over her surgical smock.

"Hi. I'm Garcia. They told me at admitting that my partner's up here, Sergeant Bennett?"

"Bennett? The policeman who was shot?"

Garcia nodded, swallowing.

"He just came out of surgery a few minutes ago. There's another policeman, a Lieutenant Fielder, with him now taking a statement. He's going to be fine. They'll be moving him from postop— Are you all right?"

The room had faded slightly, and Garcia found himself leaning forward with both hands on the counter, apparently examining the Formica for flaws.

"Would you like to sit down?" the RN said, frowning, concerned.

"No, I'm okay." He straightened slowly. "It's been a long day. When can I see him?"

"They'll be moving him to his room anytime now." She glanced at the computer monitor at the end of the counter. "He'll be in four twenty-six. I'd wait ten minutes or so. Are you sure you're all right?"

"I'm fine. Four twenty-six?"

"That's right, and you'll find the restrooms at the end of the corridor, right side."

"Really, I'm okay now, I just—"

"Mr. Garcia, you have vomit on the front of your coat."

He glanced down. Damn! She was right. It was on his gloves too. She was eyeing him thoughtfully. "It's not mine." He sighed. "I'm just keeping it for a friend."

"How nice. The bathrooms are—"

"At the end of the corridor. Right."

The men's room was dazzling, alabaster tile, stainless-steel sinks, chrome fixtures, a gleaming air drier on the wall. And not a paper towel in sight. Garcia laid his coat beside the sink, collected a wad of toilet paper from a stall, and began wiping his coat down, cursing as he worked. He was nearly done when Fielder walked in. For one A.M. Fielder didn't look bad, maybe not parade ground sharp, but not far from it. He watched Garcia

188

working with the toilet paper for a moment, then shook his head.

"God, I hate to ask. What the hell are you doing?"

"It's so much cheaper than dry cleaning, you know? How's Cordell?"

"Considering he took two rounds in the belly, not too bad."

"Two in the—?"

"It's not as bad as it sounds. The guy used a small-caliber handgun, and—"

"Guy? What guy?" Garcia tossed the wad of toilet paper toward the bowl.

"Cordell can fill you in. I just got a squeal we picked up the shooter and the woman Cordell was tailing so I gotta go, but—"

"Give me two minutes with Cordell and I'll go with you." Garcia put on his gloves, squirted a gob of Phisohex from the soap dispenser into his palms, and began washing his gloved hands in the sink.

"Forget it, Loop. That's why I came in here. Don't bother to come downtown. What you better do is come up with a reason you two were staking out that bar after getting direct orders to stay away from it."

"The situation changed. Denny Weitz—"

"Save it, I haven't got time now. You know I'd back you on an honest mistake, Loop, but this is different and you damn well—" He broke off, drowned out by the warm-air drier whining like a 727 readying for takeoff, as Garcia calmly began drying his gloves.

"Jesus H. Christ, Garcia!" Fielder shouted.

"Just a minute, Al, I can't hear you over this thing."

Fielder glowered at him a moment, then wheeled and stormed out, yanking the door open so hard it banged off the bathroom wall.

"Hey, keep that guy warm for me," Garcia yelled after him. "I'll be down after I see to Cordell."

He'd expected the room to be private. It wasn't. Cordell was propped up in bed with an IV tube running from his wrist to a plastic bag on a stand, but it was tough to pay attention to him.

189

The room's other patient, a scrawny, fire-haired teenager, was suspended in a diaperlike sling from a stainless-steel framework attached to his bed, buttocks in the air, his elbows and knees resting lightly on his mattress.

"My, my, my," Garcia said, awed. "What happened to your buddy here?"

"Caught a couple rounds of double-ought buck in the butt. Nurse said he owed his brother-in-law some money." Cordell's voice was shallow, dry as cotton.

"I think he should have paid him."

"I guess he did. Rubber check."

"No kidding," Garcia said, running his fingers over the gleaming suspension frame. "Oh, by the way, what the hell happened to you?"

"Nice you should ask. I got shot."

"It's my fault," Garcia said sadly, easing down on the plastic chair beside the bed. "I shouldn't have sent you after that little old lady alone. I knew you were overmatched. What happened?"

"A guy tailed her from the club. He was waiting on the shoulder of the road, followed her downtown with me right behind. I got cut off in traffic, and I guess he waved her over with a coned flashlight. I figured she's about to have her head removed, so I panic-stopped, beat feet towards 'em hollerin' cop and wavin' my tin, only I trip and fall on my ass and the guy shoots me."

"Why'd he do that? He figure you broke your leg?"

"He didn't say. But the dude was all business. Stayed cool, checked for witnesses, used the car roof for a rest. If the lady hadn't peeled out he would've nailed me better 'n he did. The guy's a pro and he knew I was a cop when he fired. He was even wearin' a big, shit-eatin' grin. Service with a smile. Jesus." Cordell winced, gingerly touching his bandaged midsection.

"How, ah, how bad is it?"

"Not bad. I got tangled up with some garbage cans when I fell. They figure the slugs that caught me were ricochets, deformed, didn't penetrate very far. No torn bowels or like that. They're mostly worried about infection, gonna keep me on antibiotics a

190

week or so and that should be it. If you gotta get shot . . ." He shrugged.

"Fielder said they picked up the shooter."

"He didn't tell me."

"Probably didn't want you bustin' out of here."

"No way José. I ain't goin' *anywhere*. For one thing I got a buzz goin' you couldn't buy for ten large, and it's even legal. You oughta make it downtown, though. Find out where the guy lives so I can stay away from that parta town."

"I'll see what I can do." Garcia stood up. "You want me to get you anything? A pizza maybe?"

"If I'd skipped a few pizzas maybe I could still run half a block without fallin' on my ass. Hey, Loop?"

Garcia paused in the doorway.

"I . . . I thought I was gut shot."

"That's because you were."

"No, I mean really gut shot, you know? Blown up? You ever see anybody like that? In 'Nam, I mean?"

"A few. I guess you were lucky."

"Yeah. I'm so lucky I can't hardly stand it. Why don't you get your ass downtown and leave me be."

191

CHAPTER 26

TWO-THIRTY A.M. AND THE SQUAD ROOM LOOKED NEARLY AS BUSY as at high noon. Wilk and Keller were at their corner desk, jackets off, ties loosened, working the phones. A maintenance man in white coveralls was painting the frames of the newly installed glass panels in Joad's office. And if Harry Fein was making a dent in the paperwork piled on his desk it didn't show.

"Hey, Loop, sorry to hear about Cordell," Fein offered. "Rough week on partners—"

"Dam straight," Garcia interrupted. "Where's Fielder?"

"He'n the captain are in interrogation one with the shooter and his lawyer. Guy wasn't carrying a piece so they're doin' the old soft shoe about holdin' him. You better not go back there. Joad gave orders you should wait in his office if you came in."

"Am I suspended?"

"I don't know, but you're definitely off this investigation."

"Terrific," Garcia said. "They ID the shooter yet?"

"His name's Almiraz, Ruben, and about five aka's. LEIN didn't have anything current on him, but he did time at Milan for

192

possession with intent to deliver. He's already flunked a paraffin test and they're waiting on a warrant to search his digs. Guy was staying at the Ponch, first class."

"Where's he from?"

"Driver's license says Saginaw, up in the ward there."

"What about other weapons? Did he have a knife, a razor, anything like that?"

"He had a dime bag of 'Pulco gold on him, but no weapons. Maybe they'll find something when they toss his room."

"Or maybe not." Garcia sighed. "This thing doesn't compute. Where'd they pick him up?"

"Prowlie got him in Grosse Pointe, just driving around."

"The Sims woman's address is Grosse Pointe."

"Almiraz claims he doesn't know her. His story is, he stopped to ask directions, maybe get a little action, figured Cordell for a mugger."

"Cordell said he had his shield out and Almiraz saw it. Said the guy was smiling when he shot him."

"Smiling?" Fein echoed, his eyes narrowing. "The cocksucker was smiling?"

"That's what he said. Where've they got the woman?"

"Up on six. She seems straight enough, says she knows nothin' from nothin', and LEIN doesn't even show a parking ticket on her, but— Hey, Loop, wait a minute, you'd better not go up there. Joad—"

"What's he gonna do, Harry? Hang me twice?"

She was sitting on the edge of the narrow cot in the cramped, one-bed windowless cell, her hands folded firmly in her lap, knees and ankles tightly together. She was dressed western, pearl gray embroidered blouse, tailored jeans, and embossed turquoise boots. Her face was almost boyish, small and square, accented by her dark, close-cropped hair. She wasn't wearing makeup, not even lipstick, and her mouth was a taut, narrow line. She looked spooked and vulnerable, an easy mark.

Garcia dropped into the cell's only chair, placed the small cassette recorder the matron had issued him on the floor between

193

them, and switched it on. The woman eyed it warily, as though it was alive.

"Naomi Sims? My name's Garcia, Detective Sergeant Lupe Garcia." He read her her rights from his Miranda card. "Do you understand your rights?"

"I don't need an attorney," she said, her voice tightly controlled, "but you people may need one. I haven't done anything."

"You're involved in the attempted murder of a police officer, Naomi."

"I'm not *involved* in anything. I stopped to offer assistance. I'm not from Detroit, Sergeant, I'm from the upper peninsula. And when people ask for help up there, we give it. I didn't know the man who . . . fired the shots, or that the other man was a policeman. He wasn't in uniform."

Vulnerable, right. Barbara Stanwyck in *Cattle Queen*.

"Sergeant Bennett identified himself, Naomi. He showed his badge and called out."

"The light was poor, my car was running, and holding up a badge doesn't make you a policeman. And stop calling me Naomi. Let's keep it Miss Sims and Sergeant whatever."

"Garcia. Lupe Garcia."

"Fine, Garcia. Now can we get on with this? I don't int—"

"What do you do?" he interrupted.

"What do I? You mean my job? I work at NBD, the National Bank of Detroit."

"And what do you do there, exactly?"

"I'm a bank officer, commercial loan division, Adair Street branch."

"I see." He nodded, and he was beginning to. She dealt with hassles and hardasses all day everyday. Hell, she was probably better at this than he was. He leaned back in the plastic chair, eyeing her, speculating. She met his stare dead-on. "I think we'd better change the game," he said abruptly. "No more Twenty Questions. You were winning anyway. The new game is Let's Make a Deal."

"You know, you're more than a little strange."

194

"Thank you. This is how the games goes. I've got something you need, a get-out-of-jail-free card, and—"

"But I don't have to trade anything for that. I'm no lawyer but I know you can't keep me here for long. I haven't done anything."

"All right, let me outline the parameters of what I can trade. One, we can hold you for twenty-four hours with no charge at all," he said, ticking them off on his fingers. "Two, we can then charge you as an accessory in an attempted homicide. That's a bailable offense, but we're talking half a day to find a bondsman and process paperwork, assuming your file doesn't get lost somewhere along the line, and since I've got a lot on my mind, like a partner with a hole in his belly, I might be a little careless with yours, you know? If the prosecutor won't go for charging you as an accessory, we can declare you a material witness and hold you forty-eight hours for your own protection. How do you like the deal so far?"

"You're the one," she said slowly. "The one who's been in the papers. Garcia. I didn't recognize the name at first."

"Gee, I'm disappointed. I'll have to talk to my press agent. Of course I'll have to talk to the people at NBD first, to check you out, and with three-plus days I'll even have time to fly up to wherever the hell you're from and talk to the home folks too. Have they got a paper up there? Maybe I can get us both into it. You getting the picture, Miss Sims? You'll be stuck here in this box while I'm blundering around talking to people. Your people."

"You son of a bitch," she said evenly.

"Yeah, I think you're definitely getting the picture."

"What do you want?"

"Everything. Think of it as a foreclosure. You give me everything you've got, and maybe, just maybe, you get to walk away."

"I don't believe you."

"Lady, what you believe is down near the bottom of a long list of things I don't give a rat's ass about. How about me wandering around the commercial loan division at NBD asking about prior criminal behavior? Do you believe that part?"

"Look, I really *don't* know the man who stopped me tonight. I'll take a polygraph if you like. I've never seen him before."

"Fine, I believe you. You're an intelligent woman with a responsible job, for now anyway. But you see I'm not all that interested in Almiraz anyway. He's already history."

"Almiraz?"

"That's his name, this guy you don't know. Ruben Almiraz. He's from Saginaw, did time for narcotics a few years back, probably works for the Five Families up there, not your kind of— Is something wrong?"

"No, I just don't know why you're telling me all this. I don't know the man and if you don't care about him, what's the point?"

"Oh, I care about him, but you see we've already got him for attempted murder. I just want you to understand what your buddy's gotten you into here. It's not all bright lights and redneck love songs. He killed a woman once himself, did you know that?"

"Almiraz?"

"No, not Almiraz. Your friend Lamont."

"I was wondering if you were going to get to that," she said thoughtfully. "The papers . . ." She took a deep breath. "I'm afraid I can't help you. I don't know him either."

"It won't wash, lady. My partner followed you from the Crossing tonight. I've seen you there myself."

"I didn't say I wasn't there. I go there fairly often, along with several hundred other people on any given night. You see, the only people I know in this town are from the bank, and frankly they bore the pants off me. So I go to the Crossing sometimes. It's big, it's anonymous, people ask me to dance. I tell them I work at K Mart and nobody cares. So I know who Lamont is, I've seen him play. But I've never met him, and that's the truth."

Serious poker player, Garcia thought, good enough to be a pro. And she's got the cards now. He'd felt the momentum shift when he asked her about Lamont. She'd relaxed a little, leaned back, her hands clasped on one knee. Still, there was a sheen of perspiration at her hairline. She's got sand, so if she's got the cards, why is she sweating? Has she already bet her limit? So up the ante.

196

"Do you know a kid named Denny Weitz? Works at the Crossing as a swamper, kind of a janitor, you know? Skinny? Frizzy blond hair?"

"I think I've seen him," she said, frowning. "With a mop and bucket? That sort of thing?"

"That's him. He gave me your name." He pulled the list out of his pocket and passed it over. "See? You're third from the bottom." She paled, barely perceptibly. Busted flush?

"But why would he do that?"

"I don't know. And I can't ask him. He's dead. He was murdered, hacked up and dumped in an alley by somebody who really enjoys his work."

The knuckles clasped around her knee were showing white.

"Denny gave me your name, and was killed, and my partner tailed you, and *he* nearly got killed. I'll be honest with you. I haven't got the faintest idea of what's going on. I'm blundering around like a drunk in a funhouse and people I care about are getting hurt and I don't know why. I'm in over my head and, lady, if I am, you are too. Now maybe you don't know what's happening either, but you must know something. And you'd better tell me about it. You've got to."

She met his eyes squarely, mouth firm, her color back to normal, still very much together. He'd thought she was ready to fold, but she wasn't. He'd blown it. He felt a sudden pang of nausea. He didn't have a damn thing left to bet.

"The thing is," she said, a faint tremor in her voice, "I think I may have . . . acted like a complete idiot. I can't say I care for the feeling much."

"Welcome to the club," he said gently. "So tell me about it. What happened?"

"He, ah, he gave me a guitar to keep for him. An expensive guitar, or it was supposed to be."

"A guitar?"

"They can be quite valuable, you know, ah, collectibles. Individual pieces range from three to ten thousand, depending on condition. The rate of appreciation can be very attractive compared to . . ."

197

He let her rattle on for a moment about collectibles as investments, reluctant to interrupt, letting her professionalism reassert itself. "I think I get the picture. Why did he give you the guitar?"

"He said he felt uncomfortable about leaving it at his place at night while he worked. The security at my building—"

"What I meant was—"

"I know what you meant. You meant why did he give it to *me*?" She took a deep breath, and let it out slowly, "I suppose because he's . . . balled me just often enough to think he can trust me. You know, lonely, desperate older woman, a couple of quick jumps and she'll follow you around like a dog. And he was right."

"You've been having an affair with him?"

"No. Joan Collins has affairs, or Liz Taylor. I was just getting laid, in motel rooms or, ah—" She swallowed. "Once even in the back of a van in the club parking lot. He didn't even bother to close the curtains. And I didn't care. Would you say that qualifies as an affair?"

"I think you're being a little rough on yourself. People do have flings, you know, even bank officers. So you had one. And he gave you a guitar to hold for him. Was it in a case?"

"That's right, a locked case. Then tonight at the club he told me he'd sold the guitar and asked me to meet the buyer at my apartment and give it to him. I guessed that I'd been had, in more ways than one, but—"

"What made you think something was wrong?"

"Condition." She sighed. "Dealing with collectibles isn't like buying stocks or bonds. The condition of the piece is paramount. But this buyer was going to pick up the instrument in a parking lot, sight unseen. I knew it couldn't be a legitimate deal. To be honest, I wondered about it before, but didn't want to give up my little fantasy. My God, I'm nearly old enough to be his mother."

"I wouldn't say—" He broke off. *Son of a bitch.* "You're not talking about Yarborough, are you?"

"No," she said, surprised. "I told you I've never met him and I haven't. I've been . . . going through my middle-aged crazies with Sonny Earle."

198

"With Sonny Earle," Garcia echoed, searching her face for the slightest hint of a lie, and not finding it. He leaned back a moment, mulling it over, then fumbled inside his coat and came up with the morgue photos. "Have you ever seen any of these women around Sonny or Lamont? Take your time."

She paled a bit as she looked them over, but otherwise maintained her cool. "No, none of them look familiar to me. Why?"

"Could Sonny have other lady friends without your knowledge?"

"Probably. Almost certainly. I never kidded myself about that."

"No, I don't suppose you did. All right, I'll lay it out for you. I think you're the cutout. Sonny and Lamont and possibly the rest of them are dealing drugs, probably coke. The buyer gives Sonny the cash, picks up the case from you. If anything goes wrong, you're the one who's holding. You can't burn anybody without burying yourself. It's your word against his. He probably avoided being seen with you, right? What'd he do, tell you he was married?"

She nodded, swallowing.

"It figures. And any lawyer worth a damn'll tell you to dummy up and plead you as a first offender. You probably get off with a fine and probation, they walk away clean. Not a bad setup. For them, at least."

"My God. My job. I'll lose my job."

"Maybe, but count your blessings. You see, this operation's been running for a while or Almiraz wouldn't fork over the money up front without checking the merchandise. Which means you're not the first cutout they've used. And I wonder what happened to the others."

"You mean . . . the women in the pictures?"

"I don't know," he said, frowning. "This whole thing still feels—" He reached down abruptly, switched off the recorder, and ejected the cassette into his palm. And snapped it in two. "You think you might be ready to talk about the get-out-of-jail-free card now?"

199

CHAPTER 27

Garcia stopped off at the squad room just long enough to grab a file out of his desk, then rode the freight elevator down to the Pits, the basement offices shared by Vice and Narcotics. And got his first break of the day. Jamail Hamadi, the *wunderkind* narc lieutenant, was asleep in his office chair, wrapped in his greasy bombardier's jacket, feet up, his engineer's boots resting comfortably on a pile of reports. Davonne Watts was wearing a Koss headset, working at a wiretap transcription console in the corner, her fingers dancing over the keyboard of a Selectric, translating the mumbles and dialing beeps of a wiretap tape into hard copy. She was dressed in a war surplus USAF blue jumpsuit, a Tae Kwon Do headband, and combat boots, and still managed to look high fashion.

And dangerous. A Browning 9mm automatic was on the console beside her typewriter and she was sitting at an angle that allowed her to watch the door while she worked, wired and alert even in the bowels of a police station. Garcia remembered the feeling well. He'd lived with it a long time, the perpetual adrenaline high. And the combat nerves. And the paranoia. He entered the office with both hands in plain sight.

"Mr. Cisco," Davonne said coolly, taking off the headset, "if I'd known how bad you were s'posed to be the other day, I would've been more careful."

"If you'd been any more careful, I'd still be in the hospital."

"Or coolin' out over at Dr. K's," Davonne agreed. "Jimmy, wake up. Company."

"I'm awake." Hamadi groaned. "Just resting my eyes. Hey, Loop, how you doin'?"

"Not so hot. Did you hear about Cordell?"

"No," Hamadi said, blinking, "we've been down here forever. What happened?"

"He took two in the belly a couple of hours ago. He's okay, considering, but I need some help. You interested in an easy bust?"

"Sure. I'd like to hit the Lotto too. And the odds are about the same. What've you got, Loop?"

"We were working a homicide, Cordell backed into a drug deal, and got blown away. We've got the shooter upstairs, a hard case from Saginaw named Almiraz. You know him?"

"He's Five Families," Hamadi said, completely alert now. "Works as a mule, and a hitter."

"Right, which means he won't give up anybody else. The thing is, I already know who the other players are." He tossed a file folder on Hamadi's desk. "Names and stats are all in there. I know where they are, and I can guarantee they'll be holding, *if* we can take 'em tonight."

"Tonight? Jesus, Loop, that's not much notice. It's damn near three now."

"I know what time it is, Jimmy, that's why I'm down here. Or maybe all that crap about a tame judge was just smoke?"

"It wasn't smoke," Hamadi flared, "but I don't wanna overdraw my account either. What's this guarantee shit?"

"Just that. If we take 'em, they'll be dirty. You've got my word on it. Now do you want it, or should I go wake Cordell up?"

Hamadi eyed him, reading him like a stranger, then nodded. "Okay, we'll take it. Where are they and how many?"

"Redlands Apartments over in Highland Park. Second-story apartment, outside stairway to a balcony facing a courtyard. No back entrance. Probably two guys there, maybe three. How long to get your warrant?"

"Half an hour," Hamadi said. "And I'd better roust out Cooley for backup. Do it at say, four?"

"Four's fine. Here's the apartment number, make the warrant for search and seizure. I'll meet you there," Garcia said. "I've got some other business first."

"Don't be late for the party," Hamadi said, "or we'll start without you. And, Loop, this sucker better be righteous."

"It will be. I guar—"

"—on-tee it, right," Hamadi finished. "How come anytime anybody guarantees me anything about dope, I start to sweat?"

CHAPTER 28

Hamadi slowed his black porsche 924 to a crawl as he circled the Redlands apartment complex. The place occupied half a block, a California-motel-style four-story brick building with a tile roof and wrought-iron trim, built with connecting balconies around a central courtyard with a swimming pool. Stairways at both ends of the building led to the balcony entrances on each floor. The pool area was covered with six inches of dirty snow, and littered with beer cans. The only activity was in one of the ground-floor apartments, a party in full swing, judging from the pulse of a stereo thumping through the wall and the stack of beer cases cooling outside the front door.

"I think your buddy Cisco's here already," Davonne said quietly as Hamadi pulled into the parking lot. "Isn't that his city Chrysler?"

Hamadi nodded grimly. The Chrysler was parked across three spaces, blocking in several residents' cars. Hamadi eased his Porsche up beside it, and waited. A few minutes later the narc ark, a silver MichCon Power van, pulled in and stopped, blocking the entrance to the lot. Curtis Cooley climbed out, wearing gray CP coveralls and a black wool watch cap snugged down over his ears. Hamadi and Davonne joined him at the van, and a moment later Garcia materialized out of the darkness at the rear of the building, wearing jeans and a navy windbreaker. Cooley slid open the van's side door and began passing out padded Kelvar vests.

"The apartment's on the east wing," Garcia said, slipping the vest on over his windbreaker. "No lights on or noise, but their car's here so I figure they are too."

"That who you got blocked in there?" Cooley asked, his breath misting in the icy night.

"Right. The black Nova. Okay, Jimmy, it's your party."

"We do it straight ahead," Hamadi said. "Curtis and I'll do the door with Davonne as backup. Loop, you take an M-16 and cover the show from the opposite balcony."

"It's my setup," Garcia said quietly. "I want the door."

"Get real, Loop," Hamadi snapped. "With all the shit in the papers and Cordell in the hospital, how's it gonna look if you waste somebody in there? Now goddammit, grab a piece and let's get it on before we all fuckin' freeze to death out here!"

Garcia shrugged and took an M-16 and ammo belt from the van's rack. He slammed a clip into the weapon, locked and loaded, and trotted off to the stairway without a word. Curtis grabbed an M-16 and loaded it while the others checked their weapons of choice, a Browning 9mm auto for Hamadi, the sawed-off automatic shotgun for Davonne. Hamadi waited until Garcia was in position, kneeling behind the railing on the second-floor balcony across the courtyard, then started silently up the stairs with Cooley and Davonne close behind.

216. Hamadi double-checked the number against his note, and quickly scanned the layout. The door opened to the left, which meant a light switch to the right. Using hand signals, he ran it down. Curtis in first, two steps in to clear the door and hold, Hamadi next, going right and hitting the lights, with Davonne covering from the doorway. He raised his eyebrows. Questions? Curtis was already dancing, shuffling in place like a prizefighter, wired up, ready for Freddie. And Davonne was

checking her weapon for the third time. No questions. "So let's do it," Hamadi said softly.

Curtis braced himself against the wrought-iron railing, raised his right leg, and launched a full-force kick at the door. There was a cracking sound, but it held. Cursing, he reared back and kicked it again. It didn't move.

"Blow it!" Hamadi snapped at Davonne.

She jammed the shotgun's muzzle against the lock mechanism and fired one round, punching a fist-sized hole through the door.

"*Po-lice!*" Cooley bellowed, and slammed into the door with his shoulder, ripping the safety chain out of the frame, stumbling into the room off-balance as the door flew inward. "Mother-fucker!" He tripped and went down as Hamadi hit the lights. And Davonne fired from the doorway, exploding the end table beside the fold-out sofa bed as LeeRoy Clayton clawed frantically for the .38 in the top drawer. LeeRoy screamed and rolled to the floor, buck naked, clutching his bloodied shoulder. Hamadi darted forward, kicked the .38 away, and pressed the muzzle of his 9mm into LeeRoy's ear.

"Jesus Christ," Sonny Earle said, sitting up groggily on the other side of the bed, "what the hell's goin' on?"

"Shut the fuck up," Hamadi snapped. "Curtis! Check it out!"

Cooley quickly checked the bathroom and the apartment's only closet. "Clear."

"Okay, you," Hamadi said, jabbing a finger at Sonny, "out of the bed and up against the wall, and don't do nothin' sudden, understand?"

Sonny nodded, wide-eyed, stunned. Hands raised, he slid out of bed and backed unsteadily to the wall. He was wearing only a pair of red stretch bikini briefs.

"My, my, my," Hamadi said softly, "what do you think, Davonne, wanna frisk him?"

"Not without rubber gloves," she said. "Might be Cooley's type though."

"Up yours, lady." Cooley grinned. "And shut the friggin' door, okay? These boys ain't exactly dressed for the weather."

Davonne stepped into the room and kicked the door closed

behind her. Hamadi backed warily away from LeeRoy and motioned him to his feet. LeeRoy stood up slowly, teeth bared against the pain, blood trickling from between his fingers into the matted hair of his chest. Naked, unarmed, he was still a formidable figure, a shaggy-maned, slab-muscled Viking berserker, whose wounds only made him more dangerous.

"Move over against the wall with your buddy," Hamadi said. "Curtis, call an ambulance."

"Maybe I better put on some pants," LeeRoy said, "before your nigger girlfriend starts creamin' her jeans."

"Mister, you're big and dumb and you scare the shit outa me, okay?" Hamadi said evenly, earing back the hammer on his 9mm. "But if you don't move your ass right now, I'm gonna blow your nuts off and see if your voice changes, you dig? Now get over against the fuckin' *wall!*"

Glaring, his eyes locked on Hamadi like a stalking cat's, LeeRoy moved around the bed to stand beside Sonny. Cooley called emergency and then began searching the kitchen area, rummaging through the overhead cupboards and dumping drawers. Hamadi picked up a pair of oversized, rumpled jeans from the floor and quickly searched the pockets. He tossed them toward LeeRoy, but at the last second snatched them back. And slid the belt buckle blade out of its sheath.

"Jesus, you gotta be the ex-con, right?" Hamadi snorted, examining the knife. "Hideaway blade, surprise, surprise. What is it with you guys? You gotta pack these things to prove you belong to the club or somethin'? You're lucky I spotted this. You mighta pulled it out crooked and cut your shlong off." He threw the jeans at LeeRoy, catching him in the face.

"Yo mama!" Cooley roared from the kitchen, hauling a Zip-loc bag out of the tiny refrigerator's freezer compartment and dumping the stash on the counter.

"How much?" Hamadi asked.

"Only a couple grams." Curtis frowned. "Maybe an ounce."

"Keep looking. We got Garcia's guar-on-tee, remember?"

"Right," Cooley said doubtfully, glancing around the tiny apartment.

"You ain't gonna find shit else, nigger, 'cause there ain't shit else *to* find," LeeRoy said. "And we wanna call our lawyer."

On the balcony across the courtyard, Garcia rose stiffly to his feet, shivering. His hands were numbed from the wind and the icy metal of the M-16 and he flexed them to restore circulation. Two young guys in shirt-sleeves were standing in the snow below him staring up at Sonny's apartment, drawn from their party by the gunfire.

"Yo, gents," Garcia called down softly, showing them his badge and the M-16. "Welcome to the war on drugs. And by the way, you're drafted."

"Nothin'" Curtis said, disgusted. He was standing on a chair groping inside the overhead light fixture. Hamadi had already torn the sofa bed apart and was going through the record albums while Davonne kept Sonny and LeeRoy covered. There was a cautious rap at the door. Davonne crossed over to it and nudged it open with her shotgun barrel.

"Hi," Garcia said. "Don't shoot, I'm with the band." He stepped into the room carrying the M-16 in one hand, and a black leather guitar case in the other. "Shook down their car and found this in the trunk."

"Hey, wait a minute," Sonny said. "You didn't find that sucker in my car."

"Sure I did," Garcia said blandly, laying the case on the wreckage of the bed. "I've even got two witnesses who watched me take it out. And another lady downtown who can swear it's yours. Sorry about the latches, had to break 'em open with a tire iron." He flipped open the lid of the case and stepped back.

Hamadi glanced at the tinfoil-wrapped packet neatly taped beside the guitar, and then at Garcia, measuring him. "How much?" he asked at last.

"A full key and a couple of freebies. About twenty years worth."

"Jesus, it's a fuckin' frame," Sonny shouted. "He never found that shit in my car! The woman had it, it's hers!"

"Shut up!" LeeRoy said.

"Fuck it, I'm not goin' down for this! This is your fuckin' setup. Clean machine, you said, no way to fall. Well, I'm not doin' no twenty years because you fucked up. Look, mister, we can do a deal," Sonny pleaded with Garcia, "but you gotta get me outa this!"

"What about Lamont?" Garcia asked. "Is he involved?"

"Sure, you can have anybody you want, and not just for fuckin' coke either. I'm—"

LeeRoy's arm snaked around Sonny's throat in a stranglehold, jerking him off the floor and cutting off his air as effectively as a noose. He twisted around, keeping Sonny's body in front of him as a shield. Sonny gagged, his eyes bulging, arms and legs flailing helplessly as he keened vainly for air.

"Let him go!" Hamadi shouted, drawing his 9mm, sidestepping quickly to the left to get a clear shot as Garcia shifted the other way with the M-16. "Dammit, let him go now! You got one second!"

Instead, LeeRoy slammed his bloodied forearm into Sonny's jaw just below the ear, snapping his head around with a terrible, muted *crack*.

"*Nooo!*" Hamadi fired, shouting over the roar of the 9mm,. punching three slugs into LeeRoy's torso at point-blank range, slamming him back into the wall. For a moment the Viking seemed unaffected, glaring about wild-eyed, teeth bared, holding Sonny off the floor without effort. And then his legs began to quiver, failing him, slowly buckling, and he toppled like a tree, carrying Sonny down beneath him as he fell.

"Sweet Jesus!" Hamadi knelt quickly beside LeeRoy, trying vainly to pull his bloodied arm from around Sonny's throat. "You stupid bastard, look what— Curtis! Where's that goddamn ambulance!" He gave up on LeeRoy's wrist, he couldn't budge it, and it was obvious it was too late anyway. Sonny's head was lolling at an impossible angle, his tongue clamped between his teeth. And his eyes were already empty. Hamadi rocked back on his heels, white-lipped, trying to get his breathing under control.

208

His chest was knotted with anguish, though for himself or the two in front of him, he wasn't certain.

"He shouldna done that," LeeRoy whispered, his voice bubbling and moist, as though it came directly from his torn lungs.

"No," Hamadi swallowed. "I guess not."

"Is he dead?"

"Oh, yeah," Hamadi said softly, "looks like both of you are." He took a deep, ragged breath, then rose abruptly, glancing blankly around the room as though seeing it for the first time. "You," he said, jabbing a finger at Garcia, "outside."

Garcia followed the smaller man out on the balcony, pulling the smashed door closed behind them.

Hamadi leaned out over the railing, lifting his face to the night sky, gulping the icy air like a man who'd just surfaced from a very deep dive. "It was a frame, wasn't it?" he managed at last. "You set them up."

"No," Garcia said coolly, "it was their junk. The kid recognized the case the second he saw it."

"Goddammit, Loop, don't insult my intelligence. Maybe you took that case out of the kid's car, but you put it there first. That how you're doing business now? Planting evidence?"

"I think the word *plant*'s got kind of a nasty ring to it. Rearrange, maybe. I can live with that. Look, those two clowns called this play right down the line. They were dealing, they got Cordell shot, and they set up a straight citizen to take the fall for it. So what do I do? Tell her tough shit, but the way the game works, you get burned and they walk away? Bullshit. This isn't a fucking game."

"Jesus, you've really flipped, you know that? Or maybe you were always nuts but you hid it better. So what's shakin' now? Justice according to Hizzoner El Cisco?"

"Justice?" Garcia sighed. "Jesus, Jimmy, justice is a terrific idea, kinda like Christmas. And in this town it shows up about as often. Look, I know this thing went down hard—"

"No shit!"

"But I delivered for you. You got a clean bust, two dealers and a full key. But this thing's not over yet."

209

"What are you talking about?"

"Yarborough. The kid admitted he was involved."

"Loop, that punk was so shook he would've fingered Mother fuckin' Theresa and you know it."

"Maybe, but he fingered Yarborough, and I want you to get me a warrant for him, and I want it now. The kid's statement is probable cause, but with both of our witnesses dead, we won't be able to connect Yarborough to anything unless we take him dirty tonight. We can sort the rest of it out later."

"What rest of it? You mean the killings or your girlfriend?"

"Look, we made a deal. Now are you gonna get me that warrant, or not?"

Hamadi didn't answer for a moment, his thoughts drowned by the whoop of an ambulance rolling into the courtyard, its swirling flashers reflecting off the building like a surreal lightshow.

"Terrific." Hamadi grunted, glancing at his watch. "Right on time. Okay, Garcia, I'll get your warrant. A deal's a deal. But you'll have to get backup from somebody else. I'm not gonna involve my people in this."

"Fair enough," Garcia said, peeling off his bulletproof vest. "Get the warrant to Harry Fein. Tell him I'll call in as soon as I find Yarborough."

"On one condition. You wait for Harry before you take Yarborough. Because if you take him alone, and anything happens to him . . ."

"I'll wait for Harry."

"I want your goddam word on it, Loop."

"Fine, you've got my word." Garcia shoved the vest and the M-16 at Hamadi and trotted off toward the stairs.

"Right," Hamadi said softly. "I've got your fucking word. Lucky me."

CHAPTER 29

GARCIA SWITCHED OFF THE HEADLIGHTS AS HE PULLED INTO Harry's Riverview, using every ounce of self-control he had to keep from gunning the car straight in, flashers on, siren screaming. He let the car crawl through the lot on its own, idling in low gear, but his caution was wasted effort. Jobeth's battered blue Chevette was the only car parked in front of her trailer. Lamont's slot was empty. But if he wasn't here, where—? The image of Lamont and Linda walking into the Crossing flicked across his memory. Shoulders touching, laughing together— *Damn!*

He hit the switch for the headlights and grill flashers and gunned into a tight U-turn. The tires howled on the hardpack as the Chrysler spun, and he punched the pedal to the metal as it squared around, roaring back through the park at forty, fifty— And then he instinctively hit the brakes, and the car careened out of control, skidding broadside down the drive.

The wheel came alive, twisting in his hands as he fought desperately to regain control, fishtailing the skidding Chrysler between parked cars, pumping the brakes, cranking the wheels

211

into the skid, until the machine finally bucked to a halt across the park entrance driveway, rocking on its springs. He sat there a moment, shaken, sweating, trying to think—

The door. As he'd spun the car around, the headlights had flashed across Jobeth's trailer. And there was a thin bar of shadow along the door frame. The front door was slightly ajar. So what? So maybe the lady was just careless about closing her front door. In December? In Murder City?

He slammed the car into reverse, roaring back the way he'd come, skidding to a stop with his headlights facing the trailer. It was true. The damn door wasn't latched. He switched off his headlights and waited for his eyes to adjust. Call for backup? It was probably nothing, and if Fielder found out he was here—

He jerked his .38, piled out of the Chrysler, and sprinted to the trailer. He flattened himself against the wall beside the front door for a second, then eased it open a few inches, groped around the frame for the light switch, and hit it. The lights flicked on, but there was no reaction from inside, no movement, no sound, nothing. He waited three beats, then kicked the door open and vaulted into the room, weapon in a two-hand hold, ready to—
Sweet Jesus!

The room looked like a battle zone, a complete shambles, kitchen table overturned, window curtains torn down. An over-turned lamp in the corner cast eerie shadows across the wreckage, dark fingers from a fever dream.

And there was blood. Not much, just a few dots spattered on the counter by the kitchen sink, a small crimson blotch on the door frame of the hallway leading to the rear of the trailer, and what might be smudged footprints on the threadbare carpet. Garcia moved warily into the dim passage, hugging the wall to keep from smearing the footprints, trying to avoid stepping in the bloodstains himself, but after a few paces he gave it up. The blood was everywhere, greasy globules of it glistening on the hallway walls, oozing down toward the congealing puddles on the floor, and in the end he was slipping in it with every step.

She was in the den where he'd first met Lamont, crumpled on the floor with her back against the cheap naugahyde bar. But she was barely recognizable as human now. Her naked body had been resculptured, carved into a crimson and alabaster horror of hacks and slashes. She was glaring at him through the matted tangle of red hair that hung across her eyes, showing her teeth in a twisted snarl through a laceration in her cheek where a flap of flesh had been completely cut away. *Death of a thousand cuts. Where had he heard that? God.*

One arm was stretched in front of her, reaching toward him, but not in supplication. Her hand was formed into a taloned claw, as though her fury still somehow suffused her shattered frame. She had not gone gently into the long night, and even now, her anger was almost palpable. For a moment he saw her standing in front of the sink, her back to him, washing dishes by hand, with a faint bruise showing along her jaw. *"Do you think you can handle him?" she asked.*

"I don't know. I can try."

He knelt slowly beside her, oblivious to the blood, and closed his eyes, trying to retain the picture of how she'd looked that day, angry, wary and tenaciously loyal. *"I won't quit him. Not now."* And just for a moment he heard an echo of the melody Lamont had played, a mournful country blues, a canto de muerte, a death song. But then it faded and he couldn't bring it back. He laid his gun on the floor, and pressed his fingertips gently against the base of her throat, automatically feeling for a pulse. And she *moved.*

He froze, immobilized by a heart-stopping surge of mingled hope and horror. She was dead. She had to be. No one could survive what had been done to her. But she'd *moved.* He'd felt her move.

He swallowed and tried again, the carotid artery this time, but there was nothing, and her skin was already cool to the touch. Maybe a reflex or— She moved again. But this time he recognized it for what it was. He was feeling a barely perceptible vibration through her skin. Footsteps. Someone else was in the trailer. Stalking softly toward them down the hall.

Garcia turned to face the door, instinctively shielding Jobeth's body with his own from whatever was coming. He picked up his

.38, and the weapon felt alive in his palm, slippery with blood from the carpet. He raised it to cover the doorway. And realized Lamont was already standing there, watching him from the shadows in the darkened hall.

Neither man spoke. Lamont was dressed as he'd last seen him, faded denim jacket and jeans, but his face was transformed now, alight, burning with an inner fire that blazed in his eyes. Madness. And a killing rage.

"Don't," Garcia said, cocking his weapon. "Don't even think it."

But Lamont didn't seem to hear. He crossed his right wrist over his heart, then flicked his arm forward with fluid grace, and a sliver of steel materialized in his palm, a straight razor, its blade gleaming in the dim light. With a twitch of his wrist he flipped the blade in the air, spinning it above his head like a juggler, and catching it again.

"Drop it!" But he knew it was already too late, that he'd hesitated too long, and he fired, desperately emptying his weapon as Lamont charged him, howling, swinging the razor down in a deadly silver arc.

CHAPTER 30

J OAD PAUSED JUST INSIDE THE DOOR TO COUNT THE HOUSE. THE second-floor press room was jammed with newspeople, camera crews from three local television stations, stringers from the *News*, the Freep, the *Chronicle*, UPI, at least two radio crews who appeared to be broadcasting live. He recognized most of the faces in the room, took pains to remember their first names, in fact, but there were also a number of faces he didn't recognize. National coverage perhaps? A flicker of excitement churned his belly at the thought, but he fought it down. Stage fright, he told himself, nothing more. Use it, make it work for you. A lot depended on how well he handled this mob. It was a chance to reinforce the "caring, capable cop" image he'd tried to project with his DRA speech, a chance to look attractive, possibly even electable. *If* he could get the proper spin on last night's disaster . . . He took a deep breath, forced a smile into place, and stepped briskly into the crush.

Gripping his notes tightly, he made his way down the center aisle toward the one-step dais, exchanging hellos and good-natured barbs with reporters he knew, nodding to those he didn't. The buzz of conversation rose as one of the minicam TV crews switched on their sun guns and began filming.

He took a few moments to assemble his notes at the lectern, enjoying the warmth of the floodlights, the attention, trying to see the unblinking, metallic camera eyes as windows of opportunity. At least he wouldn't have to tap dance around the usual body count questions or— A significant rise in the background noise, coughing, papers rustling, indicated he'd stalled as much as prudence allowed. Feeding time at the zoo. He cleared his throat.

"Ladies and gentlemen, you should all have been issued the official department release on last night's incidents. If there are any questions—" He grinned at the chorus of shouts from the audience. "I thought there might be. Mr. Nyquist?"

"Do you believe the suspect you have in custody, Yarborough, to be responsible for the recent slasher homicides?"

"At present he's being held on a charge of open murder, and it would be fair to say we're extremely interested in his recent activities. Beyond that I'm afraid I can't comment. Yes, Miss . . . Kujawa, isn't it? UPI?"

"It's my understanding that your suspect has an alibi for last night's murder. Can you comment on that?"

"We do have a statement from Miss Linda Kerry, asserting the suspect was with her at the time of the murder," Joad acknowledged. "However, her statement apparently can't be corroborated, and as the lady's known to be personally involved with the suspect . . . Enough said. I have, incidentally, been informed that Miss Kerry's been suspended by the *Free Press* for 'conduct unbecoming' or its equivalent. Chas Mullery can answer your questions on that. Next? Yes, ma'am?"

"Sonja Titus, WBBK, Captain. Have all of the officers involved in last night's shooting incidents been suspended?"

"They have. However, you shouldn't read anything into that. It's standard departmental procedure in any shooting, and no reflection on the officers involved. And it's a moot point to some extent, since two of the officers, Sergeants Bennett and Garcia,

216

were wounded in the performance of their duties, and are still hospitalized. I'm afraid I'm going to have to cut this short—"

"Captain?" There was a momentary hush, as Chas Mullery levered his bulk upright, in anticipation of a comment or an outright clash. Mullery's patronage of Linda Kerry was an open secret. "One last question?"

"Seniority has its privileges, Chas." Joad said, smiling warily. Mullery hadn't stopped by the office for his usual prebriefing chat, and Joad was unsure of his mood.

"Can you give us the current medical status of the officers and the suspect?"

"I, ah, was given an update just as I came in." Joad frowned, riffling through his notes, trying not to show his relief. He'd been half expecting a confrontation, but the question was a marshmallow, a peace offering. The old fox wasn't going to let some bimbo jeopardize their relationship. "The suspect, Lamont Stacy Yarborough, has been upgraded from 'critical' to 'serious but stable' condition, and is expected to recover. Officers Bennett and Garcia are expected to recover as well, though it's unlikely they'll return to active duty anytime soon due to the seriousness of their injuries. And that's it for today. Thank you, ladies and gentlemen." He strode briskly from the dais and moved through the crowd, nodding smiling, but making no further comments. Always leave 'em wishing you'd talked a little longer . . .

Al Fielder was waiting for him in the corridor, looking harried and exhausted. He'd been up all night. He fell into step with him as Joad headed for the elevator.

"Captain, I was wond—?"

"Are the forensics reports in yet?" Joad interrupted.

"Ah, no, sir, there's apparently some kind of a foul-up. I called over there a few minutes ago and they said Skowron was out doing legwork and Dr. K wasn't working today, something about a dedication ceremony?"

"The new aviary at the Renaissance Center opens in a couple of hours." Joad frowned, glancing at his watch. "I plan to be there myself. Dammit, you'd think Skowron would realize how important it is that we get this thing sewed up quickly. This town's going to be crawling with media people and—"

He broke off as the elevator door opened and a camera-laden photographer rushed out, hurrying down the corridor toward the conference room. Annoyed at not being recognized, Joad stepped into the elevator and banged the button for four. Fielder followed, looking uncomfortable, obviously building up to something.

"What's on your mind, Lieutenant? Subtlety's not your strong suit."

"What you just said in there about Bennett and Garcia. I thought they were both going to be released—"

Joad hit the emergency stop button, stalling the elevator between floors. "You're quite right," he said coldly. "They are due to be released soon. In fact, Garcia may be out already. But we'd better get one thing straight, Fielder. No matter how completely he recovers, Garcia's *never* going to be well enough to return to active duty. Unless you consider helping Bobby Pilarski at the coffee maker active duty. He was ordered to leave Yarborough alone, and he deliberately violated that order. He used narcotics personnel to go behind my back—"

"But he was right about Yarborough, when we—"

"Dammit, he lucked out! This time. And that's the only thing that's keeping me from firing his ass outright. He lucked out and got me a good bust and I can't bring him up on charges without throwing it away. But I want him gone, Lieutenant. I want his resignation and I want you to get it. Unofficially, of course. The timing's perfect. He can go out a wounded hero with a disability pension. Hell, promise him a citation if you like, but get rid of him. Understood?"

Fielder met Joad's gaze a moment, then looked away, a muscle twitching in his jaw.

"I don't think I heard your answer, Lieutenant."

"I understand. Sir. What about Bennett?"

"Use your own judgment." Joad shrugged. He pressed the restart button and the elevator hummed into motion. "If you think he'll give us problems over Garcia's 'retirement,' cut him the same deal. But tell them that if either of them goes public with this, all bets are off and I'll hit them with as many charges as it takes to bust them back to patrol. And, Fielder, I want this handled now, before any . . . confusion develops. Do it today. Any questions, Lieutenant?"

"No, sir. I guess not."

CHAPTER 31

Garcia stared out the window of his hospital room into the gray, gusty afternoon, listening to Fielder make his pitch, following the gist without really listening. Solitary snowflakes were tumbling out of a mother-of-battleship gray sky, buffeted by the wind, spinning down and down into the parking lot below. And Lamont was standing in the doorway, and the razor flicked into his palm like magic, and his eyes . . . Garcia swallowed, unconsciously tracing the line of stitches across his left shoulder, and realized Fielder had stopped talking.

"Well?"

"Well, what?" Garcia said, turning to face him, adjusting the canvas sling to keep it from tugging at the stitches. He was wearing an anonymous hospital gown and robe, paper slippers. He felt vulnerable, numb, as though his emotions were still under deep anesthesia.

"Look, Loop, I don't like this any better than you do, but I'm in the middle here, so cut me some slack, okay? What do I tell the captain? Do you want the deal or not?"

"I don't know," Garcia said honestly. "Yesterday I would've told you— I'll have to think about it. What about Cordell?"

"He can take the same offer, or not, as he chooses, as long as he keeps his mouth shut. He's not the problem here, Loop, you are."

"So maybe I should act like one. Tell him I'll think it over. Or don't tell him. Right now it doesn't seem to matter much." He turned back to the window again. Watching the empty silver sky seemed more important than anything Fielder had to say.

"Look, I'm sorry as hell about this, Loop. You know that."

"Are you? Well, I'm sorry too, Al, almost as much for you as for me. I've been wondering which way you'd jump."

"And I've been wondering if you'd ever grow up. You're really overdue, you know? Tilting at windmills is for kids, Loop, and you're not a kid anymore."

"No, maybe not. I definitely don't feel like one. I feel like I'm at least a hundred. Or more. Is that what happened to you, Al? You start feeling old?"

"Could be," Fielder said, flushing. "But I wouldn't worry too much about old age if I were you, Garcia. The way you're going you're not gonna have one. I'll see you, Loop. Let me know what you decide, but do it quick. You don't have much time."

The door closed softly behind him, but Garcia scarcely noticed. He was seeing Lamont again, standing in the doorway, the razor flicking into his hand . . . And there was something wrong with the picture, something . . . He frowned, trying to hold the image, but it faded again. He couldn't seem to concentrate, to bring it into focus. Maybe it was this sterile box of a room. They were all alike, hospital rooms, Samaritan or the Vet's Facility, the same from here to Albania. And nobody could think in one. Kreskin would forget his own damn phone number in a room like this.

Lupe crossed stiffly to the small room's only closet and opened the door. All he had were his street clothes from the night before, blue jeans, a shredded sweatshirt, his bloodstained windbreaker. Not exactly chic, maybe, but better than hanging around Albania.

221

The elevator door shushed open, but Garcia didn't step out. Linda Kerry was pacing the corridor in front of Cordell's room, arms folded tightly across her chest, eyes downcast. Her clothes were rumpled, she looked drawn and exhausted, and her hair was awry, and yet he found his breathing going shallow at the sight of her. He stood there a moment, silently watching, wanting to delay the explosion he knew would come, but then the door started to close, and he stepped out and walked slowly toward her.

She glanced up, and he felt the sting of her ice-blue eyes, like sleet against his skin. But he sensed no response in her, not anger, or affection. A frown of sincere concern at his bandaged shoulder, the sling on his arm, nothing more.

"I . . . just came from your room and they said you were checking out," she said. "I thought you might come down here. I knew you were injured but I didn't realize . . . Are you going to be all right?"

"I'll manage. How's your friend?"

"He may live, though beyond that— Look, I have to talk to you," she said abruptly.

"Yeah, I gathered. But I don't think that's such a good idea just now," Garcia said. "It's too soon. Maybe later."

"It's important and it'll only take a minute. I, ah, I want you to look at me."

"Look at you?"

"That's right. You're a professional, you're good at your job. You should have instincts, I suppose. So I want you to look in my eyes, or whatever it is you do, and listen. You know me. We're friends, and we might have . . . been more." She shook her head sharply, dismissing the thought, and took a deep breath. "Lamont was with me from six last night until well after four this morning, at the club, then at my apartment, and in my bed. I was awake the whole time, and he wasn't out of my sight."

"Wasn't he?"

"No. He wasn't."

"So why did he leave at all? Why didn't he just stay the night?"

"He ah, he was afraid to—sleep with me. Literally, I mean. He has nightmares, sometimes. Violent ones."

"I'll just bet he does."

"The point is, he was with me. He knew Jobeth would be waiting up for him, so he went back to her place, but not until after four. And you were already there. He didn't kill her. He simply couldn't have. I'll admit I'm not an unbiased witness—"

"No kidding."

"But I wouldn't *lie* for him," she continued coldly, unruffled. "Not about a thing like this. And you know it. In your head or your guts or whatever level you operate on, you must know I wouldn't." She stared at him a moment, dry-eyed, tautly controlled, evaluating his reaction. And reading it correctly.

She drew a deep, ragged breath, then let it go. "God," she said, turning away, "you know, I thought it might really be that simple, that somehow you'd— You must think I'm incredibly naive. I'll see you around, Lupe. Take care of yourself."

"Wait a minute," he said, grasping her shoulder with his good arm, "please. I know you think you're doing the right thing, but— Damn!" He winced as she pulled her arm away, and a white-hot arc of pain flashed across the stitches in his chest and shoulder.

"I'm sorry," she said. "I didn't mean to— We always seem to manage, don't we? To beat each other up."

"Maybe we just need more practice."

"I don't think so. And I really have to go. Think about what I said. Please. Just think about it."

Her voice faded and for a moment the corridor seemed to undulate around her as she walked away. He leaned against the cool tile wall, trying to control his breathing, willing the steeply tilting floor to level out. But when it did, he was alone again.

He rapped once and pushed through the door to Cordell's room.

CHAPTER 32

CORDELL'S ROOMMATE WAS SNORING SOFTLY, SUSPENDED AT THE waist by the diaperlike sling from the stainless-steel frame, his freckled face buried in his pillow, a small puddle of drool beside his mouth. Cordell was sitting up in bed, pawing through the pockets of his suitcoat. He glanced up as Garcia came in.

"You look like shit," Cordell said. "Fielder talk to you yet?"

"That's it? Not how's the arm, Loop? Are you gonna live? What are you looking for, anyway?"

"Speeders. I know I had some. Fielder must've cleaned 'em out last night while I was in surgery. Took my gun, everything." Cordell hurled the sportcoat toward a chair in the corner.

"Easy, you'll wake your buddy there."

"Nothin' wakes him up. They keep him so zonked he don't know his own name, and I'm goin' nuts in here. Oh yeah, how's your arm?"

"When they take the stitches out it'll fall off, but other than that it's fine. And yes, I talked to Fielder. Or rather I listened."

"So what you gonna do?"

224

"Definitely cancel my squash game for Saturday. After that, I don't know."

"Look, don't fuck me around, Loop. I ain't in the mood. What are we gonna *do* about this shit?"

"Hell, I don't know. I know I should be all bent outa shape about it, but somehow . . . I can't seem to give a damn. Maybe I'm just runnin' on empty. It was a long night." His breathing went suddenly shallow as he saw Lamont again, standing in the doorway, and the razor materialized in his hand, and he began to spin it in the air . . .

"Hey, man, what's wrong with you? You blown away or what?"

Garcia snapped back to the hospital room and the image vanished. "Maybe I am a little." He shook his head to clear it, which was a big mistake. It felt like it was hanging on by a thread, a single fragile sinew. "Look, Fielder told me you can lay low if you like, let things blow over. Maybe you should."

"Forget it," Cordell said, leaning back into his pillows. "If you don't know what you're doin', don't try to tell me, okay? I can fuck up my life just fine all by my ownself. How's the redneck makin' it? He gonna live?"

"He's—" There was a hard rap at the door, and Charlie Skowron poked his head in.

"Loop, you guys got a minute?"

"Christ, I must be sicker'n I thought," Cordell said. "Come on in, Charlie, but if you're here to do an autopsy, you're early. I hope."

"You might be better off if I was. I'm afraid I've got some bad news," Skowron said, stepping in hesitantly. He was wearing a light gray London Fog trenchcoat over his surgical smock, and looked as grim as one of his patients. "Look, I'm sorry to bust in like this, I know it's a bad time, but you've got a problem."

"Charlie." Cordell sighed. "A problem is bein' cut, or shot or screwed, and we already hit those numbers, so whatever you got—"

"Look, I'll lay it on you straight out. Loop, it looks like you've got a bad shoot on Yarborough. I don't have all of the lab work

225

back yet, but what I have so far pretty much eliminates him as a suspect in the Lawton woman's death."

"What do you mean, eliminates him?" Garcia said, incredulous. "I took him at the scene, with the weapon. He used it on me, for chrissake!"

"For openers, Yarborough's razor wasn't the murder weapon. The Lawton woman's wounds were made by the same weapon that killed the others, but his razor doesn't match up, and there were no blood traces on it but yours."

"So maybe he carries a spare."

"It still won't fly, Loop. There's a lot more. The woman had long fingernails, and she used them on whoever attacked her. There was blood and a fair amount of epidermal tissue under her nails, which means she must have marked her killer pretty well, probably on his face or possibly his neck. I came down to examine Yarborough myself. One, his blood type doesn't match the tissue under her nails, and two, other than a tattoo and the three bullet holes you put in his chest, he doesn't have a mark on him. He didn't do it, Loop."

"With all due respect, Charlie," Garcia said grimly, "I think we'll need a second opinion on this. You didn't figure Denny Weitz was a slasher victim either."

"You can try that route if you want," Skowron said, his eyes hardening. "Maybe you can even con the old man into going along with you again. But not me. Not on this one. I let the thing with Weitz pass because I didn't think it mattered. What's one stomped junkie more or less in this town? But this does matter. For one thing, I think I may know who *did* kill Weitz. The murder weapon came in with the guy Hamadi blew up last night, LeeRoy Clayton, one of those hideaway belt knives. It'd been cleaned up, but it still had traces of blood on it, and both the blood and the blade are matches for Weitz. And since Clayton used it to hold up his friggin' pants, he makes a helluva candidate for the Weitz killing, doesn't he? But even if he's not, the bottom line is, you shot the wrong guy here, and I can't let you burn him to cover it."

226

"Nobody's trying to cover anything, Charlie, but since you and the Doc seem to have a difference of opinion about Weitz—"

"Opinion? Garcia, he didn't give you an *opinion* on Weitz! He just overruled my findings to give you what you wanted. He didn't even examine the body. He's pulled this crap before and I always looked the other way, but—"

"Pulled what before?"

"Altered lab findings to help a cop get a righteous bust. But it's always been minor stuff, usually just raising a blood alcohol level a point or two to nail a hard-core drunk driver. He's had a thing about 'em since the accident that killed his wife, and as far as I'm concerned, any way we can get those bastards off the road is okay with me. But this is different. Look, I'm no boat-rocker. If you can handle the situation without pissing in everybody's punch-bowl, fine. I'll stall the lab results for a day or two. And if you want to talk to Klevenger about it, be my guest. He's at the DRA aviary dedication. Maybe if you ask him nice he'll even overrule me. But if he does we're gonna bump heads, Loop. I'll take this over his head, or to the press if I have to. Let me know what you decide. I'll be at the lab."

"Charlie? Look, are you sure about this? I mean—"

Skowron hesitated a moment in the doorway, then swung around to face Garcia. "I'll tell you how sure I am, Loop. I'm betting my damn job on it. We both know how this town works, and I'm not kidding myself about what'll happen if I really have to buck the old man. He's wired into city hall like a chandelier and I'll be history so fast nobody'll remember I was here. So I hope to hell there's some way you can handle this quietly. But if not, well, you know where I stand. I'll see you, Loop." He closed the door softly behind him as he left.

For what seemed like a very long time, the only sound in the room was the moist, bubbly snoring of the kid in the sling. Cordell was eyeing Garcia, his expression neutral, unreadable. "You ain't surprised," he said at last.

"What?"

"Charlie says you blew away the wrong man, and it didn't surprise you one damn bit, did it? So why not?"

"He, ah, dammit!" Garcia said, taking a deep breath. "He didn't have any blood on him."

"Blood?"

"It was everywhere, and she hadn't been dead very long. If he'd cut her up, he should have been covered with it, but he wasn't. I think I realized it subconsciously at the time, but—"

"But maybe you were lookin' to blow him away anyway."

"Maybe I was," Garcia conceded. "But the way it came down, I didn't have a choice. He would've taken me out."

"He found you in his house, with his woman dead. What the hell was he s'posed to do?"

"If Klevenger'd just done his damn job instead of trying to help, maybe I wouldn't've been so hot to nail him that I went in without backup! And maybe I wouldn't have been in such a hurry to blow him up."

"Seems to me if you'd been much slower on the trigger, you woulda needed your head sewed back on 'stead of your arm. And you had no way of knowin' the Doc had screwed up, *if* he did. So maybe it's a mess, but it's not all your fault."

"Maybe not, but like Skow said, the bottom line is, I blew away the wrong guy. And even if Klevenger admits that he gave me bum information, Internal Affairs may still figure I did it because of . . . Linda. And if he denies it to cover himself, it's my word against his, and who are they gonna believe?"

"Dr. K," Cordell said. "No question."

"You don't have to sound so damn sure about it. *Some*body on the board might believe me."

"I wouldn't lay odds. Why should they? We shoot up half the damn town, I get blown away, you get cut up puttin' Linda's new boyfriend in the hospital, and meanwhile Cheerio just keeps on truckin', business as usual. It don't look too good, you know? We look like fuckin' clowns."

"No argument there, except . . ."

"Except what?"

"What you said about Cheerio doin' business as usual. He's not, you know."

"How do you mean?"

228

"Jobeth. She doesn't fit his pattern. She wasn't in her car. She was at home. It might make sense if Lamont had killed her. I mean, he's crazy and she was handy, right? Like the old woman in the hospital. But if Lamont didn't do it, then why would Cheerio break his pattern to seek her out?"

"She hung out at that club, and we know that at least one of the other victims did too."

"But she wasn't just another victim. He hunted her down."

"So maybe he did it to point us at Yarborough and take the heat off himself. Hell, anybody that can read a paper knows the redneck was our number-one draft choice."

"It couldn't be just somebody who read about it in the paper. The stories were about Linda, not Jobeth. It had to be somebody who knows Lamont pretty well. Or maybe knows us."

"Knows us?"

"We mentioned Jobeth in our reports," Garcia said slowly. "Cheerio could've read about her there."

"What are you sayin'? You think he's a cop?"

Garcia didn't reply for a moment. He crossed slowly to the window and stared out into the softly falling snow.

"Maybe," he said at last. "The old man said he was."

"What old man?"

"The old wino. Maish. He said he saw Cheerio, or at least his car. A boat with flashers, he said. And then somebody torched him. The thing is, we didn't mention Maish in our reports. Only somebody who was actually at the scene would have known about him."

"Somebody like a cop, you mean?"

"Not necessarily. Maybe just somebody familiar with police procedures. Isn't that what the shrink said?"

"What are you gettin' at?"

"Look, suppose we're not clowns. We didn't just pull Yarborough's name out of a hat, you know. He was a legitimate suspect."

"We had plenty of suspects. Damn near a whole town full."

"But we had evidence linking him to Cheerio. Or we thought we did, mostly just odds and ends at first, but when Denny Weitz was killed, we figured we had Yarborough dead bang. We're leaning on him, using Denny as a snitch, Cheerio aces Denny, that makes Lamont our man, right?"

"Wrong. Accordin' to Skow, Denny wasn't killed by Cheerio."

"And if Skow's right, we've got another problem, because Denny wasn't killed by a drunk driver either."

"I don't follow you."

"Skow said Dr. K's touched up evidence before to help bust drunk drivers. But apparently he also switched things around to implicate Lamont in Denny's death."

"Could've been just tryin' to help out."

"Why? He doesn't owe us anything and this isn't a drunk driving case. Or maybe it is, in a way."

"What— Oh, you mean the victims, right?"

"That's right," Garcia said. "And Skow said the old man's got a thing about drunks. I wonder how big a thing?"

"Come on, you gotta be kiddin'. You sayin' Dr. K's the man?"

"He told me Denny Weitz was a Cheerio killing, knowing I figured Yarborough for Cheerio—"

"Hell, anybody in this town that can read knew that."

"But not everybody knew about Jobeth. Only somebody with access to our reports would have known about Jobeth."

"Or persons unknown who knew the redneck well enough to know about her."

"It wasn't persons unknown who fed me bum information about Denny."

"It ain't that simple. If the Doc wanted to pin the Cheerio killin's on Yarborough, all he had to do was handle the postmortem on Jobeth and fix the forensic evidence. So why didn't he?"

"I don't know. Maybe he couldn't. Skow said the woman raked whoever killed her. Maybe she marked him badly enough so that he couldn't show himself without doing a lot of explaining."

"Only problem with that is, Klevenger's supposed to be at some kinda dedication ceremony today with about ten thousand other people."

"You're right," Garcia said. "That's where he's supposed to be."

Neither man spoke for a moment. Then Cordell shook his head slowly. "It's all air, you know? Shadow dancin'. All you got is that maybe the man gave you some bum info on Denny, and you only got Skow's word for that. And even if he did, he was probably just tryin' to help. But just to play it out, let's say Klevenger is the man. Why would he want to hang it on Yarborough or anybody else? We just been chasin' our tails on this one and he knows it."

"Maybe he doesn't know it. He spends a lot of time with Joad—"

"And Joad's been talkin' like we're one step from a bust. Christ, I think the drugs I'm on must be doin' me in. You're almost makin' sense."

"So what do you think?"

"I think if I spend another five minutes in the room with sleeping beauty snorin' over there, I'm gonna pitch his sorry ass out the window. Where's the dedication thing supposed to be?"

"At the Ren Cen, but you're not coming."

"No? All due respect, Loop," Cordell said, wincing as he swung his legs over the bed. "I don't figure you could stop me even if you wasn't stitched together like a Cabbage Patch kid. Look, if he's there standin' tall, we're shit outa luck anyway, right? So it's not like we gotta leap over tall buildings at a single bound. We just gotta get a look at the guy. So why don't you just get my pants outa the goddamn closet?"

CHAPTER 33

"**I**T'S GONNA BE DOGSHIT, YOU KNOW," CORDELL SAID GLOOMILY, as they shouldered through the holiday crowd in the brightly lit pedestrian overpass above Jefferson Avenue. "The old man's gonna be here, and we're gonna look like assholes."

"Maybe," Garcia admitted. "But if we're assholes, at least this time nobody'll know it but us."

The walkway opened onto the second-floor concourse of the Renaissance Center, the sixty-story mirror-sheathed towers that loom above the Detroit River in the heart of the city, the multifaceted jewel of the Motown skyline, built as a centerpiece for the New Detroit. The concourse was ablaze with holiday lights, Christmas trees glistening with every imaginable trim hovered in space over the open walkways, suspended by glittering ribbons from the ceilings two stories above. Metallic green and red garlands and glowing streamers of light swooped and swirled between them, trailing off into infinity overhead, while Nat King Cole purred "Let It Snow" from a hundred invisible speakers.

The concourse was jammed with shoppers and gawkers,

232

ermine-coated Grosse Pointe dowagers rubbing shoulders with denim-clad teenyboppers, shop rats, and ghetto gang bangers. Cordell collared a young black uniformed guide as he pushed past.

"Excuse me, my man, we're lookin' for the Renaissance Alliance Club. Some kind of a dedication ceremony today?"

"You mean the aviary?" the kid said skeptically. "It's on the top floor in the new wing, but it's not open to the public yet. No one admitted today without an invitation. Sorry."

"Maybe we've got invitations," Cordell said.

"You two?" The kid grinned, pushing off into the crowd. "Sure you have. If you get in, tell the governor I said hi."

Garcia's eyebrows arched a notch. "The governor?"

"Nobody can say we don't fuck up big time." Cordell shrugged. "So how we gonna work this?"

"Straight ahead. We'll check it out, see if the Doc's here. If he's not, we'll run him down. If he is, we'll mix with the crowd and get close enough just to make sure he's not marked."

"And if he's marked?"

Garcia's eyes seemed to lose focus for a moment. "I, ah, don't know about that. We'll make it up as we go, I guess. Let's find an elevator."

The elevator door slid open, but they had no chance to exit. Three oversized, immaculately uniformed state troopers ringed the door. Two more were standing a few feet beyond them holding briefcases, open, with their hands inside. The man in the middle, a lieutenant with a blond brushcut, eyed Garcia and Bennett doubtfully for a moment, then stepped forward.

"Invitations, gentlemen?"

"Police business," Garcia said. "I'm going to take out my ID, so tell your friends with the briefcases not to get antsy, okay?"

"No problem. As long as you take it out slowly."

Garcia showed the trooper his badge. He didn't seem overly impressed.

"What's going on?"

"We have to see Dr. Klevenger for a minute. It's urgent. Is he here?"

"Sure. Along with about five hundred other people, but the ceremony's due to start in, ah"—the trooper glanced at his watch—"twenty minutes or so, and I can't let you go in there looking like this. We've got media people from all over the country here and you two look like refugees from a train wreck."

"Look, we may not be dressed for the prom, but we're in the middle of a homicide investigation and it really is important that we talk to the Doc. We'll be in and out in a minute and a half. Now how about it?"

The trooper hesitated, thinking it over, then shrugged. "What the hell." He grinned. "It wouldn't be a Motown party without at least one murder. But stay low, okay, and don't hold up the show. The governor has to be gone by five. Jacobson?"

A fullback-sized black trooper stepped forward with a metal-detecting wand. He made a quick pass over Cordell, then Garcia. The box let out a startled beep near his left shoulder.

"I'm afraid I'll have to ask for your weapon—"

"I'm not armed. I've got a metal shoulder brace under the bandages," Garcia explained. "You want me to unwrap 'em?"

"Just get in and out in the minute and a half, and we'll call it even. The door's at the end of the hall. Tell the doorman Lieutenant Lyman passed you."

"Right," Garcia said, "and thanks."

"Hey, ah, Lieutenant," Cordell asked, "did you see the Doc when he came in?"

"We checked him in, sure."

"How did he look?"

"How did he look? Like a penguin, how else?"

"A penguin?"

"That's right. Now do you mind? We've got customers coming."

"A penguin," Cordell muttered, following Garcia past the pair with the briefcases. "Terrific."

"What the hell, it's an aviary, right? Maybe it's 'come as your favorite bird,'" Garcia said.

"And what was all that crap about a shoulder brace?"

"I figured he might change his mind if he knew I was carrying. Besides, I don't figure on shooting anybody."

"I hope not. I think those guys were packin' Uzis in their briefcases."

The two men stalked down a broad corridor transplanted from Versailles, delicately woven tapestries, chandeliers that glistened like suspended pools of diamonds. The red-jacketed doorman stood aside grudgingly after Garcia flashed his bronze, and swung open the ornately carved oak door.

The large, elegantly appointed room was even more crowded than the concourse fifty-nine floors below. But not with shoppers. These were the city's power elite, financial and political movers and shakers. The women were dazzling, elaborately gowned and dripping with jewelry, and every man in the room, including the waiters, was wearing a tux.

"Penguins," Cordell said evenly. "And so much for blendin' with the crowd."

"Right. Well, we're here, let's find our man."

"I already spotted him," Cordell said. "He's over by the dais, talkin' to the governor. And the captain. And we're assholes."

"So maybe we don't do great police work." Garcia shrugged. "At least we're consistent. Let's say hello."

"You've gotta be kidding. Joad'll have the mounties bounce us so fast we'll need parachutes. You got a gun. Why don't you just shoot me right here and save the walk?"

"We've come this far. You want to just walk away? Without making absolutely sure?"

Cordell stared at him hard a moment, then shrugged. "You're nuts, Loop, you know that? You always have been. Just a second." He copped a goblet of champagne from a passing waiter, raised it, checked the color, then downed it with a single swallow. "California, eighty-five."

"Benton Harbor, September," the waiter sniffed.

"Close," Cordell said, replacing the goblet on the man's tray. "What the hell, let's do it. I've been thrown out of better dumps than this."

They made their way cautiously through the fashionable crush toward the dais, Garcia being doubly careful to avoid bumping his bandaged arm. Midway, he was jostled by a waiter into a slender stunner of a blonde in a simple black dress, spilling her champagne. "Sorry." Her beefy escort, a million-dollar wide receiver for the Detroit Lions, was about to comment, but met Cordell's stone-eyed stare and thought better of it.

The governor had moved off when they reached the dais, with Joad trailing behind like a spaniel, leaving Klevenger in deep conversation with an overstuffed matron whose gown probably cost a fortune and looked like a Salvation Army reject.

In contrast, Klevenger looked positively dashing in his tux, heir to Fred Astaire, fresh haircut, gold-framed designer glasses. He'd even replaced his steel pincers with a lifelike prosthetic hand for the occasion. And there wasn't a mark, not as much as a razor nick on his face. He glanced up, startled, as Garcia touched his good arm.

"Hello, Doc."

"My God, Garcia, what the hell happened to you?"

"I, ah, had kind of a close shave. Have you got a minute?"

"If this is business, forget it. For once I'm going to enjoy the circus instead of shoveling up after the parade. So have some champagne, and get the hell out of here."

"It's not really our problem, it's yours too, and it really *is* important. So is there someplace we can talk? Privately, maybe?"

Klevenger met Garcia's eyes, then glanced thoughtfully at Cordell. "All right," he conceded, "I suppose so, if we can talk on the move. I wanted to make a last-minute check anyway, but this better be good. Will you excuse me," he said to the fashionably disheveled matron. "The press of business. Come on, gentlemen, and I'll give you a tour."

"Sorry to interrupt, ma'am," Garcia said.

"Dynamite dress," Cordell added.

"Thank you," she said uncertainly.

"This way." They followed Klevenger to a double doorway at the end of the dais. It was trimmed with red, white, and blue bunting and barred with a wide red ribbon. Klevenger lifted the ribbon carefully. "Duck under, and for Godsake don't break it."

Garcia hunched cautiously beneath the ribbon, pushed through the door beyond, and stepped into Vietnam.

236

CHAPTER 34

T HE ROOM WAS IMMENSE, A VERDANT, SURREAL JUNGLE OF GREEN-ery, of tangled ferns and bushes and even fully developed trees, reaching toward the glass dome nearly sixty feet overhead. Grapevines and creepers, clinging tenaciously to the curved, steel-skeletoned walls of bronzed glass, seemed to struggle up-ward, baring their hungry leaves to the pale afternoon sunlight. Near the center of the display a realistic replica waterfall gushed and bubbled, spilling down a cairn of boulders into a shallow wading pool. A narrow, glass-sheathed walkway circled the outer perimeter, allowing strollers to simultaneously enjoy a stunning view of the frozen river and the Canadian shore nearly a quarter of a mile below, and the birds of the teeming rain forest within.

And the birds were everywhere. In the pool, bathing and preening, roosting in the trees and the larger bushes at floor level, or in flight, fluttering and gliding in the open air all the way to the skylit ceiling. Most were multihued tropical birds, with long sweeping tail feathers, ranging in size from dime store canaries to— Garcia had no idea what the larger ones were.

"Sweet Jesus," Cordell said, "looks like they airlifted this place right outa the Mekong. Just cut out a chunk of jungle and hauled it straight over. How many birds you got here, Doc?"

"Nearly seven hundred, I believe," Klevenger said, pleased at the awe in his tone. "About half of them are canaries and parakeets, 'cage birds' they're usually called, although in this aviary, we're the ones in the cage." He indicated the enclosed walkway. "Ingenious, isn't it? I've been involved in this project from the first, the planning, fund-raising, every aspect. It's been a pleasure dealing with so much . . . life, for a change. Come on, we can talk as we walk, and I'd like to make a last-minute check." He set off at a brisk pace down the corridor, with Garcia and Bennett trailing behind. "Now what's so damned important that you've tracked me down here?"

"We had another Cheerio killing last night," Garcia said, "and I shot a suspect at the scene. Lamont Yarborough. Remember him?"

"Very well. Nice work."

"Charlie Skowron doesn't think so. He thinks I took down the wrong man."

"Really? And why would that be?"

"The woman fought her attacker, clawed him. Yarborough's blood type doesn't match the tissue under her nails, and he's unmarked."

"That wouldn't necess—" Klevenger broke off, staring into the aviary at a long, low bank of shrubs near the pool that seemed to glow from within. Several large birds were circling above it, and then one lit, screaming, and began tearing savagely at the foliage with his beak. "Damn," Klevenger muttered. "Excuse me, but we seem to have a problem." He trotted ahead to a narrow service door, pulled a key from his vest pocket, and slid it into the lock.

"Hey, wait a minute," Cordell said. "You goin' in there? With the birds?"

"They don't bite," Klevenger snapped, "or at least they won't bite us, so come or don't. But either way, shut the damn door after me."

Cordell glanced at Garcia, shrugged, then followed them

238

through the door. Klevenger was already several steps ahead, snaking quickly through the shrubbery on a nearly invisible path. Garcia moved up beside him, maintaining the pace with difficulty. "What's the problem?"

"Something's wrong at the breeding cages. The custodians are all new and—" His answer was drowned by a pair of cockatoos exploding from a nearby shrub, shrieking off overhead, screaming an alarm. Garcia gave up and fell back a step.

And seemed to tumble back through the years as a wave of exhaustion and sensory overload rolled over him. Déjà vu, moving through the dense shrubbery, the air close and thick, the cacophony of the birds. Boonie patrol in 'Nam with Klevenger on point. Wearing a tuxedo. A waking nightmare, but no more than 'Nam had been. And the constant, heart-seizing fear that he'd kept buried like a body in a basement roiled up from a dark recess of his soul, suffusing him, tightening his throat, making him struggle just to breathe. He knew it was irrational, but he couldn' shake it. Perhaps it was the feeling of being watched, by a thousand eyes that acknowledged him as warm meat, moving. Nothing more. Harry Fein's eyes were like that. And Skowron's. And earlier that day, at the hospital, for an instant he'd glimpsed eyes like that staring back at him from the bathroom mirror. He shook his head sharply, trying to clear it. And banged into Klevenger.

The old man had stopped beside a long, low table, artfully draped with camouflage netting to resemble the surrounding shrubbery. Klevenger shouted and waved his arms, driving off the toucan who'd been tearing at the net. Cordell slogged up, his left hand clamped tightly over his midsection, gray-faced and sweating from the effort of the brief walk.

"What the hell's going' on?" he panted.

"Breeder cages," Klevenger explained, lifting the edge of the net, revealing a thirty-foot row of wire cages, each roughly three feet square and five feet tall, shrouded with camouflage bunting and warmed by its own infrared bulb, a Berlin wall that more or less bisected the avian. Most of the cages contained nests, with adult birds and clutches of blind, featherless young. A line of narrow plastic troughs, each a yard long, stretched along the outer rim of the table. "We cage mating pairs to make sure they breed with the proper partner and to keep the raptors from raiding the nests and killing the young. Only somebody forgot to fill the damned troughs and we gave the custodians the afternoon off."

"Look, Doc, we didn't come here to—"

"If you want to talk, talk, but since you're here you can help. I'd do it, but this damned plastic hand is strictly for show, it's not functional. I'd wind up wearing more Clorox than I'd get in the trough."

"Clorox?"

"Ordinary laundry bleach," Klevenger said impatiently. "It sterilizes the cages and the fumes keep the raptors off. There are cases of the stuff under the table. Grab a jug and get those troughs filled. The governor's going to stroll through here in twenty minutes with TV camera crews. I don't want them filming a bloody free-for-all. Bennett, why don't you get the other side? Fill each trough about an inch from the top. Please."

Garcia half-expected Cordell to blow up, but either he was too exhausted to argue or the "please" made the difference. He gave Klevenger a look, but he picked up a jug and trudged off around the wall of shrouded cages.

"Why not," Garcia muttered. He knelt beside the table, popped the cap on a gallon jug of bleach, and began filling the trough, flinching at the acrid bite of the fumes.

"Thank you," Klevenger said curtly. "The birds appreciate it and so do I, and be careful with that stuff. It's caustic. Now what's all this about Charlie?"

"He's convinced that Yarborough couldn't have killed his girlfriend, that he's not our man."

"Well, if that's what he says, I'm sure he believes it's true, but we've been under a lot of pressure from the Christmas rush, and he's blown at least one autopsy recently. I'm sure if I check his work—"

"It may not be that simple. He says he wasn't mistaken about Weitz, and he thinks he can prove it."

"Prove it how?"

"He claims the murder weapon came in last night. A belt knife, not Yarborough's. He, ah, also said that you set aside his findings on Weitz to help me get a bust on Yarborough, and that if you tried it again he'd go to the press about it."

"Did he now?" Klevenger said, a hint of color rising in his sallow cheeks. He took a pack of Players from his vest pocket, tapped the cigarette on his wrist, and lit it with a gold-filled lighter. "He, ah, may be more exhausted than I thought. I think a vacation might be in order. With a reassignment when it's over."

"That might solve your problem," Garcia said carefully, "but not mine."

"You needn't worry." Klevenger smiled faintly. "I'm sure Charlie's mistaken about the knife. In fact, I can almost guarantee it."

"Yeah, I suppose you can. One way or the other."

"Meaning what?"

"I mean you can guarantee the outcome whether he's guilty or not."

"Yes, I suppose that's true." Klevenger smiled. "But since there's no real doubt of his guilt—"

"Charlie seems to think there is."

"And I'm almost certain he's wrong," Klevenger said mildly. "The man's scum, a murderer. Or worse."

"Or worse?" Garcia echoed, glancing up at Klevenger. "What's worse than a murderer?"

Klevenger hesitated a moment, took a thoughtful pull on his cigarette, then shrugged. "I suppose a carrier would be."

"You want to run that by me again?"

"A carrier. A death carrier. Consider the problem from a medical point of view. If death is the ultimate symptom, then a person who carries the disease is more dangerous then one who simply inflicts it."

"I'm not sure I follow that."

"Take narcotics. It's a disease, a terminal one. I see the end results every day. Murder victims, ODs, gang-bangs over turf. The police treat the symptoms, muggings, burglaries, murder,

241

but they're not very effective in dealing with the source. The dealers. You were the exception, of course."

"How so?"

"You were a good cop, and you treated the problem . . . efficiently. Surgically. Four times, I believe."

Garcia stopped pouring and stared up at him.

"No offense intended," Klevenger added hastily. "Quite the contrary. I admired what you did. It was first-rate work. And I wasn't alone. You took a bad rap from the press, but a lot of senior members of the department, friends of mine, knew you did what you had to, and did it well."

"Is that how you judge a cop's effectiveness? By the body count?"

"If you were in my line of work, how else would you judge it?"

"I don't know. Maybe you've got a point. But I don't see where Yarborough fits into your little theory."

"It's simple enough. Motown, Murder City. You hear it every day, and it's true. We had more than eight hundred homicides last year. But that was only a fraction of the body count I dealt with, a fraction. Far more were killed on the road. And more than half of them by drunks."

"But what's Yarborough—?"

"Don't you see? He's a carrier," the old man said fiercely, his eyes narrowing. "He attracts people to those places, and they fornicate like animals, and swill alcohol until they're pig-drunk. And then they leave. They get into their cars and go out on the highways and destroy themselves. And other people—" He swallowed and looked away a moment, bringing himself under control. "In any case, you have nothing to worry about. Your reasons for trying to nail Yarborough may have been personal, but you did the right thing. And I'll see that you get whatever you need to finish the job."

"For purely medical reasons."

"What's the difference, as long as it's effective?"

"It doesn't make any difference to me how he falls," Garcia said evenly, "just so I get off the hook. But I guess it bugs me a little that you're blowing smoke at me about your motives. It's just as personal with you. Isn't it?"

"I've never met the man."

"Maybe not, but you met a drunk driver once. Who'd gotten trashed in a bar. And your wife died in the crash. And you lost your hand. A woman driver, wasn't it?"

"I'm surprised you remembered," Klevenger said quietly, looking away. He seemed to shrink, visibly, unconsciously hunching his shoulders against the memory of pain. "It . . . was a long time ago."

"What happened to the woman? Did they prosecute?"

"That would've been difficult. She died in the crash."

"So she was never punished for what happened?"

"Hardly. I read the reports afterwards. Her blood alcohol level was nearly one point eight. She probably never felt a thing."

"But she has since, hasn't she?"

"I—" Klevenger broke off, eyeing Garcia oddly, and the moment of vulnerability passed. "I wouldn't know," he said at last. "I'm no expert on the afterlife. If there is one."

"Come on, Les, you know what I'm talking about. And it's just you and me and a thousand birds here. I've killed people when I had to. And so have you. Haven't you?"

"Your wound must be worse than I'd thought. You're hallucinating."

"I don't think so. For instance, I didn't *remember* a woman driver'd killed your wife. I guessed. And I'm guessing that if I dig up the accident report, I'll find that her bra was lying in the backseat. That she'd probably been—how did you put it?— 'Fornicating like an animal.' And hadn't bothered to put it back on. How'm I doing?"

"It doesn't really matter, does it? Even if it was true, it wouldn't prove anything. You can't touch me, Garcia. And I can make you very sorry if you try. Are you about finished? With the bleach, I mean?"

"Yeah. With the bleach."

"Then we'd better collect your partner and get back," Klevenger said, dropping his cigarette and grinding it out underfoot. "It wouldn't do to keep the governor waiting, would it?"

"No, I guess—" Gills. For a moment, when Klevenger glanced

down at his cigarette, there'd been dark lines on his neck. Like gills. But now there was nothing. So why—? The cages. He'd been touched by the infrared light from the cages.

"Is something wrong?"

"I, ah, I don't know," Garcia mumbled, swaying as he stood up. "I feel a little wobbly."

"Maybe you'd better sit down."

"Yeah, I—" Garcia stumbled against Klevenger, leaning on him, moving him closer to the cages. And the gills reappeared. The tracks Jobeth had gouged with her nails. He brushed the area and it smeared slightly, discoloring his fingertips. Makeup! Klevenger prepped bodies with it every day. He was an expert.

The old man flinched at his touch and jerked away from him, stunned, instinctively covering his wound with his palm. "What are you doing?"

"What happened to your neck, Les?" Garcia said softly. "Nick yourself shaving?" He met the old man's eyes for a moment, and it was like staring straight into the pools of hell. And then the world exploded as Klevenger snatched a trough of Clorox and pitched it full in his face.

The pain was instantaneous, incredible, a blistering sheet of liquid flame that seared his skin, setting his face ablaze. Garcia reeled back into the cages, blinded, trying to brush the smoking liquid away from his eyes. A lightning strike of agony flashed along his forearm and he felt the grate of metal on bone. Scalpel! He lashed out blindly to ward off the old man's rush and felt his fist make contact, but then the blade bit deep in his chest, and he staggered back, tangling in the shrubbery, his legs going numb, failing him, and he was falling, down and down.

He tried to call a warning to Cordell but the caustic fumes surged into his lungs, scorching his throat, strangling his shout to a croak. His consciousness was waning, fading. A tidal wave of darkness thundered toward him, roaring like a freight train, carrying him into the night. And he welcomed it, the dreamless dark, an end to the agony. But not yet. Not like this!

Clawing at the branches of the shrub with his good arm, he struggled to his knees. Water. There was water in the fountain. Where was the damn fountain?

He lurched to his feet and stumbled forward, blundering into the breeding cages, chest-high. The caged birds were screaming and the others took it up, a crescendo of rage that mixed with the roaring in his head. The cages. He was between them and the fountain. It was behind him somewhere. Where was Cordell? And Klevenger? He couldn't see and it didn't matter. Only the water mattered.

He turned away from the cages and staggered into the brush in the rough direction of the fountain, listening desperately for the sound of water, deafened by the shrieking of the birds.

The lip of the pool caught him at the knees and he plunged into it face first, gashing his forehead on a boulder, the soul-numbing ache of his shoulder so deep he could barely lift himself clear of the water. He drowned his face in it again and again, frantically trying to quench his burning eyes. Better. Not much, but better. He got to his knees, wiping the water away with his sleeve, but it didn't help. It was like looking through a shattered, rain-soaked windshield. His eyes were tearing so badly he could only glimpse vague, fantastic shapes. He couldn't see Cordell or Klevenger at all, couldn't hear anything but the birds, colored blurs whirring through the air around him.

He fumbled his .38 out of its holster, but the slash along his forearm had turned his arm to lead, and it was all he could do to keep from dropping the weapon in the pool. Still, it was something solid, something familiar in the chaos, whether he could aim it or not. Resting the weapon on his bandaged arm, he staggered cautiously out of the pool.

He could make out the glow of the breeding cages a few yards away. Cordell must be on the other side of them somewhere. He moved unsteadily toward the glow, keeping the weapon in front of him. A flower pot crumbled under his left foot and he went down hard, slamming his shoulder into an urn, gasping at the blaze of agony. And he dropped the gun.

He fumbled frantically in the dirt, one-handed, fighting back the pain and the black wave of despair that threatened to drown him. Without the gun . . . but he found it. His numbed fingers brushed over it, half buried in some loose soil. He wiped it off against his shirt as best he could, then crawled to the breeding cages and pulled himself to his feet.

Nothing. He couldn't see a goddam thing. If anything, his vision was getting worse, fading to red. He could barely make out the glow from the cages now. Slipping the gun back into its holster for a moment, he tried to spread his burning eyelids with his fingertips. No help. And they were still swelling. If they closed completely— He jerked the gun out again.

"Cordell!"

His voice was louder this time, but the only answer was the screaming of the birds as more of them exploded into flight around him.

"Cordell!" He was down. Had to be. And that crazy bastard was out there with him. The image of Klevenger raising the nearly severed head of Louise Barrett flashed across his memory.

"Put the gun down, Garcia. There's no need for this."

The voice seemed to come from somewhere near the cages, out of the dark. He swung the weapon in its general direction, but he couldn't see a thing. Despair knotted his belly like a punch. If Klevenger was up—

"Cordell!"

"He'll be all right, Garcia, if you let me help him. I'm willing to help you both. I'm just not willing to go to jail. And there's no reason why I should. You must see that. We want the same things. Let me help you."

"What about Louise Barrett? Can you help her? Or the others?" Keep him talking. Where is he?

"They were drunken sluts, Garcia, trash. I see three or four a week downtown, and their wreckage. They leave those places and kill themselves and anyone else who happens to be in the way. Like my wife. Like me. And last fall, when I saw her again . . ."

"Saw who again?"

"My wife. Or rather the body of a woman who looked so very much like her. Whose life had been destroyed in the same, senseless way. I knew I couldn't let it continue. I just couldn't. And I began taking—preventative measures."

246

The voice was moving. More to the left? The ceaseless shrieking of the birds made it impossible to tell.

"But they weren't drunk. Or at least two of them weren't, the nun and Jobeth. You must have changed—" Something clanked to his right and he wheeled to face it. Nothing. he couldn't see anything at all in that direction.

"You can't see, can you?" The voice was almost behind him now. He swiveled slowly toward it, trying to spot a movement, a shadow, anything.

"Garcia, if I wanted to harm you I could do it, but I don't want that. You're one of the few who might understand. But if you don't let me attend to your eyes you're going to be blind. Permanently. Put down the gun. Maybe I have made . . . mistakes about the women. We can talk about it."

The voice was definitely closer now. Where was Cordell? He couldn't have moved far in the shape he was in. Had to be somewhere near the cages. Do it. Now.

"This is quite a setup you built here, Les. Thanks for the show. And kiss it good-bye." He raised the .38, aiming it upward, toward the side of the room facing the river, and squeezed the trigger. The gun roared and bucked, nearly jumping out of his numbed hand, and a ceiling panel exploded and blew out, collapsing in an avalanche of snow and shattered glass.

"Noooo!"

He sensed movement, farther to the right then he'd expected, a blur of motion, charging at him out of the dark. And he waited, knowing he couldn't fire until— But he was too close! Suddenly Klevenger's face seemed to loom out of the blackness, and the scalpel was coming down, and he fired into the blur in front of him, again and again, clumsily emptying the gun. And then Klevenger was on him, slamming him back into the breeding cages, bearing him down as the table collapsed and they tumbled into the tangled wreckage. Garcia tried to swing his weapon, but his arm had no strength left, and the room was waning, and he was spinning, whirling hell-bound into the darkness, pursued by the savage screaming of the birds.

CHAPTER 35

T HE PURE, CLEAR VOICES OF THE MUMFORD HIGH GLEE CLUB echoed down the corridors of Samaritan Health Center in lyric fragments: the baby child is born, *in excelsis Deo*, good will toward men. In the emergency room , an exhausted intern hammered furiously on the chest of a fifteen-year-old crackhead from Parkside, trying desperately to restart his heart while the spitting cobra tattooed on the kid's chest writhed and recoiled with every blow.

In the ER lounge, three of the boy's Silver Cobra homeboys, looking krush and bad in their pearl sateen jackets and Tae Kwon Do headbands, sprawled across the bright plastic furniture, shucking halfheartedly back and forth, high-school handsome, hard and hollow as iron pipe, jiving Christmas Eve away waiting for word on a warlord. And the pudgy, rumpled security guard watching them from the corridor offered up a silent Christmas prayer to his truelight Bible Baptist savior: *Please, please, Lord Jesus, get them punkass little bastards outa here. Thank you, Lord. Amen.*

248

In the darkened fourth-floor patients' lounge, Lamont Yarborough sat alone, huddled in a wheelchair, wearing a gray hospital dressing gown that hung on his gaunt frame like Dachau pajamas. A solitary strand of miniature Christmas lights provided the only light in the room, winking merrily from a skeletal plastic pine on the windowsill.

Lamont was hunched over a small acoustic guitar, his face a waxen mask of concentration as he forced his reluctant fingers over the steel strings by sheer effort of will, wrenching a halting, discordant melody from the instrument. It was a children's song, child's play, but his hands were trembling and his forehead was beaded with perspiration from the effort.

The melody faltered. Biting his lower lip, he began again, but stumbled over the same passage, and stopped. He flexed his fingers to relax them, observing their tremors dispassionately. And realized he wasn't alone anymore. A dark figure was standing in the doorway, silhouetted in the light from the corridor.

Neither man spoke for a moment, each assessing the other in silence, waiting. Then Garcia stepped in, closed the door behind him, and leaned against it. He looked only slightly better than the man in the chair, his left arm in a canvas sling, his chest and shoulder heavily bandaged beneath a chino jacket. His face was patchy and raw, slick with smears of ointment, and there were uneven blond streaks in his hair. His eyes were feverish, exhausted.

"My, my, my," Lamont said at last, "look what we got here. The ghost of Christmas present."

"Hello, Lamont. So how you been doin'?"

"I've been better. And things ain't exactly lookin' up. What is this, my Christmas roust?"

"No, I was . . . in the neighborhood."

"Visitin' your partner? Or did he already croak?"

"No, he's still hanging on. I think he'll make it. Too stubborn to die, maybe."

"Sorry to hear it. So what do you want? If you're lookin' for your lady friend, she's gone home to her people for the holidays. And I, ah, don't figure she'll be comin' back."

"No? Why not?"

"Her career's pretty much trashed here and that's what she's heavy into. I expect I'll get a letter about it one of these days. Maybe you will too. Too bad. She was a class act."

"You don't seem all that broken up about it."

"No real cause to be. Nothin' heavy there. The lady was just slummin', whether she knew it or not. I was like a . . . declaration of independence, you know? A walk on the wild side. Never figured it any other way. It was a sweet ride, and now it's over. And I got other things to worry about, so why don't you take a hike? I'm tryna get some practice in."

"I heard, from out in the hall. You sound a little rusty."

Yarbourough glanced away, staring out the darkened windows at the city night. Parkside by streetlight. An unhealthy flush crept slowly above the collar of his robe. "That's right," he said after a moment, his voice tightly controlled. "I forgot, you're the music critic. Well, maybe I am a little rusty. Or maybe I'm havin' some minor problems from some bullet holes I picked up someplace."

"Too bad about that. But it's not like I had a lot of alternatives at the time."

"Trashin' my life was just parta your job, right? All in a day's work? Bullshit. Maybe you can smoke everybody else into believin' that, but I'm not buyin'. It was personal. You wanted me, and you set me up for a fall. Only I'm not the only one who went down."

"You were set up all right," Garcia acknowledged, "but not by me. Mostly, you were just in the wrong place at the wrong time. You were on top of my suspect list when Klevenger needed somebody to draw us off, and you've gotta admit you looked good for it. You're not exactly Snow White, you know? So maybe you got a rough deal, but I've seen rougher. I see 'em every day."

"That's a real comfort. I'll mention it to Jobeth next time I bump into her. 'Tough break, babe, but hey, the man was only doin' his job.' Think she'll go for it?"

Garcia swallowed, but said nothing.

250

"Right. I don't figure she will either. And even if she did, I wouldn't. We aint' finished yet, Mex, you and me. Maybe I'm stuck in this chair for now, but I won't be forever. We got a day comin', and you can take that to the bank."

"Yeah, well, you do what you think you have to, Lamont. But as far as I'm concerned, it's over. I've asked the department to drop the assault and weapons charges against you, and we're picking up your hospital tab. You're supposed to be a bright guy, take some advice. Quit while you're behind. Walk away."

"Maybe I would if I could walk. And maybe if I sit in this chair long enough I'll mellow out. But I wouldn't bet on it. If I was you I'd keep lookin' over my shoulder. Now why don't you take a walk. Leave me alone."

"No problem." Garcia turned to leave, but paused in the doorway. "Look, I know it won't mean much to you, but I want you to know that I'm sorry about . . ."

But Lamont wasn't listening. He'd begun to play again, hunched over the guitar, wrestling with a melody. Not the children's song he'd been playing earlier; this one was more intricate, a mournful country blues. His technique was ragged, and painful, and each note was an effort, but still the song was recognizable. And eerily familiar. Garcia waited, listening, until it was finished.

"You told me once you forgot that one."

"I guess it came back to me. Things have a way of doin' that, you know. Comin' back. And I've got a pretty good memory. Too good, maybe, since I mostly remember things I'd rather not. Sometimes I feel like I know a thousand years' worth of songs, all of 'em blue. And I'll remember you, Garcia, count on it."

"I'll remember you too. But don't give up on that song. I like it."

"Good. Maybe I'll play it for you again sometime. Like at your wake."

"What's wrong with right now?"

"Now? Why should I?"

"Because I might not be able to hear it at my wake. Or maybe

251

you won't be there. Besides, it's Christmas Eve and I'm the only audience you've got, right? So why not?"

Lamont stared at him for what seemed like a very long time, then shrugged. "It won't make any difference, you know."

"I know. Play it again anyway. Please."

Garcia closed the door softly behind him as he left, but the indigo melody managed to escape and follow him, weaving itself into the holiday harmonies of the Mumford High chorus, echoing down the deserted Samaritan corridors and out into the night. And somehow he could hear it even more clearly in the cold, mercury vapor glare of the parking lot. The icy river wind seemed to pick up the tune and whisper it over the murmur of crosstown traffic. Blues for Murder City. A sad song for a hard town. Not a bad song, though. Not bad at all.